[handwritten signature] Edwina Martin-Arnold

Good With His Hands

T.T. Henderson
J.M. Jeffries
Barbara Keaton
Edwina Martin-Arnold

[handwritten: Enjoy :)]

Noire is an imprint of Parker Publishing LLC.

Copyright © 2009 by T.T. Henderson, Barbara Keaton, Edwina Martin-Arnold and J.M. Jeffries
Published by Parker Publishing LLC
12523 Limonite Avenue, Suite #440-438
Mira Loma, California 91752
www.parker-publishing.com

ISBN: 978-1-60043-063-3
First Edition
Manufactured in the United States of America
Cover Design by Jaxadora Designs

Good With His Hands

T.T. Henderson
J.M. Jeffries
Barbara Keaton
Edwina Martin-Arnold

Good With His Hands

Hot Spot
By
T.T. Henderson

OTHER TITLES BY T.T. HENDERSON

Ambrosia
Passion
Path of Fire
Something So Right (After the Vows Anthology)
Tattooed Tears
Too Much Hennessy
Tangled Webs

DEDICATION

To my big brother, Terry, who thinks too much...but not enough of himself. You are one my favorite people in the whole world. Luv ya'.

"At one time we too were foolish, disobedient, deceived and enslaved by all kinds of passion and pleasures...But when the kindness and love of God our Savior appeared, he saved us, not because of righteous things we had done, but because of his mercy."

Titus 3:3-5

Chapter One

Byggie Quinn could think of dozens of better ways to spend her Sunday. Going to church with her older sister and her bad-ass kids wasn't one of them. Her Blackberry rang as they entered the building.

"Uh-uh. Don't even think about pulling that I-gotta-work-emergency bit, Byg," Her sister, Selena scolded as she nearly shoved her ten and twelve-year-old sons through the door.

"If Aunt Byggie has to leave, can I go with her?" Quinton, the oldest asked his mother.

"Hello?" Byggie answered her phone while watching Selena glare at her son the way their mother used to do. Byggie would never tell her, but she was still intimidated by that look. It had the required affect. Quinton's face went from hopeful to hang-dog in two seconds flat.

"Byggie it's Steve Carter. Did I catch you at a bad time?"

"No. Now is good," she said, turning her back as her sister's glare turned in her direction.

"Good. Good. I need you to fly to Phoenix next week. We're opening an office there next quarter and I need you handle finding us a facility."

"Phoenix, huh? What're we putting there? New call center?"

"No. Operations. We need to set up IT and some other back office functions for Business Resumption planning. You know the drill."

"Understood. When do you need me out there?"

"You know how the board is when they make a decision—it needs to happen yesterday. Can you be there Tuesday for meetings with our realtor and some of the city planners?"

"Yeah. No problem, Steve. I'll make it happen."

"Great. That's one thing done."

"Hey, Steve?" Byggie said.

"Yeah?"

"You do know it's Sunday, right?"

"Yeah. So?" It was just like him not to care or be aware that most people took the day off.

"Just a friendly reminder, even God took a day off every seventh day."

"That's 'cause he didn't have to worry about keepin' a job, Quinn. We're all livin' in Donald Trump's world nowadays. One day you're sipping champagne in a million-dollar Penthouse suite and the next, you're plunging toward earth clinging to your tattered golden parachute. You know that."

Most folks would've taken that to be a joke, but Byggie knew her boss didn't have a sense of humor about such things. Steve was Chief Operating Officer of OMG Financial and with the market being as volatile as it had been, he was constantly worried about staying in the good graces of the CEO and Board of Directors.

"If you're so all about keepin' to the Sabbath, why're you answering your Blackberry?" Steve challenged.

"You know me, boss. I'm scared I'll miss somethin'. Besides I am at church right now."

The man laughed on the other end of the phone. "Make sure you get out before lightening strikes."

"Forget you," she said in mock anger. "I'll get my itinerary together and e-mail it to you tomorrow."

"Thanks, Byggie. I can always count on you."

She ended the call and spun on a high heel to face Selena. The boys had gone off to their respective Sunday school classes and her sister's glare had nowhere else to go but here.

"What?" Byggie shrugged. "I'm done with the phone. It's going in my purse. See?" she dropped it deliberately into her bold red leather Dolce. "Give me a stinkin' break, alright?"

Selena shook her head, sighed and headed toward the sanctuary. She snatched the bulletin out of the greeter's hand with impatience. Byggie offered her an apologetic smile and offered a gracious "Thank you" as she took her own. She'd been irritating Selena since they were kids, but mostly because Selena irritated her first...and secondly, because Byggie derived some small pleasure at making her older sister lose her flippin' mind.

Byggie followed Selena to the section they always sat in, the upper level on the right. They found seats just as the choir and band began playing. She always enjoyed the music, even though it lasted far too long. She examined the three-inch designer pumps she was wearing. They were designed to be stylish, not endure a marathon praise and worship session. She leaned over to place her handbag on fold out chair, taking time to ensure her Blackberry was on "vibrate". She rose and tugged on the skirt of her dress that had ridden up just a bit.

A gorgeous man was entering the aisle. He quickly averted his eyes, but not before Byggie caught him staring at her assets. She smiled at him, feeling a spread of desire warm inside her.

He set his Bible down on his chair and began to sing and worship. Byggie continued to stare at him with interest. He was tall, medium brown, with one of those well-manicured beards that framed his handsome face. His hair was also closely cropped. She was a sucker for a well-groomed, handsome man.

Byggie continued to stare at him even after her sister hissed a warning in her ear.

"You don't pick up men in church, Byggie," she whispered hotly.

"Why not?" Byggie countered. "You said this was the best place to find a good man and that one looks plenty good to me."

"Honestly, Byggie. I don't know why you're not struck down right here, right now," Selena folded her arms, unable to enjoy the music.

"Me neither, sis," Byggie teased. "Maybe I haven't done anything quite scandalous enough."

"Hmpf," her sister replied, as if that wasn't even a remote possibility.

Just then, the man turned and stared directly into Byggie's eyes for a long moment then jerked his gaze away.

Smiling, Byggie picked up her handbag. He was as good as hers. "Be right back," she tossed the words at her sister and made her way down the aisle.

Trey Reed had been six months and nine days celibate thanks to the Life Group he'd joined at church. They had promised him freedom from sexual addiction, and to his amazement, the group and his newfound faith had done miracles in curbing his appetite for frequent, meaningless encounters. For the entirety of those six months he was all about getting his praise on Sunday mornings, but today he was finding it hard to ignore the beautiful distraction standing to his right. She was chocolate decadence. Five foot nothin', probably weighed a hundred and nothin', had arresting dark brown features and deliciously sexy curves.

She shifted her weight from one gorgeous leg to the other, swaying to the choir. Each time she swayed, he could smell the scent of her perfume and he could feel old desires stirring. He felt her eyes still on him, even though he'd turned away. Trey breathed deeply, closed his eyes and threw his hands up into the air. "Lord, you know my weakness. Can I ask you to give a brotha a hand today?" he pleaded silently.

As if he'd just conjured her with his prayer, she was next to him, touching his arm, sending disruptive currents through his veins. He looked into those gorgeous deep brown eyes and fell immediately and profoundly in lust. "Can I scoot past?" she asked. "Got an important call to make." She offered up her Blackberry as evidence as she smiled, sweetly, but intently.

Trey nodded and stepped back to grant her wish. At that moment, he'd have granted her just about anything. He watched with guilty pleasure as her nice apple bottom moved past him toward the end of the aisle—Sistah's form was incredible.

Three-second rule, Trey. Three-second rule, he reminded to himself, averting his eyes upward quickly. A look more than three seconds long is bound to go wrong.

The woman paused then and looked back. "Would you mind helping me with something real quick?"

It took a moment for Trey to register the question—he was suddenly imagining what it'd be like to kiss those pouty lips. He struggled to shake off the thought. "I'm sorry?"

"I-need-your-help," she said each word deliberately, as if speaking to a child or a half-wit. But Trevor didn't mind. He was too enraptured by her playful smile and dark, smoldering eyes. She wanted more than just a helpful hand, he was sure of it.

"Awright," he said. Everything within him was saying this girl wasn't nothin' but trouble—exactly the kind of girl he always fell for.

"This way," she said turning. She made quick haste getting out of the row.

Trey could no more avoid being pulled by the playful jiggle of her bottom than metal could avoid the pull of a magnet. Warning signals clanged in his head.

Chill, he told himself. This was church and this was a churchgoing woman. She probably just wanted some help and here he was making it into an erotic fantasy.

When they exited the sanctuary, her hips grew a more pronounced sway. Then again...

Trey followed even as he wondered if this was a test set up by his Life Group. Was this part of the twelve step process, he wondered. Were they testing him to see if he would fail?

They stopped at the door of the family restroom. Trey looked at her quizzically.

"Don't be scared," she said sweetly. "I need your help in here. I promise I won't do anything you don't want me to."

Trey could feel his pulsing throb in his hands and his temples. He couldn't think of a single thing he wouldn't want her to do. It bothered and excited him, sending his heart racing the way it did when he was about to fulfill his deepest desires. High from the adventure of the moment, Trey entered the restroom and watched with interest as she closed and locked the door. He leaned back against the large counter and crossed his arms, trying to play it cool. "So what can I help you with, pretty lady?" Had his voice just cracked a little?

"Well, unless I miss my guess, you're a man who likes a little fun in his life. Am I right?"

Trey gave a noncommittal shrug. "Depends." He didn't know why he was tryin' to play like he was all hard-to-get. The way his heart was pounding and his palms sweating, she had to notice how much he was into her right now.

"The thing is, my sister's been draggin' me to church with her and her kids every Sunday tryin' to get me saved or somethin'." She reached around him to place her trendy red purse on the countertop. She lingered there a moment. Just long enough for him to have her sweet scent tease his nostrils.

Seduction, he guessed. How fitting. "So, it's not working? You're not saved?" Trey asked, trying to find a hint that he'd misread the woman's intentions and this was just an innocent encounter.

"No. And it's a pity really." She clasped her hands behind her back. Her breasts became more pronounced beneath the stretchy fabric of her dress. "I like to be successful at things. But getting' saved doesn't seem to come as easy for me as climbing the corporate ladder." She moved her eyes up and down his body as if she was sizing him up.

"What do you do?" Trey asked, realizing there was no innocence in the woman. He'd read her right from the get-go. It was decision time—to stay was to give in to his addiction, but to go didn't seem right.

"I'm the executive vice president in charge of corporate properties for OMG Financial." She ran her hands along his crossed arms. "What about you, honey?"

Trey flexed his muscles under her touch. "I'm a maintenance engineer. I think I service two of your properties here in town."

She looked amused. "You clean the toilets in my buildings?"

"I fix them if they break. I don't clean a damn thing," he offered, a little put out. "I also maintenance your AC systems and inspect your electric panels for hot spots. It's very dangerous work."

A perfectly manicured eyebrow arched. "Hot spots, huh?" she asked, amusement unmistakable in her tone. "I've got one I'd love for you to inspect." She widened her stance, forcing her snug fitting skirt to stress at the seams. "Ever since my sister's been bringin' me here I've been fantasizing about having sex in here with a good lookin', God-fearin' man."

Trevor couldn't hide his smile. "I've had the same fantasy," he confessed. certain now that he was being tested. Equally certain that he would fail.

"So, what's your name, good-lookin'?" Her voice was beyond sultry as she moved a step closer.

"Trey," he said as his eyes fixated on her perfectly round breasts. His breathing quickened, his head grew light. It came too easy; the flirting, the need. "What's yours?"

"Byggie," she backed against the door.

Trey nearly laughed. "Byggie? Are you serious?" The woman was petite. He doubted she stood five-foot tall even wearing three-inch heels.

"I may be short, but I assure you I'm more woman than you've had in a long time."

"Oh, I see how it is. You all bold and sassy-like, huh?" This time Trey moved closer to her, warming to the game, feeling his old groove coming back. "I'm down with whatever you want to show me, Miss Lady." Tomorrow. He'd give up casual sex tomorrow.

Her dark eyes lit up and she turned slowly until her back was to him and her bottom skimmed his crotch. "This dress has one zipper," she smiled over her shoulder at him, "and I ain't got a thing on underneath."

Trey exhaled slowly. The first step of his twelve-step program to fight sexual addiction was to admit he had a problem. He damn sure had a problem right now—and she had the prettiest ebony skin he'd ever seen. Trey had unzipped the dress without thinking. He slid his hand down the silky softness of her dark chocolate skin then up the front. Her breasts were warm and heavy in his hands. In one move, he slipped the dress off her shoulders and scooped her up in arm, turning her to face him.

"Oh my," she cooed. "You're a smooth one, Trey."

Trey couldn't help but feel a bit smug. "Too bad you're not wearing a bra," he teased, "I can work magic on one a those bad boys."

"And cocky," she added turning her attention to the bulge in his slacks. "I like that," she whispered sexily.

Trey felt her hand move between their bodies, caressing and massaging him to rock hardness. Maybe it was his brief celibacy, but he hadn't been so excited about the possibility of having sex with a woman in a long time. He bent his head to taste the delicious-looking lips only to be met with a smooth, brown cheek.

"We don't know one another well enough for kissing on the mouth," she explained.

"But I really want to kiss you," Trey said, moving for the soft spot where her neck and shoulders met. "I'm really good at it." He trailed more kisses up her neck and just under her chin to prove his point. "You wouldn't be disappointed."

"I have no doubt about that, sugar, but it's kind of a rule I have. Kissing on the mouth makes all of this a bit too personal, don't you think?"

He searched her eyes then and saw what she wanted him to see. That this wasn't a lifetime commitment, just a one shot fantasy that was never to be repeated. She cupped her breasts in her hands as if they were an offering. "But feel free to kiss anything else you like, baby."

Sex with a beautiful woman, with no strings attached—it was perfect. Surely God could forgive him for a small indiscretion. He'd been good for six months, for heaven's sake.

Accepting her "gift", Trey pulled the dark tip of a breast into his mouth. The nipples hardened against his tongue as he sucked firmly until the nipple hardened against his tongue. He released it, circled it with his tongue then pulled it back inside his mouth, loving the way her skin seemed to melt in his mouth. He repeated this on her other breast and then it happened. She uttered the most beautiful sound a woman could make...a sudden hitch of breath followed by a shuddering, "Oh."

Oh yeah. She was his.

Chapter Two

His mouth was hot on her skin. Byggie closed her eyes and laid her head back against the door as he trailed hot kisses along her belly. "Yes," she encouraged him. "That's it." She wanted to say his name, but couldn't recall it—Taye, was it? It really didn't matter. All that mattered was how he was making her feel. His hands massaged her bottom. His tongue was like fire on her skin and all Byggie wanted was to feel this way for as long as she could.

"What's that?" he asked.

"What?" Byggie opened her eyes and looked down at him. "I didn't say anything."

He nodded. "Yeah, you did. You said this is heaven." He smiled then. "Told you I was good, didn't I?"

He looked like a ten-year-old all of the sudden, all proud of hitting a home run at a little league game. She didn't know why men always had to puff out their chests and beat on them like gorillas—and at such inappropriate moments. "Yeah, sugar, you're the best. And you know what? I'd be willing to bet you can find something more creative to do with your tongue. What do you say?"

A sobering look slowly stole across the man's handsome features. His hands fell to his sides as he moved away from her.

Byggie groaned. "What?" she asked, irritated. "Don't tell me you're offended."

Troy or Ty or whatever his name was, shook his head and gave a small, disgusted laugh. "You are something, lady. You know that?"

"What's that supposed to mean?" Byggie narrowed her eyes at him, growing more irritated. Suddenly, she felt her nakedness and grew uncomfortable. "If we're not going to do this, could you help me with my dress?"

He gave her an unreadable look before taking her dress in his fingers. Slowly he stood, lifting the fabric and covering the curves of her body. He stood looking down at her, holding the fabric in place while she put her arms through the holes. Then gently, he turned her until her back was to him. He zipped the dress deliberately.

Byggie felt as if her whole fantasy had just re-wound.

His hand remained on the small of her back as silence filled the space between them.

Suddenly, Byggie wanted nothing more than to go home, go to bed and pull the covers over her head. Her face burned. It made her angry that he'd made her feel—dirty.

"I'm sorry," he said softly, as if reading her thoughts. "I shouldn't have followed you here."

She whirled around, anger filling her veins. "What, this is all my fault now? You're all innocent here you poor Christian man being led by a temptress of Satan?"

His eyebrows lifted. "No…I didn't mean—"

"Well, you can save your lame-ass apologies for someone else, mister. I don't need anyone to feel sorry for me!" She snatched her handbag from the sink and yanked open the door. The nerve of him—judging her. This was why she didn't come to church. Everyone was always so damned high and mighty.

She didn't want to look back at the man, and she sure couldn't stomach the look her sister would give her if she went back inside the sanctuary. Byggie pulled out her Blackberry and called a cab and headed straight outside to wait on it. A moment later, the man followed her. He was really pissing her off and she told him so.

"I'm not trying to make you angry," he said. "This wasn't your fault, I'm in Recovery see and—"

"Recovery?" Byggie stopped pacing the sidewalk and stared at him. "You're on drugs?"

He shook his head. "Worse. I have a sexual addiction."

Byggie didn't even know what to make of that. "I didn't know there was such a thing," she said truthfully. "But can I ask you a question?"

He shrugged. "Sure."

"What's so bad about sex? I mean, really. As long as two people consent who's getting hurt, huh?" She was still steamed by his following her. "Why do you people always have to make others feel bad about doing something that God created to make us feel good? I don't get it."

He scratched his well-manicured head. "You know, I don't have a good answer for that. All's I can tell you is instead of making me feel good, after a while I just felt empty and depressed after havin' sex, you know?"

Byggie could feel a headache coming on. "No. I really don't know." She answered, massaging an aching temple.

"Yes you do." He leaned against a light post and put his hands in his pockets. "You know exactly what I'm talkin' about."

"Why are you talking to me?" she shot at him. "What makes you think that you and I could possibly have anything in common?"

His eyebrows lifted in that way he had when she surprised him. "What makes you so sure we don't, princess? Just 'cause I'm in maintenance and you got a fancy job title? Shoot that don't mean a damned thing when you think about the fact we was both in that bathroom ready to tear each other apart."

"But we didn't did we?" Byggie narrowed her eyes at the man. "Today we might be in the same place, but tomorrow morning at eight o'clock, you'll be plunging toilets somewhere while I'm making multi-million-dollar real estate negotiations. I wasn't looking for a lifetime with you, man, just a couple of minutes of fun. You shot that deal all to hell."

"True dat," he said, pursing his lips and nodding as if he hadn't considered it. "And you know what? That means something."

"It sure does." Byggie was relieved to see the Taxi entering the parking lot. "It means you just missed out on livin' a fantasy you would've remembered for the rest of your days, baby. Gotta go." She hopped into the cab that smelled too much like pine and old cigarettes. She couldn't wait to put some distance between herself and that man. It suddenly occurred to her that Selena wouldn't know she'd left and it wasn't like she could call her—the woman never had her cell phone on in church. Whatever. She'd leave her a voicemail.

Trey stared at the cab as it headed out of the parking lot. "Byggie." He whispered the name into the warm mid-morning wind, loving the irony of such a tiny package carrying a nuclear explosion of personality. Feisty. Yeah, shorty was sexy as hell.

Back inside the sanctuary, he moved back into the aisle he vacated what seemed like hours ago. The woman down the aisle eyed him suspiciously as he moved his Bible from the seat and sat down. It took him a minute to realize she was probably Byggie's sister and that she'd probably seen them walk out together. He smiled at her weakly, hoping to allay any fears that he was some sort of rapist or murderer.

The woman frowned deeper.

"Please open your Bibles to Titus 3:3," the pastor instructed.

Trey did so obediently, trying not to meet the woman's accusatory glare.

"Here is where you should turn if you're fighting any kind of addiction, overeating, smoking, drugs, you name it," The Pastor spoke to the passage laying open on Trey's lap.

"It says, 'At one time we too were foolish, disobedient, deceived and enslaved by all kinds of passions and pleasures.' Sound familiar to anyone here?" He asked.

Man, that always happened. It seemed like whatever Trey was struggling with, the message he got was right on the money.

"Verse four says, 'But when the kindness and love of God our Savior appeared, he saved us, not because of righteous things we had done, but because of his mercy,'" the pastor continued.

Is that what had happened, Trey wondered? Had God saved him from his lust today? If so, at what cost? He thought back to the look in Byggie's eyes when he'd apologized to her. She'd stung him with her nasty insults. But behind it, he swore there was something else, something less bold, less fierce that fascinated him.

"What did you do to my sister?"

Trey jumped a bit at the whispered demand. He realized then that it was Byggie's sister hissing in his ear. "Jesus, lady, chill. I didn't do anything to her. She left."

"You shouldn't take the Lord's name in vain like that," she scolded. "And what do you mean, she left?"

"I mean...she left. Took a cab and—left."

Her eyes narrowed. "Why did she leave? What happened?"

She was about one nosey heif—uh, woman.

"Nothing." Trevor decided that was the best answer. If Byggie wanted her sister to know what happened, she'd have tell her herself.

"Fine." The woman leaned back a bit. "I hope you're not lying to me," she warned.

Or what? She was no bigger than her sister. Trey could snap her like a twig. "I don't have a reason to lie to you, awright? I think she wasn't feeling well and went home." If this was how she always acted, Trey suspected Byggie would never tell her what happened in the church bathroom.

Service ended and Trey headed toward the church gymnasium where his friend and sponsor, Daniel Webber pastured to teenagers. Trey admired the old dude. Personally, he didn't have much patience with kids, especially teenagers. They were always poppin' off like they knew everything. They were much better off with a person like Daniel who had patience.

"Hey, man, what's goin' on?" Danny's face lit up as he hugged his friend and gave his back a friendly pat. "You had a good week?"

"An interestin' one," Trey chuckled. "If you got a minute, I'd like to tell you what just happened."

"I got time," Danny checked his watch. "The wife always has to socialize before we can get out of here." He put an arm around Trey warmly and walked toward one of the Sunday school rooms. They sat at one of the round tables. "So what happened?"

Trey proceeded to tell him about his encounter in the bathroom. He left out the woman's name, but confessed to everything else. "I don't know man, I'm sure it means somethin' that I stopped, but the way she looked when I did—I don't know. I feel terrible that I upset her."

"Wow." Danny leaned forward, placing his elbows on his knees. He was a dark-skinned black man with gray hair at his temples. He was good-lookin' for an older guy. He was in his fifties, but had the physique of a man of about thirty. He spent a crazy amount of time in the gym working out everyday. "That's a new one on me, I'll tell ya. Right in the church bathroom, huh?"

Trey nodded. "Crazy, right?"

Danny shrugged. "I dunno what's crazy and what ain't, son. But let me ask you this...what was it that made you stop?"

It was just like Danny not to trip on anything Trey said or did. Like always he just got straight to the heart of things.

Trey leaned forward on his knees, mimicking Danny's posture as he tried to remember exactly what it was that got to him at that moment. "I was feeling excited...you know and smug, like I was proving once again that I could have any woman I wanted. She...she made this sound and I knew I had her, knew I could make her scream my name even though we was in the church bathroom. I think I said somethin' to her like I told you I was good, or somethin' like that." Trey found it embarrassing now to tell the story. Was this what was important to him, really?

Danny didn't say a word, just waited.

Trey cleared his throat and continued. "She looked at me and then said something rude. She talked down to me like I was a child."

"How'd you feel when she did that? Angry?"

"Naw, man. See that's what's weird," Trey struggled to find the right words to explain, "I stopped because of what she said, but I wasn't mad at her. I was surprised, you know. It was like all of the sudden I could see myself through her eyes and what she saw was a nuisance. Here I was thinking I was all that and she was thinkin' 'get it over with dude so I can throw the memory of you out like yesterday's trash.'"

"You saw yourself differently in that moment and it made you stop?"

Trey nodded. "I started to count how many times I'd felt the same way about a woman after I'd slept with her. I hated the way they tried to make a relationship out of a moment. I was about getting' to the next moment so I'd say anything, do anything, to make them leave me alone. Then I'd throw the memory of them away."

Danny put a kind hand on his shoulder. "Sounds like you found your match."

"Yeah," Trey chuckled. "You know the craziest part, man?"

"What's that?"

"All I can think about now is how I can make a relationship out of this moment. It's sick, right?"

Danny's eyes were warm with understanding and good humor. "I don't know about sick, son. But make sure you get yourself healthy before you go diving into a relationship with someone else. Hear?"

"I can roll with that," Trey agreed. "Thanks for your time, man."

Danny was the closest thing Trey had ever had to a father. His old man had left him and his mama when he was a baby. He'd seen him from time to time, but mostly he didn't think about his sperm donor father. His mama on the other hand was great, but fragile. He could never tell her the things he'd shared with Danny and his Life Group. She'd likely wonder how he came out to be as trifling as his dad. Trey never wanted to disappoint her the way his father had.

Trey checked his watch. Speaking of his mama, he'd better get over to the hospital. She'd never forgive him if he didn't bring her Sunday breakfast.

Byggie had slipped into her most comfortable sweats and fuzzy socks and was halfway through a pint of Ben and Jerry's when her sister barged through her front door.

"What's going on?" Selena asked, tucking the keys back inside her purse. "Why'd you leave church so suddenly?"

"I had a headache," Byggie was only half lying. She did have one by the time she'd left. "And by the way, big sis," she pointed her spoon at her sister. "If you don't start knockin' before you come in my house, I swear I'ma take that key away from you."

"So what? I have a headache every day of my life," she said, ignoring the knocking part. "You think that's a good excuse for leaving and making me worry about you?" Selena moved around the town house straightening her mail on the entryway table, picking up the paper and putting it into the recycle bin in the kitchen.

Byggie shook her head. The woman never stopped moving—her body nor her tongue. The last thing she wanted was another fight. "Sis why don't you sit down and rest for a minute? Have some ice cream." She offered up what was left of the pint.

Selena stood in front of her, hands on her hips, anger hardening her face. "What? You think ice cream is going to make all your troubles go away?"

She used to be so pretty, Byggie thought, trying to remember when she'd changed. Oh yeah, it was when her husband left her last year. That's when her sister's face had taken on a permanent frown. "Selena, next to sex and chocolate, ice cream is a woman's best friend."

"Right. I'll remember you said that when your hips spread six inches." Selena's eyes searched the room. No doubt trying to find a speck of dust she could destroy.

Byggie looked at her still slender hips. "Maybe you're right," she said, quickly putting the lid on the ice cream and heading for the freezer. "No more ice cream or chocolate. But you realize that just leaves sex, right?" She shot her sister a mischievous grin, hoping to coax a smile from her.

Selena just sighed. "You don't take anything seriously, Byggie, except that job of yours."

"And you, sister dear, take everything way too seriously," Byggie tapped her sister's nose as she moved back to her lounging position on the couch. "Besides I love my job. Did I tell you I'm going to Phoenix next week?"

"No." Finding nothing to clean, Selena finally sat down in a chair. She looked exhausted.

"That's why Steve called me today. I need to go find a property to move some of our back office operations into."

"Don't you ever get tired of traveling?" Selena asked, letting her head fall back against the chair.

"Heck no. I don't know what I'd do if I didn't have a challenge all the time."

"You could settle down. Get married. Have kids."

Byggie just stared at her sister. "No thanks, sis. Your kids are the best birth control I could ever think of."

"They're not so bad," she defended.

"Like hell," Byggie countered. "Your little angel Keenan jumpin' off that bridge on a dare, breakin his leg and costin' you all that money in hospital bills was bad, girl. Admit it."

"He said he had to do that in order to get some respect. He was getting beat up every day before he did that. The next day he walks in with his cast and he's like some sorta Grade School hero. I think it took guts to do that. In fact, he reminds me of you as a kid, Byg."

"I was never as bad as Keenan." Byggie argued. Still, she had to smile. She'd gotten many a whippin' for doing things just to prove she could.

"What about marriage?" Selena asked. "That out for you, too?"

Byggie nodded. "That's your fault too. I thought you and Kelvin were invincible, right? Like nothing would ever come between you."

"So did I." Selena's voice sounded small and tired.

Not wanting the mood to get too maudlin, Byggie switched subjects. "I still wish I'd a been with you when you rolled up on Kelvin and his floozie and beat the two of 'em down that flight of stairs." She smiled at the thought of her sister getting the best out of both of them. "I would've taken pictures and put 'em on You Tube."

"Byggie that's not funny," Selena said even as a smile lifted the corners of her mouth. "I swear I was temporarily insane at that moment. Like an outta body experience."

"I think it was great. They both deserved it."

"It wasn't very Christian-like."

"No, but it sure as hell was Quinn-like." Byggie laughed hard.

Selena couldn't hold back any longer. Soon they were laughing so hard Byggie's stomach and cheeks ached.

"Stop. Stop, sis," she wiped tears from her eyes. "I can't take it." She was breathless.

Selena's laughter subsided. "Oh. You know, I haven't laughed that hard in a long time."

"You should try it more often," Byggie said. "It's good for you."

"Yeah." She stared at the ceiling a while before shifting in the chair. "I guess I'd better go check on the house. No tellin' what those boys've done to my kitchen. When I left they were making grilled cheese sandwiches."

"Well good luck with that." Byggie walked her to the door.

Selena stopped and turned when she reached the door. "So what happened with that man at church today, Byggie?"

"What man?"

Selena lifted an eyebrow. "You know what man. Don't play."

"Oh, that man. Well, nothing happened. We talked a bit, that's all," Byggie had a hard time swallowing after telling the lie, but what her sister didn't know wouldn't hurt her. Then it occurred to her that he might've gone back and said something. "Why? Did he say something that made you think something happened?"

"He sure did," Selena stated firmly.

Byggie could feel a slight panic rising, followed closely by anger. "What did he say?"

"He told me that nothing happened."

"Well, then what makes you think something did?" Byggie asked, confused.

"Because all men lie, Byg. We both know that. As for you, I'm disappointed that you didn't tell me the truth."

Byggie sucked in air knowing just how busted she was. "Trust me, Sis. You really don't wanna know the truth. Let's just leave it at that."

"Fine," Selena said, opening the door. "Just remember. One day you'll be judged by your actions."

"I realize that. In the meantime, could it not be by you?"

Selena started to say something, thought better of it, and closed her mouth. "Hope your trip to Phoenix is a good one."

Byggie was grateful her sister chose to end the day on a good note. She'd had enough drama for one day. Even after a half pint of ice cream, she couldn't seem to forget the way the man's hands had felt on her body. "Thanks. Hope you have a good week, too."

Closing the door, Byggie headed back to the fridge. Maybe finishing the pint would help her cool the hot flush she got just from thinking about him.

Chapter Three

Trey loved traveling for work. He made decent money, but having to kick in to pay for his mama's hospital bills prevented extravagances. He always found time to do something fun whenever he traveled, loving how different every place was from the next.

When he'd told his mama he had to make a quick trip to Phoenix she'd asked him to take pictures of the hot air balloons. He reminded her that the balloons flew in Albuquerque and usually not until October. He'd gone on the Net and found out there was a Jazz concert at the Phoenix Botanic Gardens while he was there. He'd promised to find something special at the concert to bring back for her.

But, first things first. He had a building to inspect. Thankfully the hot day hadn't reached the basement where he was performing his inspection. Trey found the long electric switchboard. The gray metal boxes always reminded him of extra large school lockers. He rolled out rubber mat and pulled out a short screwdriver. He powered up his Thermocam, infrared camera, the one his nephew claimed looked like a remote control, and placed it back into his tool belt.

This was one of the most important things to check, the breaker panels. OMG wouldn't want their systems to overload or short circuit. Unfortunately, he couldn't turn off the electricity to do this check. It had to be energized to check for hot spots. Carefully, he stuck the flathead in the space at the top of the first control panel, searching for the interlock. It was the only way to open the panels while the power was still on.

Careful to avoid the hot wires, he moved the screwdriver by millimeters in one direction. Finding no purchase, he moved it the opposite directions slowly. And then, there it was. He'd found the safety switch, which he pushed down gently to released it.

"I love it when a plan comes together," he said absently, channeling an old episode of MacGyver.

He pulled his screwdriver out just as carefully as it went in then opened the panel revealing a bank of busbars. These housed copper wires that distributed power to various parts of the large office building.

Pulling out his infrared, he moved it along the wires to test how hot they were. Most were showing a normal red range, but one bank of wires was white hot. They were the wires feeding the buildings offices and work areas. Not good. One long day with everyone on their PC's and it these bad boys would trip fore sure.

He holstered the camera and made a note for the potential owner of the building, OMG. He finished inspecting every one of the boards, then in turn went back to close the safety panels. The last one didn't close properly. He pushed a bit harder, but the latch refused to catch.

He cursed. He didn't dare slam it. That might create sparks, which was never a good idea around hot electrical wires. "Time for the trusty screwdriver," he said, and pulled the tool from his belt once again. Holding the door closed, he felt around once again for the safety switch, this time to make it lock. He found the switch and applied gentle pressure. "Come on, sucker," he insisted. He jiggled the tool ever so slightly.

There was a pop. The switchboard bank went silent. The building lost all power.

Shit.

Trey pulled back the handle of the screwdriver. The metal had completely disintegrated. A sense of dread filled him as he watched the lazy curl of smoke drift carelessly upward toward the smoke alarm.

Shit. Shit. Shit.

The loud sirens nearly deafened him as he ran for the outside doors just as the sprinkler systems went off in the upper floors.

Trey pushed his way outside and slammed the door behind. He cursed and searched for his phone. He needed to make sure the fire department didn't show.

A moment after he hung up with the Phoenix Fire Department, a trio of people ran out of the building's front door. "I'll be damned," he whispered. There was Miss Chocolate Decadence herself, soaking wet, along with a woman and a man he didn't recognize. He approached them, recalling now that she said she worked for OMG. "Sorry about that," he started to walk toward them.

Byggie stared hard at him as she wiped water from her face. Even with her hair slicked to her head and her dress soaked, she was pound for pound the sexiest woman Trey had ever seen. "That was my bad...Byggie, wasn't it?"

"You know this man?" the man with beady blue eyes and white hair asked.

Byggie looked from the logo on his work shirt to his eyes. Recognition finally registered. "You're with our vendor. I'm guessing you were doing an inspection?" she directed this question at Trey.

He nodded smiling. "That's right. Trey Daniels," he offered his hand in turn to the woman and man. He discovered the woman was a realtor, Cindy Shockey and the man was City Council Chairman, Chuck Martin. "Nice to meet you all. My company sends me out for the rush jobs. I did the downtown site for you this morning," he gave a nod to Byggie, whose dress was now revealing the hard tips of her breasts. Three second rule, Trey. Just three seconds. "This one I was just finishing up."

"So there's a problem with the electricity in this building, Mr. Daniels?"

The realtor woman pushed her wet matte of blond hair away from her face. "Is that why the power went out?" she asked.

"Well it had some real hot wires, that's for sure, but nothing that couldn't be fixed before you took possession." He risked another look at the stunning Byggie. "That's if you go for this building."

"Did you set the sprinklers off?" Byggie asked. She pulled at her black slacks that were clinging to her curves like Saran Wrap on an apple.

"Oh that. Yeah." Trey explained the mishap with the safety panel. "I called off the fire department just before you folks came out."

"Your screwdriver vaporized?" the Councilman asked.

"Yeah—damndest thing." Trey held up the remaining handle for inspection.

"You're lucky you didn't get electrocuted," the realtor added.

"Naw," Trey shook his head. "I grounded myself. I was standing on a rubber mat."

"Well, why don't we all get dried off and go over the offers on both properties tomorrow." Byggie took charge. "Mr. Daniels when will you have your inspection reports to me?"

Trey shrugged and looked into her dark eyes a moment longer than he should have feigning to calculate the time it would take to finish his reports. In reality he was imagining ripping off that clinging black suit and licking the cool water from her warm skin. "Usually takes about forty-eight hours," he said.

"Since you caused water damage in this one, let's say you make it twenty-four?" Her dark brown eyes were blazing with anger and impatience.

"Awright." Trey let a slow smile take hold. "If you tell me where you're stayin' I'll have them faxed over tomorrow morning."

"I'm at the Westin. I need to get there and get changed," she offered to her companions who offered similar comments.

"I'll get 'em to you first thing, then," Trey offered as they started toward the black Lexus parked in the lot. "Sorry about the sprinklers and all. Shame there's never a church bathroom around when you need one."

Byggie shot him a warning look before climbing inside the sedan.

Trey couldn't erase the smile from his face as he watched them pull away. What were the odds of him meeting up with her while he was in Phoenix? And as luck would have it, he was also staying at the Westin. This was turning out to be a great work trip.

This had been the worst work trip ever.

Byggie stripped off the wet business suit and hung up the pieces on the shower bar to dry. First her flights were late getting in last night. Her suitcase was nowhere to be found so she'd had to delay her meeting time with Cindy and Chuck while she went shopping for another suit at the mall. The first building was an absolute disaster, requiring intense renovations in order to be functional and then there was the second building. It had potential and everything was going well until the power shut off and sprinklers shot on. But the absolute last thing she expected to find on the lawn was Mr. Best-Sex-She-Never-Had.

Coincidences this big just didn't happen. She'd obviously conjured him up with her unrequited desire. She stared at her wet self in the mirror. "You had to go and have wet dreams about that man and look at what happened," she chided.

If she could just sleep with him once maybe he'd become a distant memory. That wasn't likely to happen since he was swearing off sex. "You sure know how to pick 'em," she whispered at the woman in the mirror. She felt restless, wishing she could do anything but wait on clothes to dry. She went to the closet and put on the Heavenly Robe before noticing the blinking red light on the hotel phone. It was a message informing her that her suitcase was at the front desk. "Yes!"

She called promptly to have them bring it to her room. "Hey, is there a fun event going on in the city tonight?" she asked the front desk person before releasing the call. "Anything close by will work."

An hour and a half later, she was feeling much better—drier—when she arrived at the Phoenix Botanic Gardens. She marveled at the green bark of the large tree that stood at the entrance of the gardens. She'd never seen such a beautiful tree. Breathing deeply of the dry air, she found it a bit cooler than she'd expected. Byggie pulled her wrap over her bare arms, wishing she'd packed a dress with sleeves. Still, the gardens were beautiful as she wend her way on the brick path through various cacti and other desert plants and flowers toward the ticket booth.

The concert hadn't started yet, but Jazz filled the air just the same. She entered the enclosed area finding a bar to the right and a small stage on the left. The backdrop of the stage was a majestic and towering bluff. The sky darkened as the sun made it's slow, but exquisite exit in a blaze of purple, yellow and orange hues. If she had a date, the night would be perfect.

She got a merlot from the bar then scanned the area for an empty chair. It seemed all the Jazz lovers had arrived early and there wasn't a single chair in sight. A camera clicked and flashed to her right.

Turning Byggie, stared at the man. A very familiar man. "Unbelievable," she breathed. "Are you stalking me or what?"

Trey checked the picture he'd just taken. "Gorgeous," he confirmed, turning the camera so she could see. "And, no. I'm not stalking you."

It was a great shot of her surrounded by leafy plants and sparkling lights.

It looked like a photo straight out of a travel magazine. "It is a pretty place," she agreed.

"Who was talkin' about the place?" he asked, taking another shot of her, this time straight on.

"That's an awfully forward remark for a man who's sworn off women," Byggie scolded him. The nerve of him showing up here lookin' all fly? His silk collarless shirt displayed the width of his chest and muscles beneath it like a work of art. The fact that she wanted him even more right now made her irritable.

His eyes were dark and sparkled under the garden's lights. "I'm trying, but you're making it hard on me."

Trey looked so sexy and sounded so sincere. Byggie wondered for the second time if she had conjured him. It seemed the moment she'd thought about needing a date, he was standing next to her. Then again, he could be following her. "How is it that you pop up wherever I am nowadays, Mr. Daniels?" she asked coolly.

"Call me Trey and I guess I should point out that I was here first." His tone was matter-of-fact, his eyes brimmed with confidence. "And as for how we keep ending up in the same place…well, maybe that's divine providence, Ms. Byggie."

"Don't call me Ms. Byggie." She wrinkled her nose. "That makes me sound old or somethin'."

He leaned comfortably against a tree. "Since we're destined to be together, at least for tonight, I'll call you whatever you like."

The way he looked straight into her eyes when he said it, made Byggie lose her track of her thoughts for a moment. "Call me Ms. Quinn…or Byggie. Just not Ms. Byggie."

"Byggie." He said it soft and low, like he'd just discovered some long, lost treasure. "I like that. Suits you, even if you ain't no bigger'n my twelve-year-old niece."

"If we're going to be friends, don't start crackin' with the short jokes." Byggie took a sip of wine and searched the crowd. Her shoes were beginning to pinch her toes.

"Looks like we'll be getting started in a minute," Trey noted the band practicing on stage. "Why don't you take my seat? Unless…you're here with someone." He looked around as if the thought just occurred to him.

It would serve him right if she had been with someone, but happy for his offer, she decided to say nothing. Byggie eased her chin up a notch. "I'm here alone, but I am getting tired of standing in these heels," she offered truthfully.

"Fine, then I insist," he led her halfway down a row, removed his jacket and held the chair as she sat.

"Thanks. Although it really is the least you could do to make up for how you've treated me," she jabbed.

He looked at her like she was crazy. "Is this still about what happened at the church?"

Byggie nodded with emphasis. "That, plus the fact that you've now caused water damage in the office building I was going to buy."

"Aw, hell naw." He shook his head and looked around as if he wanted to find a weapon. "I'll be right back and we'll set this business straight."

For a moment Byggie wondered if he was seriously angry. He wasn't crazy enough to hit her in front of all these people, was he? She felt inside her purse for the small container of pepper spray she'd bought at Wal Mart and carried around wherever she went. If he messed with her, she was willing to give as good as she got.

Trey was back in minutes with a chair in hand. He had half the row scooting their chairs to allow him to place it next to Byggie. He threw his jacket over the back of the chair and turned intense eyes in her direction. "Awright, first off, have a seat."

She obeyed.

"You should be thankin' me Ms. Quinn, not givin' me shit," he said, plopping into the chair beside her.

"For what?"

"First, for findin' two major flaws in that building that'll help you negotiate the price down and second, for treatin' you like the lady that you are and not some two-dollah ho." He said it just loud enough to send curious glances their way.

"Keep your voice down," she whispered between clenched teeth. "And do me a favor."

"What?"

"Give up on liquor while you're givin' up on things. It's obviously made you lose your everlovin' mind."

"You're right. I have lost my mind, 'cause lately it's always thinkin' about you." He tossed back the half glass of wine like it was a shot.

Byggie was stunned by his confession. Her heart did weird flips in her chest. She eased her grip on the pepper spray and took a healthy swallow of her own libation. "Oh," was the only reply she could manage.

He slumped in his chair and stared at his empty wineglass, twirling it between his fingers. "That was a helluva thing to say, huh?" He seemed as surprised as she did.

"I'll say." Byggie took another sip of wine, feeling the power shift between them. He might've given up on sex, but she hadn't. She crossed one leg over the other carelessly. The movement allowed the fabric of her wrap dress to fall away and reveal a healthy amount of leg. Byggie got satisfaction watching his face as he swallowed hard trying to avert his gaze from her legs. "Still thinking this is divine providence, us running into each other?"

He cocked his head in contemplation. "That or the damned devil's after my soul." The announcer was on stage, making introductions of the band and the evening's Jazz singer. "I need another drink. Would you like one?" Trey offered.

Byggie took the last swallow of her drink and offered him the empty glass. "Merlot, please." She watched him leave, enjoying the long stride of his legs, the confident way he carried himself and the way he didn't think twice about paying for two rounds of drinks.

Sighing, she wondered just how far she could tempt him. The man smelled like sex to her, and she wanted him in the worst possible way. He turned and smiled as he headed back. He was handsome, not in a movie star way, but in a real man, real life kind of way. By the time he'd returned, she'd made her decision. Tonight, she'd do everything in her power to get him in her bed. "Thanks," she said, taking the drink he offered, making certain to run her fingertips along the back of his hand.

His eyes burned into hers for an intense moment and she hoped he could read his destiny in her eyes. You'll have to give up sex some other day, Trey Daniels. Tonight you're mine.

On stage, the woman with a sultry Billie Holliday-esque quality voice began singing. It was glorious, the music, the night and the feeling stealing over her as the wine warmed her insides. Trey proved to be a great date. He was knowledgeable about Jazz and had interesting historical insights into the pieces the woman sang. He was surprisingly complex for a man who inspected buildings and plunged toilets for a living.

There were three sets before intermission and by then Byggie had managed to scoot her chair closer to him, to lean in while he spoke, and feign enough of a chill for him to place his arm comfortably around her shoulders. It was nice here with him and she was reluctant to break the spell even though she really needed to go to the restroom. She excused herself, noting that Trey didn't seem anxious to lose her company.

"Did you need anything from the bar?" he asked.

"No thanks. If I have another drink, you'll be carrying me out of here," Byggie said truthfully. She'd never been a big drinker, finding it far more appealing to keep her wits about her at all times.

Byggie fell in line at the women's restroom, but for once didn't mind the wait. She was feeling a bit heady and very happy at this unexpected turn of events. Trey had been whispering about Jazz in her ear and she found the sound of his voice pleasingly male and deeply sexy. He'd been letting his eyes slip over her body, her legs, her mouth and her eyes as well. He wanted her. She could feel it. It was going to happen. She was going to have him. All she had to do was figure out how to get him to her hotel room.

After relieving her inflated bladder, she walked back and smiled smugly.

He was standing by their chairs, hands in his pockets looking incredible. A smile lit his face as she approached. It made her feel warmer than the wine. "Did I tell you that I'm a bit surprised to find you out tonight?" she asked, wanting to keep him talking.

"Why's that?" he asked, holding her chair as she sat.

"You promised to have reports in my hand first thing tomorrow morning. Since I've compressed your deadline, I thought you'd be slaving away."

"I never miss a deadline," he bragged. "You'll have your reports. But I always make time for fun wherever I go." He offered her that insanely sexy smile. "Looks like we have that in common."

"I work hard, Mr. Daniels, but I play even harder." She cut her eyes at him.

"I told you to call me Trey," he corrected, taking his seat. "And for the life of me, I keep thinking you've got something on your mind you're not telling me." His eyes searched hers, looking for an answer.

Byggie laughed. "If you paid closer attention, Trey, you'd know good and well what I was thinking." She crossed her arms, forcing her bosom up higher. "But then again, that wouldn't be a good thing."

"Why?"

"How would a woman keep secrets?" she baited him.

He kept his gaze even. "Why would you need to?"

Byggie leaned closer to him, close enough to whisper in his ear. "Because I've been thinking nasty thoughts. Thoughts, I'm sure you wouldn't approve of."

She could hear him swallow hard as he pulled back slowly to look at her. "You're right. Maybe you should keep those thoughts to yourself. I'm having a hard enough time keeping my own thoughts in check."

Smiling, Byggie ran a hand down his clean-shaven cheek. "The great thing about this, Trey, is that you don't have to fight so hard to be good. I'm giving you permission to be bad."

"I know, but this means something," he insisted. "You and me meeting twice in a week. It has to mean something."

"It does," Byggie said, running a finger over his lips. "There's something so powerful between us, it can't be denied. You can feel it, can't you?"

"Yes." He closed his eyes and grabbed her wrist. He kissed the palm of her hand so desperately she wished it were her mouth—of course that would break her no kissing rule.

Byggie's heart raced with excitement, her palm heated beneath his lips. She couldn't imagine a better ending to the night than having him make love to her. Suddenly, she couldn't wait for the concert to be over. When the music began again, she let her wrap fall off her shoulders so Trey could get a good glimpse at her cleavage so he wouldn't forget how badly he wanted her.

It was excruciating waiting the additional half hour for the concert to finish. They walked out of the gardens close together. Trey stopped at the gift shop near the entrance. "I need to buy something for my mom," he explained.

"Oh. Okay." Byggie tried to hide her disappointment. Her panties were now damp with wanting him. She followed him inside the bright, cheery store.

"I buy her something from everywhere I go," Trey explained as he perused the shelves of the small shop. "She keeps them along the windowsill of her hospital room."

"Your mom's in the hospital?" Byggie asked. "What's wrong with her?"

"Cancer." He said it simply. "Final stages. If she doesn't respond to this round of chemo, they'll move her to hospice."

"I'm sorry," Byggie said, meaning it.

Trey shrugged. "She's got a real good attitude. But what she really wanted to do was travel. When my dad left, she was too busy working, cleaning houses, cleaning buildings, to keep me in school. When I graduated from college and saved a little money, I took her to Italy and the Holy Lands before she go too sick. So now, it's tradition. I buy her something whenever I leave town and I tell her everything I see so it's just like she was there with me."

"That's sweet," Byggie suddenly felt a bit guilty about wanting to get him out of her so quickly. "What does she like?" she asked, joining him in his search for the perfect gift.

His eyebrows lifted as he smiled at her. "Something specific to the area, but nothing cheesy like a mug, a T-shirt or key chain."

"Sure," she replied, uncertain as to how she felt about finding a souvenir for the man's dying mother. It was unexpectedly sobering.

Shopping turned out to be surprisingly entertaining. They took turns showing items to one another only to get a "thumbs down" or slash across the neck in disapproval. Finally, Byggie settled on a potted pink cactus that was truly lovely. "Nothing says Phoenix like a cactus plant." She held up the tiny beauty in her palm as Trey examined it.

"She'll love it," he declared.

"Good."

Trey bought the plant and one of the Jazz CDs they had for sale before leaving the small gift shop.

Byggie took a deep breath outside, wondering how to get back to the subject that had been on her mind all night. "So, I've got my rental if you need to be dropped anywhere." She pulled her key out of her bag.

Trey pulled a key from his pocket. "Got a ride, but thanks." He walked her to her rental car. "See you at the hotel."

"What? Nooo." She searched his face to see if she'd heard him right. Was it really going to be this easy?

"You said you were staying at the Westin. So am I." He flashed a brilliant smile. "Seriously freakie deekie, huh?" Before she could respond, he closed her door and trotted toward his own rental car.

Byggie started the car and sat there for a moment looking into the clear night sky. "Divine providence?" she asked, tentatively. Her breath fogged the window slightly, but she took it as a good sign that there were no other signs from the Almighty to provide an answer.

"Whatever it is," she sang to herself. "I'm all for it."

They arrived at the hotel at the same time, finding parking spots close to one another. Trey, the consummate gentleman, walked her to her hotel room door.

"Well, this is me," she offered, shuffling unnecessarily in her purse for the card key. It was just where she'd placed it, in the zippered portion of her wallet. "So it seems we have—unfinished business." She tapped the card against her chin. She hoped she didn't sound as desperate as she was feeling.

Trey nodded slowly as if testing the theory in his head. "Could be," he agreed. "So what do we do about it?"

Do you have to ask? She wanted to take him by his lapels and drag him into her hotel room. Instead, she placed a hand on his chest and ran it over his solid muscles. "You know—we should—finish it." Her hand slid down his flat belly to his slacks. Oh happy day, he was hard as a lead pipe. "But only if you want to," she added quickly.

His arm was around her waist in an instant, he pressed her to the solid wall of his body and before she could take another breath, his lips were on hers, pressing urgently and insistently, demanding entry.

His kiss was strong, demanding and incredibly sensual. Byggie let his tongue inside. He tasted of red wine and spice and everything nice. She brought her arms around his shoulders and felt her feet lift from the floor as he tightened his grip around her. Byggie couldn't stop the moan from leaving her lips. It was the best kiss she could remember, she reveled in it, wanting it never to end.

Trey loosened his grip and let her feet touch the ground again. He pressed gentle kisses on her lips, her cheek, her neck until she almost lost her mind.

Finally, he pulled away. His breathing was hard, his chest heaving. "There," he said simply. "We've settled that."

Byggie was confused. "What?"

"We kissed," he said as if it explained everything. "Now, it's personal between you and me."

Damn him for making her forgot with that incredibly powerful kiss. She nodded. "You're right. It's very personal, Trey." She turned to open the door, bending the card key as she jammed it into reader.

"Byggie Quinn," he spoke quietly in her ear.

She closed her eyes, loving the way her name sounded in his voice, loving the warmth of his body on her back. "There's only one way to finish the business between us. Marry me."

Surprise made Byggie's eyes fly open. She pushed him off her. "What the hell? You know you don't want to marry me any more than I want to marry you, Trey. I want sex, not some frigging romance movie," she said it so fiercely it hurt her throat.

Trey's forehead was wrinkled, his eyes deep, dark and serious. "I never thought I'd say this, Byggie, but I want the romance movie, awright? Never before, but tonight I do. I've never felt about a woman the way I feel about you. I want you to be my wife."

"Oh for heaven's sake." Byggie sighed and turned a full circle of frustration. "How long have you been off sex?" she demanded.

"Six months, four days and fifteen hours," he said like a true recovering addict.

"That's why you think I'm so special," she reasoned. "You're sex-starved and I'm a veritable buffet. But that's okay. I'm here, man. Take me, lick me, sop me up with a damned biscuit!"

He kissed her again gently, on the forehead, like she was a two-year-old. "I'll see you in the morning," he said walking away with a pained expression.

"You've got some serious issues, Mister," she shouted after him.

He didn't respond.

Byggie stared after him as he headed toward the elevator bank. For the first time, she noticed the object in his hand. He'd kissed her incredibly, thoroughly, mind-blowingly, holding a pretty pink cactus the whole time.

Chapter Four

"Good morning."

Byggie didn't bother to put down her USA Today to answer him. Last night his voice had been the answer to her dreams. This morning, he reminded her the dream had turned into a nightmare. "What's so good about it?"

Trey sat opposite her at the small table in the hotel restaurant and placed his breakfast in front of him. "Buffet is great. Is coffee all you're havin'?" he asked.

She could hear the clink of his knife on his plate. It was getting on her nerves. She moved the paper so he could see how angry she was. "Could you take your little plate and go somewhere else?"

"Could." He pushed a forkful of sausage and egg into his mouth. "Not gonna."

She leaned across the table. "You are a damned stalker, aren't you?"

Trey just smiled as he chewed. His cheek bulged with eggs and sausage. His beautiful lips glistened with grease or butter—something that looked delicious and kissable.

Byggie despised herself for wanting to be his napkin.

Trey finished the small glass of orange juice. "I'm going for some more juice. Wanna refresh on that coffee?" he offered genially.

Byggie snapped her newspaper back in front of her face.

"Got it," he said. He was gone only a few moments. "Look, if it makes you feel any better," he began, taking his seat once more, "I had to take a cold shower when I got back to my room last night."

It made her feel a little better, but she wasn't about to let on.

"Didn't work," he sighed. "I got in the bed and just started thinkin' about that kiss. Damn woman you can kiss. Anybody ever tell you that?"

Byggie was no longer paying any attention to the words on the paper, but she didn't admit it.

"Anyway, the more I thought about you'," he continued as if there wasn't a newspaper between them, "the hornier I got and the next thing you know I got a tent goin' in the bed and nothin' to do with it."

Curiosity made her drop the corner of her paper. "A tent?"

"Yeah." He pulled his napkin over his hand and lifted his thumb beneath it. "A tent."

"Oh. You had a hard on," she stated crisply. "Serves you right."

"Needless to say, I had to go in the bathroom and give myself some much needed relief."

Byggie smiled behind her paper. "Like I said—serves you right."

"I thought about knockin' on your door about a half dozen times. Once, I even started toward the elevators."

"Don't tell me." She lowered the paper, giving up the pretense of reading altogether. "God spoke to you and told you to turn around."

He lifted an eyebrow and cocked his head. "God doesn't speak to me. Not so's I can hear Him anyway. But I knew it wasn't the right thing to do."

Byggie sighed and put the paper aside. "Listen. Whatever issues you've got, Trey, from now on, I just need you to leave me out of them, okay? This little game you're playin' isn't fun all right? I don't have time for it."

"You're right. I really need to get myself straight before I..." he let the thought drop. "Anyway, I'm willing to keep things strictly business between us. That marriage proposal thing—"

"Psshh. That was no proposal," Byggie jumped in quickly.

"Anyway..."

It was a response, she noted, not an agreement.

"I figure I'm all right with us being friends for now. How about you?" He offered his hand across the table.

"Fine." In a way it was a relief. She'd almost lost her mind over one kiss last night. She'd all but begged the man to come in to her room and sleep with her. What if he had? It wouldn't be good to have a man around who had so much influence over her. That kind of thing was dangerous.

"Solid." He rubbed his palms together "So, you ready to see my reports?"

"You really got them done?"

"Told you—I never miss a deadline."

Byggie pushed aside the remnants of her cold coffee and pored over his inspection reports. To his credit he stayed quiet the whole time—well he was a bit noisy about his eating, but at least he didn't speak.

"Looks like the building on West Washington will take the fewest cosmetic fixes."

"Yeah, but the one on Third has the best infrastructure."

"The one you caused water damage to with your brilliant evaporating screwdriver trick?" she asked wryly.

"No need to thank me." He spread his arms broadly as he got a smug grin on his face. "Now you know the sprinkler system works and that the circuits are too hot. You can argue down the price because if you can't plug in all your computers and phones without worry of overload then the place is no good to you. It'll cost plenty to fix that problem. Oh and you need to get some gas for the back up generator. It should've gone off when the power shut down. I checked it out when ya'll left. Generator's fine. Needs gas is all."

Byggie stared at the man incredulously. "You do know I have to pull up that carpet and replace every bit of it, right? You know how much that's going to cost?"

"Got a pretty good idea." He shifted to pull out his wallet and a card. "But I gotta cousin can put some new stuff in, won't cost near as much as those contractors you use right now."

Sighing, she took the card. "You've got an answer for everything, don't you, Mr. Daniels?"

"Mr. Daniels?" he started. "I thought we were friends."

"You're right." Byggie held her hands up in surrender. "Thank you, Trey. I'm impressed with how thorough these reports are. I'm going to take them and negotiate a nice price for OMG." She lifted her briefcase from the floor and placed the papers neatly inside her portfolio. She checked her watch. "I've got an appointment with my realtor in a half hour. I've gotta go."

Trey rose and offered his hand. "It was a pleasure doin' business with you," he said graciously.

"You too." Byggie shook his hand, but was immediately sorry. She remembered how good those hands had felt last night.

Trey pulled her closer, keeping a firm grip on her. "And just so you don't keep dissing it, my proposal was real," he said quietly. "I do intend to marry you and I do intend to tap that tight ass of yours first chance I get after the I do's."

His dark eyes were intense as he spoke. Byggie felt intense desire swirl between her legs in an instant. She really hated that he could do that to her. "I thought we weren't going to do this," she swallowed hard, trying to read his eyes. Was he crazy for real? Or was he just trying to drive her crazy?

Trey took a step closer. "Oh yeah. We are sho nuf gonna do this." His voice was a hoarse whisper. "Best get used to seein' me."

Byggie fought for control. "I don't have anything to say about this?"

His lips covered hers. "Yes. That's all you have to say."

It wasn't until he released her, that she could feel the tile beneath her feet and the hot flush of embarrassment for being an unwitting participant in a public display of affection.

"Have a safe trip back." Trey kissed her cheek before leaving the atrium.

Byggie collected her purse and briefcase that hung limply from her fingers now. She dodged glances of strangers self-consciously as she made her own way out of the area toward her room. Her panties were damp and she had to change them before heading out for her meeting.

Chapter Five

"So how you doin, son?"

It was the same question his mama asked him every Sunday when he visited her at the hospital. Juaneba Daniels amazed him. She never complained even though cancer was eatin' her alive and she only had a couple of months to live according to the doctors.

"Doin' all right, Mama." He pulled the bed table over and laid out the food he'd brought with him. I brought your favorite. An omelet and some biscuits from Shoney's down the street. Oh, and I brought you this pretty cactus from Phoenix."

"Oh, isn't that nice?" She turned the little pot in her trembling hands. "Always wanted to see Arizona. Heard they've got beautiful sunsets there."

"They do," Trey acknowledged, remembering how nice it had been to be with Byggie under a blazing purple and orange hued sky played to the sounds of Jazz. "It was surprisingly pretty considerin' it was desert. That's why I found that cactus. I thought they were all green."

"So did I," she said. "You're so good to me." She put the pot down next to her food. "And if this don't look delicious," she seemed genuinely pleased to see the food, but Trey knew she'd eat very little of it.

"If I had to eat another hospital meal, I would've screamed." She said the same thing every week even though Trey knew better. His mama loved the food here and the attention she received from all of the nurses. He guessed she'd worked hard enough all her life to deserve for someone to wait on her hand a foot for a while.

Trey brought out a white container with his favorite, pancakes and sausage and settled into the chair next to her bed. "So, what's the scoop around here?"

For a woman who was pretty much confined to her bed, his mama knew an awful lot about what was goin' on all around her.

"That pretty Mexican nurse that does the morning shift, Rosa, well she had to take a few days off. Turns out her son had a car accident—he goes to college out in Tennessee—didn't hurt himself, thank the good Lord—anyway, her replacement was an absolute monster. Every time you ask for somethin' she rolls her eyes, and makes those sucking noises with her tongue. You know how I hate sass. So by Tuesday, I'd had about enough of her attitude—"

"Took you that long?" Trey teased.

She shooshed him and gave a wave with her now bony hand. "I said to Nurse Sass, 'Now listen here, Miss Thang. We're all sick and dyin' around here and the last thing we need is a nurse who makes our last days on earth a livin' hell.'"

Trey chuckled and wiped at a drip of syrup at the corner of his mouth. "What'd she say?"

"I'll be darned if she didn't roll her eyes and stomp her way outta my room. Makes you wonder how she ever got a job around sick people."

"When does Rosa come back?"

"Oh she's back already. You can bet I tole her how much I appreciated her." She took a tiny bite of omelet and sat back against her pillow. "Mm. This is great, baby. Thank you."

They ate in silence a while, watching the television without sound. His mama loved to watch the news. The man whose house she cleaned for twenty years always was watching the news, that's where she got hooked. Her favorite channel was C-SPAN—pretty much the channel most likely to put you to sleep as far as Trey was concerned.

"They been talkin' about companies that are goin' to stop matching contributions to 401(k) accounts. You still got one a them at work, baby?" she asked.

"Yeah and it's losing money right now. Thing is, you don't lose money unless you pull it out right now. I figure I got time to let it ride. It'll come back up."

"Hmph. Sounds like gamblin' to me," Juaneba said a little breathless.

"What's the matter? You in pain?" He moved to her side.

"It's not bad, baby. Not bad."

"Why you wanna lie to me," he teased. "Press the button and get some a that good morphine. Go ahead."

"You know this stuff is highly addictive?" she chided.

"I know, but I swear I won't tell anybody my mama's a druggie, awright?" He put his hand in the air as if swearing in. "Now go ahead."

Reluctantly, she pushed the button. Almost immediately her breathing relaxed.

"That's better, isn't it? We both know you ain't scared of getting' addicted. You just don't wanna miss anythin' that's goin' on. Just 'cause you're nosey doesn't mean you need to suffer."

"Suffer?" she shot back sleepily. "This ain't nuthin'. Sufferin' is not havin' no grandbabies around to spoil." Her eyes were bright as she spoke. "Sufferin' is dyin' and leavin' you all alone, baby. I hate the thought of that."

Grief squeezed at his heart. Trey lifted her hand and pressed it to his lips. "I'll be awright, mama," he whispered onto her paper-thin skin. "Don't you worry about me." He hoped he convinced her, because he sure wasn't fooling himself. He had no idea what he'd do when she was gone. "Can I ask you somethin', Mama?"

"Sure, baby."

"You remember telling me that you wasn't the marryin' kind?"

"Yeah, baby." her eyes began to droop a bit as the medicine took effect. "What about it?"

"What made you say yes when Daddy proposed? I mean ya'll were married for twenty years before he died and I can't remember ya'll having anything in common."

Juaneba chuckled sleepily. "We didn't. He liked to run the street, go bowlin', play cards, run his mouth all night. I liked it better at home, cookin', makin' the house nice—except I always wanted to travel. I tole you that, didn't I?"

"Yeah, you did," he said.

"But yo Daddy and I had somethin' between us that neither one a us could deny."

"Love?" Trey asked.

She shrugged her frail shoulders. "More than that, baby. I can't really explain it. Just he was so sure he wanted me, is all. There's something 'bout that man...wantin' me so bad...got me all caught up in him." The drugs finished the job and she sailed off into a deep sleep.

Trey sat watching her for a while before letting his eyes wander to the small, brightly colored cactus. He wondered what Byggie was doin' right now.

Sitting back into the easy chair he folded his hands and thought about being married to the tiny, but powerful high-powered executive. He wondered if she would have babies with him.

Babies? Where'd that thought come from? He'd spent his entire adult life tryin' to make sure he didn't have babies with any of the women he slept with. On more than one occasion, he'd gotten on his knees and thanked the makers of Trojans brand condoms. 'Course that was BJ— Before Jesus.

Nowadays, he sank to his knees to thank God for pretty much anything good that happened to him—like his recent promotion at work. His boss said Byggie Quinn had everything to do with his decision. And most of all for his ever waning need for meaningless sex. He hadn't craved another woman since he'd met Byggie Quinn. And it was all right to want her since he had every intention of marrying her.

Better to marry than to burn, the Good Book said. Trouble was, every time Trey thought of Byggie the flames burned hotter so the wedding would have to be soon. But first things first. He had to get her to say 'yes.'

Trey lay his head back and let the hypnotic sound of the machines whirring and beeping lull him into drowsiness. In that moment between awake and asleep, it occurred to him what he had to do.

♂ ♥ ♀

"There's a Trey Daniels to see you, Ms. Quinn."

Byggie didn't know quite how to read the feeling in the pit of her stomach. By the time she'd arrived home from Phoenix she was furious at Trey Daniels. No man did this to her, played with her like she was some damned toy. Byggie wanted to make sure his boss knew he was never to work around her or her company ever again.

Maybe what she was feeling was guilt. She'd called his employer and told them that he'd done a fine job with her inspections, but that she was uncomfortable with his conduct. She refrained from providing more details. She hadn't want the man to lose his job...just lose her as a client. So why was he here now? To apologize? Cuss her out? That was more likely.

Well, she never backed down from a fight. "Send him in, Casey." She told her assistant then sank back against the wings of her ergonomic chair and propped her two hundred dollar heels on her desk. Whatever Trey Daniels wanted, this time she'd be ready for him. He was in her territory now.

Trey walked inside very relaxed, wearing that knock out grin of his and carrying a spectacular bouquet of flowers. Not many men could make a plain blue work shirt and Dickie's work pants look sexy. But Trey pulled it off somehow.

Byggie smiled. "Here to apologize?" she beat him to the punch.

Trey looked confused. "For what?"

Was he kidding? "You're the last person I expected to see today—or ever," she offered truthfully. "I told your boss I didn't want you coming around here anymore."

Trey frowned. "Really? According to him, you raved about me. He gave me a promotion. Said your recommendation put me over the top."

It was Byggie's turn to be surprised. She removed her feet from the desk and sat up in her chair. "I guess I did say you did a good job on those reports. I negotiated a great deal on the property. But, I told him I was uncomfortable around you." It was all she could think to say at this turn of events.

"Hm." He studied the flowers a bit longer. "With this promotion I don't get to support this site anymore, so if you really don't want me coming here, that worked out for you." His eyes threw accusations her way.

"It's for the best, Trey." She tried to remain matter-of-fact. "So the flowers were—"

"To thank you," he finished her thought. He glanced at the flowers, and bounced them around a bit. "Guess there was no need, huh?"

Guilt started to creep into her gut. Byggie fought against it. "No." Her tone hard, but she was determined to hold the upper hand.

"Hm." He stood there assessing her for a long moment. Finally, unceremoniously, he dropped the gorgeous bouquet into her wastebasket.

Byggie was beginning to grow damp under her armpits. "Look, if there's nothing else, I really do need to get back to work." She pulled open a file and pretended to be interested in the fact, figures and charts on the page.

"All right," Trey finally spoke. "I'll let you do that, but remember—you owe me."

"For what?"

Trey walked deliberately over to her desk, leaned over, and lowered his voice to a whisper. "For stealing my damn heart." His eyes sought hers and stared straight into her soul.

For all her bravado, Byggie could feel her upper hand slipping under his magnetic gaze. She struggled to regain control. "See, it's this craziness that made me tell your boss to reassign you. If I make another call, you could lose your job."

Trey chuckled and perched himself on the edge of her desk. "You wouldn't do that."

Byggie narrowed her gaze in warning. "Don't be too sure."

"Then what's a brothah gonna do when we get married?" Trey reached out to caress her hand. "Let you pay all the bills yourself? Now that just don't seem right."

His lips touched her palm and Byggie about wet herself. What was it about this man that made her react this way? She pulled her hand away and tucked it beneath crossed arms. Sitting back, she tried to slow her breathing, even the pace of her erratic heartbeat. "We're not getting married. We don't even know one another and besides that, if we don't sleep together how will we know it'll be good between us?"

The smile slipped from Trey's lips. He stood and offered her a hand. "Come here." His tone was deep and sexy, his eyes darkened with lust.

There was some sort of spell he was working on her, why else did she stood at his command? Why else would she walk into his open arms? Byggie didn't take orders from anybody, but there was something inviting about the way he held out his arms and the way his eyes roamed her body like a fat man at a buffet. \

In an instant, she was captured in his embrace, enticed by the smell of his cologne and held captive in his dark, lustful gaze. His leg slid smoothly between hers, hiking up her skirt, grazing her panties as his hot breath and warm lips trailed kisses along her neck. The way he made her feel was sweet agony—raw ecstasy.

He pulled her closer and whispered to her. "Can you feel that?"

She could. His penis was hard and long beneath her pelvis. "Yes," she responded, hoping like hell today he'd end his stupid streak of celibacy.

"Nowadays, this only happens when I think of you or when you're around. You don't have to wonder if it'll be good between us, baby, I'll offer you my guarantee."

"You sure think an awful lot of yourself, Trey Daniels."

Trey slid her closer, his thigh between hers hitting the exact right spot to send shudders through her body and make her cry out.

"Oh, baby, I like it when you make that sound," he groaned, bending his head to give her a long, deep, slow kiss. The kind of kiss you only see at the movies, the kind that made you wish for a man who could make you feel on the inside the way the actress seemed to look on the outside—delirious.

Delirious was exactly how Byggie felt when Trey's kiss ended. Delirious and warm and giddy and—completely vulnerable. Byggie hated feeling vulnerable. "See, this is why this thing you want—this relationship you keep asking for, won't work," she spoke, softly, honestly.

"What're you talkin' about, woman?" Trey looked completely confused. "This here is clicking on all cylinders as far as I can tell." He gestured back and forth between them.

Byggie backed her way out of his arms, missing their warmth immediately. "You make me feel weak," she admitted, "out of control. "I don't get drunk, I don't do drugs, I don't even take gas at the dentist because I hate the feeling of being out of control."

"What's wrong with being out of control every once in a while?" he countered, taking a step in her direction.

Shrugging, Byggie backed further away. "When people lose control, they act different. Some act stupid, some act like they don't have morals and others...others beat the shit out people they love and then act like they couldn't help it because they were under the influence."

To his credit, Trey chose to say nothing at that little revelation of her past. "My father beat my mother to death when my sister Selena was eleven and I was nine. We were taken out of our home and forced to live with strangers. We fostered in different homes until we graduated high school. I got a scholarship and went off to college and asked Selena to come live with me. But she went and fell in love with a man who treated her like crap then messed around on her. But even now she thinks about going back for more."

"What's that got to do with you and me?" Trey asked. "Just because things didn't work out with your parents or your sister doesn't mean it can't for us. My mom and dad were married fifteen years before he died. He never a lifted a hand to her, always treated her like a lady. My mama's still crazy about him...can't wait to see him when she...when she passes."

It didn't escape Byggie's attention that his voice cracked when he talked about his mama. "I'm a cynic. A realist. A skeptic, call me what you like, Trey. It's just that you've put some kinda magic spell on me and I don't trust you not to use it again."

His smile returned. "Well, you trusted me enough to tell me about it.

That's something, isn't it?"

Byggie shrugged, not knowing what to say about that.

Trey reached inside his pocket and brought out a red velvet box adorned with a delicate white bow.

Panic streaked through Byggie like a bullet train. "That's not what I think it is, is it?"

Trey pushed it into her hand. "If you think it's a promise, then yes."

"A promise?" Byggie stared at the box. It seemed to grow hot in her shaky hand.

"Yeah. A promise that I'll marry you one day. That I'll love, honor and cherish you from that day forward."

"You'd better be kiddin' me," she warned, her voice hoarse.

"I'll also promise you the best sex you ever had." Trey kissed her on her cheek and began to back toward the door slowly. "But if you do decide to marry me, Byggie Quinn, it's forever. We ain't havin' none of this divorce crap. So think about it. Come to church with me Sunday, we'll spend the day together. You can meet my mama."

Swallowing past a big lump, Byggie felt her panic grow. "You want me to meet your mom?" That was a pretty big step.

"Don't worry if she'll like you or not. She won't. Doesn't think anyone's good enough for me." He was smiling that dazzlingly handsome smile as he headed out the door.

Byggie tried to find the right words to yell at him, but came up empty. Heart pumping, she sat back in her chair and stared at the little red box. What idiot of a man left a ring—because certainly that's what was in there—with a woman who'd just told him she didn't want to see him anymore?

She stared at the box off and on for the rest of the day. She stared at it as she answered e-mails, tapped it up and down as she pored over reports, and spun it between her fingers as she sat on conference calls. But she didn't open it.

She packed her laptop and files, intending to put together a report at home over a frozen dinner.

Byggie stared at the box a moment longer, before picking it up and turning it in her hand. She couldn't leave it here, she reasoned. She had to get the thing back to Trey before he got the wrong idea and thought she was actually considering his back-ass-ward proposal.

Finally, she dumped the box into her trendy bag then retrieved the vase of flowers from her desk. She'd pulled them from the wastebasket and placed them in water moments after Trey had left. Not because they meant anything to her she'd lied to herself, but because it would be a shame to waste something so pretty.

♂ ♥ ♀

Despite the distraction of the heavenly scented flowers, the still unopened red velvet box, and the lingering scent of Trey Daniel's cologne on her skin, Byggie managed to finish her report at exactly eight thirty-six—only seconds before Selena dashed inside her apartment.

"He called, Byggie. I dunno know what to do." Selena whipped off her coat and was sitting across from her sister at the small dinette set in two seconds flat.

Sighing, Byggie packed up her folders and placed them back into her briefcase before her sister could start sorting them into neat stacks. "First of all, you've gotta chill, Sis. Second, who called?"

"Adrian."

"What's that Big Head Baby Daddy of yours want now?" She pulled her legs up and crossed them in her chair.

"He wants to get back together." Selena covered her mouth with her hands. Her eyes were bright with hope and excitement.

Byggie's heart broke. "You're not seriously thinking about taking him back, are you?"

"He said he'd go to counseling at the church this time," Selena looked happy for the first time in a long time.

Byggie didn't want to burst her bubble, but she'd been there the last time the dirty dog had left her for another woman. How long had it taken Selena to get out of bed? To start taking her kids to football and basketball games again? To keep from collapsing in tears every time she thought of the man? "Selena, honey," she started cautiously, "remember how you felt the last time he said he was coming back, but didn't."

"I know, I know. But this time he's changed."

Taking her hands, Byggie looked into her sister's desperate, but pretty eyes. "I know you want to believe that, probably need to believe it, but how do you know it, honey?"

"I prayed on it, Byg. The Lord gave me peace about it."

Byggie dropped her head. What was up with this blind faith that everyone around her kept on about. "Okay, but listen, before you take him back, make him prove to you that he's serious."

"How do I do that?" Selena seemed interested.

"Don't sleep with him, make him wait."

Selena's brow furrowed. "Why would I do that? It's been so lonely sleeping without him, Byg. You don't know how much I've missed him. All I can think about is having his arms around me and never letting go."

"I get it, Selena," and she did. Since that afternoon, she'd all but craved the feeling of Trey's strong arms embracing her, "but your marriage has to be more than a physical thing. The two of you have to find out about one another again, to find out what you like about one another. But both of you have to be in love." Byggie stopped and thought about the words coming out of her mouth. Was this what Trey was trying to do? Make them force one another to find out more about the other without having sex get in the way? Her eyes glanced at the box that was now sitting on top of her table. Maybe he wasn't so crazy after all.

"Why do you love him, Selena?" Byggie asked, truly interested in the answer. What made a woman want to give her life to a man for the rest of her life?

"Why?" Selena looked surprised at the question, but stared off into the distance as she formed her answer.

"I know you think love makes me blind, Byggie, but it doesn't. Really it's kind of the opposite. I see everything about that man so clearly. All of his faults, the way he tries to act so macho all of the time, even the reason he chases after other women. It's because he hasn't found what he needs inside himself. He sees this man in the mirror and every day finds him inadequate—not good enough. He's been working at a job he hates making enough money to keep in kids in hundred and fifty dollar tennis shoes, but he thinks he's a failure because he owns a Ford instead of a Lexus, he has a three-bedroom house instead of mansion. He's got friend who made it to the NBA and all he can do is squeak out a few games at the YMCA. All he's trying to do is erase the pain when he goes chasin' after them bimbos.

"But when he looks at me, there's real love in his eyes, I feel it in my soul. We validate each other's existence by saying 'it's okay for you to be you and me to be me'." Her eyes came back into focus. "I'm explaining it badly, but when you really connect with someone, you'll know what I mean."

"I saw what it did to you when he left you, Selena. You're telling me he can still validate you and make you feel loved after that?"

Her eyes teared up as she spoke this time, "When he betrayed me, Byggie. It hurt like hell and I sure don't want that to ever happen again." She wiped tears from her cheeks. "But when he loves me, he loves me so right that the world doesn't exist outside of his arms. Without him, I can't figure out how to move on. I'm tired of trying to figure out how."

"Oh, honey," Byggie took her into her arms and listened to her soft sobs. In her heart of her hearts, she knew this is why she was fighting Trey Daniels so hard. She wanted badly for the attraction between them to be just about sex. That would make things easy. But he wanted more than that. He wanted love—a commitment. Byggie knew that it would be too easy to give in to Trey. No other man had affected her the way he did.

As her sister cried in her arms, Byggie looked again at the little red box and knew more than ever, that it, and the man who gave it to her, had to get out of her life once and for all.

Chapter Six

It had been two full weeks in an office job and life sucked. Trey was ready to go back to doing maintenance. His days were filled with meetings, teleconferences and meetings with clients about their needs. He didn't like that the same guys who'd gone out to have a beer with him two weeks ago were avoiding him now and whispering the word "management" behind his back like it was a dirty word.

His mama's doctor had called that Saturday to tell him that the chemotherapy had done nothing to slow the progress of the cancer as it ate away at her liver, kidneys and now, her brain. Trey was making arrangements with the hospice to care for her and keep her pain manageable for her remaining days, possibly weeks, of life.

He dropped his head into his hands and fought back tears. Every time he thought about losing her his heart filled with so much pain it felt like his chest would explode. It had been the two of them for so long, he didn't know what he'd do without her.

Squeezing the wetness from his eyes, he opened his mail to take his mind off his misery. He picked up a FedEx package. He ripped it open, tilted it and out tumbled the red box he'd given to Byggie. There was no note with it. Nothing.

"Shit," he cursed and shoved the box into his pocket. She hadn't even opened it. The least she could've done was wrote a note saying "Kiss my ass" or something. He'd looked for her at church the day before. She hadn't showed.

Well, if she didn't want him, forget her. He was tired of trying to make a relationship out of nothing. Besides, he didn't have the strength. He'd been fighting depression night and day since the doctor had told him the news. His mama was gonna die. And despite all his prayers and positive thinking, there wasn't a thing he could do stop it. He shoved his fist in his mouth to muffle his sobs.

"Oh no. Oh, I'm so sorry."

Trey hadn't seen her approach his cubicle. He swiped at his eyes and struggled to compose himself.

Byggie reached for his hand over the Fed Ex package. "I didn't mean to hurt your feelings."

He pulled back quickly. "This isn't about you," he bit out angrily, "so save your apology."

"Oh." She sat back quietly waiting for further explanation.

Trey didn't offer one.

Understanding dawned on her face. "Is it your mom?"

Trey was touched that she remembered. He nodded, but offered nothing further, not trusting his voice.

"Is she..." she struggled to find the words, "Did she pass?"

"No." He avoided her eyes, feeling the sting of tears pressing at the back of his own. "But the chemo didn't work."

"I really am sorry," she said softly, rising to her feet. "I didn't mean to bother —"

"Stay." He hated that it sounded like begging. "No. Nevermind." He waved her off.

Byggie bit her lip and shifted her weight back and forth. She looked good in her gray business suit and blue silk blouse. But then, she always looked good. "Wanna have lunch? I came to explain why I gave the ring back."

Trey blew out a long breath. Did he really want to hear this? Naw, but he didn't feel like sitting in that damned cube crying about his mama either. "All right. I know a place down the street." He hadn't eaten in like two days, or something.

The wind was soft and warm as they walked toward the deli he liked. He wished he could find words for a polite conversation, but they wouldn't come.

Byggie placed her soft hand in his.

Trey's heart leapt at the small gesture and he wrapped her fingers around hers tightly. There didn't seem to be a need for words after that.

When they arrived at the deli, she asked what was good and he told her he was partial to the Rueben sandwich and the Cobb salad. She ordered the salad. He ordered the sandwich. They sat a small table near the window and watched people walk by as they ate. Then, out of the blue, she asked, "Tell me about your mother. What lasting lesson did she teach you?"

Trey thought about the question as he chewed down the cheek full of corned beef and bread. "I learned never to say the word 'can't' around her."

"Why? What would she do?"

"Well, one day I told her I was too sick to go to school...this was when I was in high school. She figured out pretty quick I wasn't sick at all, just didn't wanna go to class. She asked me why and I told her because I didn't get my paper done and I was gonna fail the class no matter what.

"She told me to get my sorry ass out of bed. Said she wasn't going to work until I did."

Byggie giggled. "What'd you do?"

"Well, I knew I was in trouble then. Mama always went to work, come hell or high water. So, I got up and went to the kitchen where she was waitin. Before she could say anything I told her the class was at 1:00 and I couldn't get my paper done because I didn't have enough research on the topic...the economies of China and America or something. I had much attitude.

She told me, 'If you gonna fail, Trey Jermaine Daniels, then fail fabulously. Don't half ass it.'" She made me write that paper then and there and told me to write what I remembered and make up the rest.

"Fail fabulously, huh?" Byggie chuckled. "So did you?"

"Naw." Trey sipped his Coke. "Got a B minus on the paper, passed the class with a C."

"Good lesson," Byggie nodded.

"What about you?" Trey asked. "You remember much about your mama?"

Byggie nodded and pushed her salad around the plate a bit with her fork. "I remember thinking that she was very sweet—too sweet for my dad. And I remember the way her back looked, all straight and rigid when she would get between Daddy and us. Especially when I was arguing with him, which was all the time. I didn't like that she got between us. I wanted him to hit me like he hit her just so I had an excuse to hit him back.

"At night, I'd plan exactly how I'd do it, shove his nose with my palm, poke his eyes with my fingernails, knee him in the groin then kick him in the head when he finally fell to the ground. I was angry when he went to jail for murdering my mom, because I knew I'd never get the chance."

"Seriously?" Trey looked at her sideways. "I didn't know you had such a mean streak, woman. It's probably a good thing you sent me back my ring." He pulled the box from his pocket.

Her mood changed immediately. "About that—"

"That's all right. I don't wanna hear it," he said dismissively. Trey pushed aside what remained of his Reuben. Placing the box on the table between them, he pulled at the white ribbon until it came free of its bow and slid down the red velvet. He opened the box and admired the sparkle of the square cut diamond surrounded by dozens of smaller stones. "Did you wanna look at it before I take it back?" He turned it so she could see it clearly. "I thought I made a pretty good choice."

Byggie's eyes grew round as saucers as she stared at the ring. "It's beautiful," she finally managed. "I knew it would be."

"You know, you could try it on if you want," Trey pulled the treasure from the box and reached for her left hand. It was shaking. He was happy. That meant he was having some effect on her.

"You're not fighting fair," she whined.

"I'm not trying to take advantage of you." He said the words sincerely as he gazed into the wonder of her dark brown eyes. "All I want is what we have." He pushed the ring onto her finger. It fit perfectly. "There's some seriously strong chemistry between us, Byg and I don't want it to stop. I want more nights with Jazz in the air. I want more lunch dates where we just sit and talk. And I want someone who doesn't make me feel weak when

I cry. I want you, Byggie Quinn. Be my wife, but do it because you know you want it."

"Aw, hell, Trey. I want for this to be for right. I want it so bad, it's just so hard to trust… Promise me you're not crazy." Her eyes searched his.

"I'm only crazy when it comes to you. So what do ya say? You ready to do this?"

"What if it doesn't work out?" she asked.

"Then let's fail fabulously, baby. Let's not half-ass it."

She closed her eyes and took a deep breath. When her eyes opened, they were wet with tears. "I'll marry you, Trey. But you darned well better make good on all these promises, you hear me?"

The wedding was held in the hospital chapel so Trey's mama could see him married. Byggie had fallen instantly in love with the sharp-tongued, sharp-minded old woman and had cried as hard as Trey when she passed a week later.

Selena had come with her bad boys and their Daddy, but she looked ten years younger and way happier as she basked in the undivided attention he was paying her. Maybe it would work out this time, Byggie decided.

It had taken a few weeks for Trey to finish taking care of his mama's bills and putting her house up for sale. Plus, they both had to put in for vacation. They were very lucky to find a last minute vacation package to Jamaica and so here they were, husband and wife, in Ocho Rios.

Trey had been holding her hand, caressing and kissing her the entire trip. He'd built the anticipation of this moment up until all Byggie could think about was how quickly she could get him inside of her.

Her heart was stampeding in her chest. She placed a hand over her chest trying to calm it down as she stared at herself in the hotel bathroom mirror. She ran fingers through her short, sassy hair and looked down her body, hoping the lacey corset, sheer stockings and clear high heels would drive Trey crazy. She sucked in a deep breath and threw the door open to the bedroom and struck a seductive pose.

Trey stopped midway through his pacing. He stood straighter, stared open-mouthed at her. Finally, a small "daaaamn" made its way out of his mouth.

Byggie smiled at his reaction, but was distracted by the handsome planes of his chest that peeked out beneath his black satin robe. He had on matching drawstring pajama bottoms. The smell of soft cologne and hard sex drifted across the short space between them.

She stepped back into the bathroom and motioned him forward with a crook of her finger.

He was quick to obey the silent command.

Byggie was in his strong arms a moment later, her mouth open to his needy assault. She felt herself being lifted out of her heels as Trey pressed his hard erection against her belly.

Byggie grew deliriously light-headed as they tasted and explored one another, wondering if she'd ever felt this good in any man's arms before. There was something more than sex going on here. There was a meeting of two lives, the melding of two bodies. She moaned and let her head fall back as his kisses moved to her breasts and his tongue warmed her nipples beneath the lace.

"Oh, Trey," she said over and over again. Byggie wound her stockinged legs around his narrow waist.

Trey's fingers drifted between her legs and finding nothing to stop him, pushed his way inside her folds.

Byggie cried out again, clinging to his shoulders as he pushed his fingers in and out of her as his thumb circled her clitoris in heavenly circles. It was too much. It was not enough. Byggie moved with the rhythm of his hand, growing greedier by the second.

She didn't know when it had happened, but her breasts were now bare as Trey's hot mouth alternated between them. His hand never stopped pushing in and out, circling around and around, making her cry out over and over.

Byggie's breaths came in short bursts as she pushed against his hand and came to the brink of climax. Before she exploded, Trey backed her up to the long sink and she felt the cool granite beneath her naked bottom. As his hands released her, the memory of their first encounter flashed through her brain. Her concern quieted quickly as she watched him pull the string on his pajama bottoms. Black satin fell in pools to the floor and Trey's erection stood magnificent in the lighting of the fancy bathroom.

Byggie wanted it inside her to finish the job, but couldn't resist sliding her fingers up and down the soft skin that covered his hard length.

His moans of pleasure brought her down from the sink and onto her knees. She couldn't fit his entire length inside her mouth, but took as much of him in as she could.

He sucked breath between his teeth and gripped her shoulders hard as his head fell back. "That's good, baby. That's so good," he chanted.

It made her happy to satisfy him, to make him feel as good as he was making her feel. Byggie sucked up and down the length of his chocolate hard-on and reached around to cup his hard butt. He filled his fingers with her hair and moaned with more urgency. "Oh my God," he whispered.

Byggie blew on the hot, wet chocolate hard on and Trey cried out again. She smiled. She'd never had this much fun pleasing a man before. Probably, because none had been as vocal or thankful before.

"That's enough, that's enough, baby." Trey reached down and slid her up to standing. His belly hairs tickled her stomach. "You're gonna make me come."

"Isn't that the point?" Byggie stared up at the gorgeous black man that was now her husband.

"It is the point," Trey agreed. "But I want you to come first."

"Really?" she looked into his eyes. They held warmth and sincerity and something more. "Do you love me, Trey?" she asked suddenly, not knowing where the question had come from.

"Since the moment your fine behind walked past me in the church aisle," he said without skipping a beat. "Don't act like you didn't know," he whispered in her ear before lifting her and carrying her toward the bed.

He lay her down and bed felt cool after being near the heat of his body. Trey slowly pulled the corset the rest of the way off her body. All that was left was the sheer black crotch-less stockings. "Those can stay," he said with a grin. "That shit is sexy as hell.

Byggie felt heat and wetness form between her legs.

"'Course I need a little more room to operate," he said as he gently moved her knees further apart. "Perfect." He ducked his head between her thighs.

"Ohhh!" Byggie clutched large handfuls of comforter into her fists as Trey worked some sort of blissful magic with his tongue. "What're you trying to do, kill me?"

Trey looked up at her, wearing that crooked grin. "Naw, babe. Just trying to make good on some promises I made. How'm I doin' so far?"

He was doing great, but she couldn't tell him that, he'd get a big head for real. "I ain't complainin'," she offered non-commitally.

"Hmmmm." Trey frowned. "Guess it's time for the big guns, then." To her delight, he directed that magnificent erection toward her throbbing opening and pushed inside with one strong, stroke.

The explosion inside of her had her grabbing the comforter, arching herself off the bed and screaming his name at the top of her lungs. He rode her fast, pushing inside her again and again, making her climax go on for long seconds, long enough for Trey to find his own ecstasy. He tensed, cried out and spasmed violently inside her until finally, they both collapsed into a shuddering, panting, sweaty pile on the bed.

"Jesus, that was good," Trey panted into the pillow. "What're the chances of us doing that again?"

Byggie could still feel him throbbing between her legs. She stared past his shoulder to the ceiling. Her vision was a bit blurred. "Just as soon as they room stops spinning," she said, surprised at how much she still wanted him.

"Thank you," he whispered. His breathing slowed, his weight grew heavy on top of her since he didn't bother to roll off.

Funny, she didn't mind at all. She ran her hands up and down the smooth dark skin of his back. A moment later the buzz of his soft snores filled the air.

A soft breeze blew from the ocean and into their open balcony doors. The sound of the waves lapping rhythmically in the distance added a sense of calm and peace to the late afternoon. Happier than she'd ever been, Byggie Daniels fell into a contented sleep beneath her husband.

Trey awoke suddenly in the night. It took him a moment to realize where he was. But soon took in the sounds of the ocean and let his eyes adjust to the dimly lit room. It took less time for him to become aware of the soft warmth of Byggie beneath him and grow hard with desire. It had taken an incredible amount of will power to keep her out of his bed before their marriage. But now that she was his wife, he planned to make up for lost time.

He kissed her cheek. A slight smile lifted her lips, but she was still soundly asleep. "You are so fine," he whispered, kissing her lips, her eyes, her neck. By the time he reached the soft mounds of her breasts, he could hear her breaths catching and could feel her moving beneath him.

"What time is it," she asked sleepily.

"Time for seconds," he said, letting his tongue roll lazily around a hard nipple before taking it into his mouth.

"Mmmm. I didn't think you had it in you," she teased.

"Don't worry about me, babe. For your sake, I hope the room's stopped spinning because I can't wait much longer." To prove his point, he pushed himself into her hot, warm folds.

She rose up to take him in like she did before.

It felt so good, Trey had to stop to gather control before continuing. He lifted himself off her chest to get a deeper thrust. Why'd he wanna go and do that? It felt too good. So good he about lost his mind.

Byggie liked it to. She said as much before she pushed her pelvis up to meet him, stroke for stroke. "That's it, Trey. Right there, keep hitting it right there," she pushed with greedy urgency.

Trey bit his bottom lip and did his best to hit that spot every time. 'Cause the harder he hit it, the more she squeezed herself around him. The more she squeezed, the better it felt. He'd always enjoyed sex. Always. But with Byggie the experience was something new. They talked to own another, teased with another, pleased one another as their bodies connected. Each time he moved inside her, it was as if he was becoming a part of her, a part of her life, not just a moment in her life. It was the connection he had to her that was making this special. He wondered if

Byggie felt the same way.

"Oh, Trey, Trey, Trey..." She was bucking beneath him now, pulling the covers taut over his bottom, screaming his name.

Trey smiled, loving the way she screamed, loving how unashamed and free she was as she wrapped her legs around him and instructed him to give her what she wanted.

He'd prided himself on making women scream before, but now, with Byggie all he wanted was to make her happy. Lord knew he was a having a great time.

"Now, Trey. I'm coming now. Hit me now," she pleaded and pulled him deeper.

"All right, baby. Here we go. Hold on." Trey couldn't control himself anymore, didn't want to. Not when she was going crazy like that beneath him. He rose to his knees, lifted her bottom in his hands and thrust hard. His hips slapped playfully against hers in rapid succession. His eyes were glued to her face, watching as she gasped for air, called his name and finally opened her eyes.

Their eyes locked, making time stand still.

Trey's heart pounded hard in his chest. It was full for the first time in his life. "I love you," he said.

"I love you, too," she whispered hoarsely.

And suddenly, the sex became surreal.

They moved together gazing into each other's eyes. He released her bottom and moved to intertwine their fingers. Trey's blood grew hot, his head felt light, and his entire body buzzed with electricity. He'd never felt this way before, never.

"Trey?" Byggie's eyes looked glazed in the dim moonlight that filled the room.

"Yeah, baby."

"If I forget to tell you after—"she caught her breath, "f-f-for the record, you're incredible at this."

Trey couldn't stop the smile. "So are you, babe." He kissed her gently on her lips. "You're my Chocolate Decadence." He began to move with more urgency.

Byggie panted and moaned, "Okay, all right, okay," until finally, she arched hard beneath him. Her head moved backward into the pillow, her eyes squeezed tight with the intensity of her orgasm.

She tightened around him, growing warmer and wetter. Trey couldn't hold back a second longer. Plunging deep, he buried himself to the hilt inside her and felt every drop of his essence force its way out. From that moment on, everything he had, heart, body and mind, belonged to her. Maybe it always had.

His soul he left for God whom he thanked that night for letting him see what he truly desired. By some miracle, he'd been able to take a moment and make it into a real relationship and he'd completely lost his need to look, touch, taste or feel other women. No one had been more surprised than his mentor, Danny back at the church.

"You were right, Mama," he said to the darkened room. "Persistence pays." The wind blew the curtains inward as if in response. "Anyway, I hope you're doin' all right up there and that you're not feelin' any more pain," he continued. "And if you happen to see Dad, tell him I said 'hey.'"

The sound of island music and ocean waves drifted up from the beach. A beach Trey suddenly wondered if they'd ever see. He wasn't sure if he'd be lettin' Byggie out of the hotel room for the next seven days. He smiled remembering how good their first two rounds

Mr. Telephone Man
By
Barbara Keaton

Other Titles by Barbara Keaton
Love For All Seasons
Nights Over Egypt
Cupid
Blaze
By Design
Homeland Heroes & Heroines Anthology Vol. 2 (Wishing For Tomorrow)
An Unfinished Love Affair
All I Ask

Chapter One

"What do you mean the building hasn't been wired?" Victoria Morrison jumped up from the seat, its back slammed angrily against the thick glass plate, and began to pace around the office like a panther. She forced herself to control her anger. Actually, she wanted to scream like a banshee for already the project was nearly $3 million in cost overages, regardless of the fact the project was a year ahead of schedule and there would be a bonus four times that amount. Still.

"That wiring must go in before anyone even thinks of mixing dour rock and plaster." She blew out, raking her hands over her long black pony tail. "Bobby, I suggest you find that Mr. Mays and get this issue solved now. It seems as if he's got a cadre of incompetent folks working for him. Tell him if I have to find someone else I will not be pleased."

Vic hung up the phone and hooked it back on her waist, then she looked across her expansive office to the small scale model of the building she and her sister, Maxine, were in the process of developing. This project was coming in on time or she was going make sure there was hell to pay. She walked back to her desk and sat in her large leather chair.

The feel of her cell phone vibrating on her hip snatched her attention. She looked down at the caller id and frowned. It was Scott.

Putting her powder blue Timberlands encased feet on her desk she answered the phone. "Yes, Scott?" She had tried just about everything she knew, short of a shot gun, to get him to move on with his life. They had dated for nearly two years and during that time Scott had talked a lot about them getting married, combining their lives and their love of construction. And just as Vic began to warm up to the idea of possibly marrying him, she'd caught him in bed with his business partner. So much for thinking about getting married.

But what surprised her most was that she had dared to ask him why he found it necessary to sleep with another woman. While admittedly she had been smitten with Scott, found him handsome and quite social, she had not felt that spark Max was always talking about. So she was not quite ready for the response he'd given. He had told her he needed a woman who was a little more giving with her emotions. Vic was surprised by his admission. But when he added that she wasn't as feminine as he'd like, she was truly outdone. Admittedly, she wasn't into wearing frilly stuff twenty-four hours a day, but she didn't consider herself masculine—she just worked in a masculine industry.

Not prone to dramatics, Vic had wanted to slap Scott upside his head; instead, she straightened her back and walked out of his life without another word. That had been a year ago.

When she ran into him at the monthly meeting of Black Contractors Inc. last week, he'd started calling her daily asking could they at least be friends. To her, that wasn't something she was able to do and was quite unhappy that he even felt she owed him that much. Hell, she fumed; she didn't owe him a damned thing! So to answer his question, as Madea would say: Hell to the naw!

"Scott, I'm really busy today." She sighed loudly when what she wanted to say to him was "find you some business." Vic held the phone for several more moments as Scott droned on about an upcoming event and his needing a date. She knew the event, BCI's annual fundraiser, but she would be going it alone.

"So, how about it, Vic. Want to go together?"

"No, that won't be possible. I'm going with someone else." The lie slipped past her lips effortlessly. She didn't want to admit that she didn't have a date for the black-tie event. Why she couldn't admit to it she didn't know. "Hey, I've really got to run, Scott. Take care. Bye." She quickly rang off and then thought of just how much his words had affected her once she really sat down and gave them some serious thought.

Scott, like her first serious boyfriend, was attempting to change her. Had wanted her to become a stalker, knowing histrionics wasn't her bag. What she wanted was a man who accepted her for who she was and to bring out the one thing she hid well—her insatiable appetite. And just when she thought that maybe if she gave Scott a little nudge, the heat in the bedroom would turn up a notch or two. He was okay in bed, but his love of the missionary position and his refusal to engage in oral sex left Vic wondering. She had only had one man before him and he didn't know his way south, either. Vic was curious, but not to the point where she'd be the giver and never the receiver.

So, she'd thought she would surprise him, dressed only in a trench coat, armed with a "how to book," massage creams, and a few toys. Damn, had she been the one surprised. And then he had the audacious audacity to insinuate that she had driven him into the arms of that blonde, surgery queen she caught him hammering. Doggy style! Heck, the woman had had more plastic and enhancement surgery than Joan Rivers and still didn't look as good as Joan—and that was saying a whole lot.

Okay, she knew that she could be a little rough around the edges, but when you played in a man's world day in and day out, you had no choice but to inherit some balls of steel. But just the same, she wanted a man who could hold his own in and out of the bedroom—and Scott couldn't do either.

And to add to it there were those men who had been too intimated to approach her and had spread the rumor that maybe she like women. And while it often came with the territory, those who questioned her sexuality would be surprised. If they only knew.

Vic chuckled as she thought about the Rundu coffee table book she kept in her bedroom. The book boasted some of the most tasteful and gorgeous men in America dressed in absolutely nothing. She had often daydreamed about the various men, wondered how it would be to lie beneath, her legs wrapped around the man's waist, his face buried in her bosom, his lips and tongue paying homage to her nipples as their pelvis.

The sound of the phone broke into her daydream.

She cleared her throat before responding to her executive assistance. "Yes, Brooke?" She forced the images from her mind and gave her full attention to what Brook was saying. Vic nodded as Brooke went on to inform her of an issue at another construction site. "Okay, call Bobby and ask him to handle it for me and also tell him that I will reach out to Mays Communications."

Vic placed the phone on its receiver and then kicked off her work boots. She removed her sweat socks and then proceeded to slide her toes back and forth across the full, plush area rug that ran the length of floor under her desk. She closed her eyes, loving the feel of her bare feet on the rug as an image of a man massaging and kissing her feet appeared in her mind.

Vic moaned slightly and wiggled her toes; the nails painted a wicked red called "Hot Stuff." In her mind's eye she could feel the large hands travel slowly up her well-formed legs, caressing her calves. She couldn't wait for this project to be over. In six months she would head to Turks and Caicos for two weeks. Too bad she didn't have a steady date.

Her head came up at the knock then the sound of her office door opening. Only two people would knock and then enter without prompt: Dad and Max. This time it was Max.

"Hey, Vicki, how's it going?"

Vic watched as her big sister waltzed into the office, her sleek Versace summer linen pants suit fit her in all the right places, her shoulder length, honey streaked hair, hung perfectly about her pear shaped face. They favored enough that they could be twins, but Vic had dark, smoky grey eyes and Max's were hazel.

"Nice shoes, Maxi." Vic pursed her lips and then pointed her finger downward. "Girl, when did you get those?"

Max sat in the padded, cloth seat across from Vic's desk then placed her feet upon the desk.

"Macy's had this sale and you won't believe how much I paid for these."

"Are those Ferragamo's or Bandolino's?" Vic eyed the shoes—she and Max wore the same size. "You know you going to have to let me play in them at least once."

"They're Ferragamo's and I guess I can let you borrow them at least once." Max wagged her feet from left to right before crossing them at the ankle. "So, what's new around here?"

"That wireless contractor," Vic said as she moved from her office chair to one situated next to Max. "Can you believe we're ready to lay the rest of the foundation and put up the walls, and they haven't even begun to lay the fiber optic wiring for cable, phones and internet; nothing." Vic's eyes were wide. "This is going to put us behind schedule—and you know how much I hate that."

Max nodded. "Sure do. Just don't let it drive you nuts, okay, baby sis." She rubbed Vic's shoulder. "So, what else is going on?"

Vic smiled at the nickname her sister called her by. Three years separated them but that was about all. Victoria and Maxine had always been close and once they'd gone into business together they found themselves really leaning on each other's expertise.

Max was known as the beauty and the brains, in charge of massaging and hand-holding their clients, scoping out new possibilities for Morrison Construction, and managing all projects from start to finish. Vic was the hands on partner. She would scale the building, leaving no tile unturned, and then go about the day-to-day onsite operations, making sure codes and materials exceeded expectations. Vic could hang drywall, wire a place for electricity and lay foundation—there wasn't anything she couldn't do.

For over an hour, the two sisters talked about the various projects they'd had going on, with the residential/commercial development being one of their biggest. At the end of their impromptu meeting, the sisters hugged, with Max reminding Vic they were having dinner with their father at his favorite Italian restaurant.

"That's about it." She rose when Max did and walked her over to the door.

"I know you're going to be inspecting today's work but please don't be late." Max kissed Vic on the cheek. "I'll see you later."

"Will do." Vic returned the kiss.

She loved her job and her life was almost perfect. Vic was missing that one thing, though. She'd yet to experience what Max had called "toe curling, slap yourself," sex. She hadn't met the man to make her toes curl like a pretzel and then want to slap herself silly. And she wasn't sure if she ever would.

Vic sighed loudly as she returned to her desk and turned her attention to the construction site she was personally working on.

A twenty-story building with commercial business on the first two floors, the third through seventeenth floor would have three to four condo units each and the top floor a penthouse condo. The twelfth floor had been completed and featured three finished, fully furnished condos. Two of the condos were being used as models for potential buyers. The third condo, which was the largest, was Vic's home. Though the building was close to fifty-percent complete, nearly ninety-five percent of the units had been sold.

Her thoughts went to that Mays guy. She had looked him up on the internet and saw his picture. The older gentlemen's eyes and tan face didn't scream scammer. This was the man he father had worked with years ago, telling of Mr. Mays's migration to the US years ago.

Vic knew there had been a break down somewhere and she needed Mays Communications to step up their game. Because of them she didn't have cable. When she wanted to watch her flat screen, Plasma TV she had to play DVD's. And if she wanted to keep abreast of local and national news, she had to tune her radio to the local AM news station and hope for the best.

Vic had moved into the building for two reasons. It allowed her to keep a closer eye on its progress and she loved the layout of the condo, which occupied the entire floor. She'd had Max design the condo's floor plan and amenities with her in mind.

She thought about the rest of the project. Vic knew that her love of construction was rare among women, but she didn't mind. The crew she worked with, many who had been with Morrison's from the beginning, or their father's had, knew her to be a fair taskmaster and a perfectionist. Once she had tore out substandard drywall that had been installed by a subcontractor. She had amazed her crew when she took the sledge hammer and busted the walls before she personally purchased and then hung new drywall.

Vic turned her office chair to face the window and looked out on the beautifully landscaped grounds. She'd worked on the construction of the industrial park, which consisted of several buildings of various sizes intended for mixed use—from storage to manufacturing to office buildings.

She glanced at her watch. It was time for her to head over to the work site before showering for dinner with Max and Dad. Vic placed her work boots back on her feet and grabbed her hard hat. As she headed out the door, she caught her reflection in the mirror near the door. She paused and looked at herself, the minute freckles across her face, the dark eyes, and the round nose. Taking loose her hair, she allowed it to flow around her shoulders. Rarely, because of her work, did she wear her hear around her shoulders. This, she mused, would be something else she'd do once she gave up the day-to-day grind of construction. Vic shook her head. Who was she kidding? She would never give up the love of building something with her own hands.

Vic steadied her hard hat between her knees as she secured her hair with a barrette, shrugged her shoulders then headed out to the work site.

Chapter Two

"Papa, I mean no disrespect, but you should not have allowed Jose to even attempt to service the Morrison account. Why didn't you call me?" Lennox Mays said to his father as he sat down in a chair and pulled it close to the bed.

Miguel Mays had pulled a muscle in his back and due to the extreme pain was forced to take muscle relaxants and stay off his feet for two weeks. That was three weeks ago. His son, Lennox, had been out of town at the time the wiring for the Morrison account was scheduled to begin.

When Lennox returned he thought all was under control only to find out that they were on the brink of not only losing a lucrative account, but tarnish their stellar reputation. Mays Communications didn't believe in unsatisfied customers. In the forty years they'd been in the communications and telecommunications business, they hadn't had one unsatisfied customer. And Lennox wasn't about to start now.

"Who do I need to meet with?" he asked his father. He watched the man who had taught him everything, from how to be a savvy business man to a well respected human being, struggle to pull his self up into a sitting position.

"Easy, Papa, don't get up." Lennox said as he placed his hand gently on his father's shoulder. He gave a slight smile when his father settled back.

"Find Vic Morrison," he said. .

"Will do and where is Jose? I need the specs and to know who the installation crew will be before I head over there."

For an hour, Lennox talked and worked out the logistics with his father and younger brother, Jose, once he appeared at the family home. By the time they'd finished, the sun had begun its descent into the horizon.

Had he'd known about his father's condition, he would have left Miami sooner. He'd been there overseeing the installation of fiber optic wiring, telecommunications and cable wiring for a sports arena. "I'm going to head over to the site and find Vic Morrison," Lennox said as he stood. "I'll also offer a discount and we're going to have to eat the cost of some of the wiring. If the site is as far along as you say, Jose," he looked at his brother who nodded at him. "Then we're going to have a lot of crow to eat. And I don't eat crow well." He leaned over his father and kissed him on the cheek.

"Good boy."

"Adios, Papa, hasta manana." He spoke in his father's native tongue and then nodded at him. He noticed his father's tan face, weathered by age, and his deep set eyes, so much like his own, reminded him of a brilliant amethyst—but the color changed with his moods, which if you knew him, was the only indicator of any emotion.

Lennox smiled to himself as he left the bedroom his parents shared. The one person who got emotion out of Manuel Mays was Lena Rawlings-Mays. He chuckled as he mentally recalled the story of how his parents met.

At the age of 20, Manuel Jesus Mays had been a merchant marine from Puerto Rico when the ship he was assigned to docked off of Lake Huron and finally ended in Chicago. He'd met Lena Rawlings when he took an English language class at a local community college. According to his father, he had been smitten with the black American from the moment he saw her. And for forty-two years they'd been inseparable.

Lennox wanted what his father had—a loving mate, someone to watch over him and be by his side when things got rough and someone who had an appetite. Yet, all Lennox seemed to attract were the women who wanted to be seen on his arm.

Lennox found Jose standing outside his parent's bedroom.

"Buenos noche, mi hijo. Call me tomorrow."

"Will do," he replied to his father and then headed to the door. "Jose, please come with me."

Lennox and Jose walked to the front of the house they'd grown up in. "Okay, while I appreciate your intentions, I'm disappointed that you didn't tell anyone when things got too tough." Lennox sat on the stool near the kitchen island. He rubbed his large fingers across his short, wavy hair and down his goatee. He then began to flip through the papers that showed the specs for the wiring installation.

"That's what we are here for, Jose—we are family and we support each other." He watched as his brother hung his head. He didn't want to chastise his younger brother, fourteen years his junior and the youngest son, but he did want to impress upon him that there was no shame in asking for help. To Lennox, the shame was in not asking and then covering up the fact. And unfortunately, Jose's refusal to ask for help could possibly harm their reputation.

"Brother, I know you're the perfect one."

"That's ridiculous." Lennox rose to his full six-foot two-inches and met his brother who was at least three inches shorter. Their eyes met, with Lennox's narrowing. He spoken evenly, his voice held a slight hint of annoyance. He then quieted. His parents had always talked about how controlled he was, from his anger to even his joy—he was slow to show emotion. And because of it, his fiancé broke off their engagement. She'd said he wasn't passionate enough about their relationship or the planning of their nuptials. He didn't understand all of that.

"Well, that's how I feel sometimes." Jose glanced away and sat on the stool vacated by his oldest brother.

Lennox shook his head. He'd been young and impetus once, but he didn't recall feeling as if he was walking in anyone's shadow. He wanted to understand what his brother was feeling.

"When have we ever asked you to be anyone other than who you are?" He tapped Jose on the hand that was resting on the island. "You have a great head for numbers, Jose." He tapped him on the shoulder. "And that's why we want you to manage the financial arm. Is there anything wrong with that?"

Jose shook his head.

"So, let's chock this up to an experience. But next time I'm out of town and Papa is injured you call me immediately. Comprende?"

"Comprende." Jose stood as Lennox pulled him into an embrace.

"Thank you, brother." Lennox grabbed the keys to his truck and headed out the door. He shook his head and prayed that what damage Jose had done could be undone.

The thought of meeting such a man of stature was still at the forefront of Lennox's thoughts when the large structure came into view as Lennox turned down the street. He parked his truck across from the structure and then noticed the beginnings of the first two floors. According to the specs Morrison had provided, this was the commercial area that would house a coffee shop, a doggie day care and spa, a gourmet grocery store, a dry cleaning business and the management offices.

He stepped out of the truck and then leaned back as his head bent to take in the rest of the structure. He saw the exposed steel beams and exhaled a sigh of relief. While the base foundation had been set, the remaining floors had yet to be laid. As his eyes continued its visual assessment, he noticed two upper floors were completed.

"So much for wishful thinking." He murmured as he walked across the street. As he stepped onto the sidewalk, he glanced to his right and noticed the advertisement for the intending condo units. He guessed that the two floors were where the sales office and models were located.

Lennox knew it wasn't unheard of to create two floors as a means of selling out while construction continued on the remaining structure. It relates to positive cash flow.

Lennox glanced at this watch. It was after five-thirty. He muttered a curse. The likelihood of anyone being around was slim. He walked back to his truck, replacing his white Nike's for steel-toed boots, grabbed his hard hat and then headed back across the street, this time to the rear of the site. If anyone was at the site, he may be able to find them there.

Coming upon a large steel door, he saw an intercom nearby. Lennox pushed the button and waited. After several moments, he pushed it again. After several more moments and no response he decided he'd come back first thing in the morning. As he began to walk away, he heard a voice. He rushed back to the intercom.

"Yes, can I help you?" asked the voice.

Lennox tilted his head slightly to one side. The warm, husky timbre wasn't one likely to belong to a man. "Umm, yes. I'm looking for Vic Morrison."

"Who's calling?"

He cleared his throat. "Lennox Mays from Mays Communications."

Second ticked by as he stood waiting for a response. He opened his mouth to say something further when he heard the sound of the automatic lock disengage. Lennox opened the door and then listened as a voice instructed him to take the elevator to his left to the seventeenth floor.

Following the directions of the voice, Lennox stepped into the waiting elevator. He watched the numbers on the panel of the construction elevator signal each floor. He noted that a key was needed for the eleventh and twelfth floors.

"Must be the sales floors."

With a jerky stop, the elevator came to a halt on the seventeenth floor. The doors opened and Lennox stepped out onto a concrete floor, the exposed floor plan gave him a generous view of the city of Chicago. Ahead of him, he saw the back of a person, leaning over a large piece of particle board supported by two construction horses. As he got close enough to make out the form, he saw a long pony tail poking out from under a white hard hat, black letters across it spelling out the name Morrison.

"If you don't have a hard hat, there's one over there," came the same voice he'd heard over the intercom, only this time it seemed softer, with a hint of annoyance. He saw the slender finger point to a stack of hard hats arranged on top of another make-shift desk.

"No, thank you, I've got my own. I'm looking for Vic Morrison. I need to …" his voice trailed off when the figure turned to face him, her skin a deep warm mocha, with a dab of cream, and eyes so dark and mysterious he felt as if she were hypnotizing him. Her ample chest was covered in a flannel shirt and her just right hips were covered in denim. He wished he was that denim.

A small hand jutted out toward him. "I'm Vic Morrison. And you are from Mays Communications?"

Lennox wanted to beg that cat that had just run away with his tongue to bring it back. He couldn't talk. Couldn't move. Couldn't get his thoughts to form complete sentences. All he could do was grasp the offered hand and hold on.

"Expecting my father?" Vic asked as she stepped even closer. "I'm Victoria, Vic for short, and my dad is Victor."

Lennox nodded and continued to look into her sooty dark eyes, which slanted giving her a somewhat exotic expression.

They stood there, less than three feet from each other, their eyes absorbing the other. Lennox knew that he had to say something for if he didn't she'd think he'd gone daft and Mays Communications didn't need any more negatives; nor did he want her to think him daft. Suddenly he wondered why it even mattered what she thought of him personally, as long as he was able to salvage the bruised relationship between the two companies.

He nodded his head. "Actually, I was." His own voice sounded foreign to him as the words came out on a heavy breath. He hoped he hadn't sounded like an obscene phone caller. He hadn't realized that his hand still held hers until she tugged it free.

You trippin', his mind screamed.

"Sorry to disappoint you, Mister Telephone Man."

Lennox blinked and like a douse of ice cold water, his mind cleared instantly.

What did she call me? Telephone man? Mays communications is more than just telephones—*we are a full-service communications company, able and willing to install every form of communication known to man and then some.*

"Mays Communications," was his simple reply as he shook his head slightly from side to side.

"Okay." She waved a hand and thappeaen crossed her arms under her breasts. The simple act only served to enhance an already full bust line. Lennox felt an odd sensation begin to roll in the pit of his stomach. He forced his eyes to meet hers.

"Ms. Morrison, I know that our company is way behind the schedule you've set, but I'm willing to make some concessions to salvage this relationship."

"Like what?" she replied as she turned her back on him and returned to the makeshift desk.

Lennox's eyes traveled from the white hard hat, past her small waist to the wicked roundness of her derrière. Instantly, images of his hands roaming and plying her derrière, her smooth voice moaning in his ear, invaded and overrode all thoughts and threatened to give him an erection. She had to have some special powers—he had never gotten a hard on just looking at or thinking of touching a woman's ample behind.

The sound of her clearing her throat brought his eyes up to meet hers.

"Umm, I'd like to see ..." he started and then paused, giving his mind time to clear itself of the sultry image and refocusing on what he was there for: to salvage a business client not seduce the client. "Let me rephrase that. We are willing to absorb the cost of the initial wiring, work twelve plus hours a day until the base is complete and then grant a twenty percent discount on the overall wiring itself."

He watched her dark eyes soften as a slight smile crossed her face.

"Okay, Mr. Mays, you have yourself a deal." Vic said. "We are truly behind schedule and I'm going to need you and your men to work nearly non-stop for the next two weeks to get the basic wiring installed before you work on the satellite wiring, the wiring for Wi-Fi, cable, telephone, etc." She looked up at him and motioned him closer with her index finger. "Here are the specs as it stands now." She handed him a copy. He glanced at her side profile and swore that she had exhaled deeply, as if she had been holding her breath. Lennox resisted the urge to sniff his underarms. Her sultry voice caught his attention.

"We've already started our part, as you can see, so you've got to catch up. Think you can handle that?" she asked.

Lennox could only nod his head.

"Well, if that's all, I'll expect your crew here at six am. Here's the code that will allow you entrance into the building and here is a remote to activate the rear gate." She tossed the remote which had been sitting on the make-shift table in his direction and watched as he caught it in mid-air. She tilted her head slightly to one side before she continued. "The rear gate is locked every evening at six." Her eyes met his, her hands resting on her hips. Lennox fought to keep his eyes trained on hers.

"Got it," he replied. "We'll be here first thing."

"Great. Do you need anything else?" She asked, her dark eyes settled on his, her expertly arched eyebrows raised.

Lennox shook his head no before responding. "I'm just pleased that we're still able to do business. You have our full apologies for the mix up. There will be no more."

"Glad to hear it," Vic stated.

They stood still, one looking at the other in abject silence. For some reason, Lennox wondered if she had a boyfriend, someone she snuggled up to at night. For if she didn't ….

Lennox was the first to break the silence. "Well, I guess I need to be heading out." He held out his hand to her and observed as she slowly placed hers in his. He held it, the small hand, with short nails, was soft but cold. He resisted the urge to place his free hand over her cold one. Instead he released it and stepped back. "We will be here first thing in the morning. Good night, Ms. Morrison."

"Night, Mr. Mays."

Lennox nodded his head, turned on his heels, and walked to the elevator. It was only after he got on and faced forward did he see that she was watching him. He recorded the image of the lithe woman with the dark eyes and small hand as a brand onto his mind.

He'd been in business a long time and had met many a woman, but he had never met one that vexed him to the point of silence. And he wanted to know what it was about one Victoria Morrison that had rendered him mute and more than mildly curious.

Chapter Three

Vic blew her breath out in one long, continuous huff. Here she was expecting a man about the same age as her father, and instead she found herself looking at the finest brother she'd ever laid eyes on. And his eyes! They were the most arresting, striking, color she'd ever seen. They didn't look real, the deep, golden honey color was so clear and, she had to admit, quite beautiful. She had no idea that Manuel Mays had a son, much less one that doggone fine. She guessed him to be at least six foot two, weighing in at a wondrous 250 pounds—just her type. Unlike Maxi, Vic liked a man with some real meat on his bones, and the meat on that brother's bones looked well-defined, she thought as she mentally recalled the way his white t-shirt fit across his broad, muscular chest. And when she put her hand in his—Lord help her. She wanted to pull him closer, rub her nose along his face and inhale the woodsy aroma of his cologne mixed with a very manly, masculine scent. Vic wanted to melt. He was better than the Rundu men.

And as she watched him she wondered just how many women he had at his beck and call. Umph, she huffed to herself, why did she even care?

But business is business, she reminded herself, and due to the Mays's, a portion of their construction was incomplete and she couldn't have that. But he hadn't flinched when she suggested his crew be on site by six in the morning. She liked that. He didn't even take umbrage to her calling him Telephone Man; he just stood there with that unreadable expression on his face. The only time she detected a hint of something was when his eyes turned an interesting dark shade of gold.

Vic left the seventeenth floor and headed to her condo. Stepping into her home, she was met by her miniature Pincher, Little Bit. She picked the pint-sized dog up into her arms and nuzzled the dog right under her neck.

"Hey, Little Bit," Vic crooned as Little Bit began to alternate between licks to Vic's neck and yaps, which on any other dog would have been a full-fledged bark. "How's my baby today?" she asked as she carried the dog through the unit.

She placed Little Bit on the floor as she made her way toward the kitchen. She looked out among the large open area and was quite satisfied with the way Maxi had decorated. Maxi had one hell of an eye for interior decorating and had done wonders to Vic's place, using gold and green colors as a means of warming up the place without making it too busy.

After feeding Little Bit, Vic headed to her bedroom and disrobed before heading into the attached master bathroom to take a shower. She had one hour to shower and dress before she'd be late for dinner with Dad and Maxi.

After her shower and applying her favorite scented lotion, Vic chose a black, pencil skirt and a white, capped sleeve blouse, adding a large red belt to her waist and a pair of red, high heeled sandals. She twisted her hair into a chignon then grabbed a clutch purse as she rushed to the construction elevator. She exited at the basement where several construction vehicles and her drop top Volkswagen Cabriolet were parked.

As she headed to the restaurant, Vic couldn't seem to shake the image of Lennox Mays from her mind. From his yellow hard hat, to the fitted shirt, down to the way his jeans hugged his thighs, Vic found herself wondering, quite scandalously, how he'd look in a pair of boxer briefs. It had taken all of her control to make sure her eyes hadn't lingered too long on his crotch.

Arriving at the restaurant, Vic rushed inside and found her father and sister sitting in their favorite booth. Waving, Vic joined them and planted a kiss on both of their cheeks before sitting.

"Sorry I'm late. I had a visitor."

Max looked up from dipping a piece of bread into freshly grated parmesan cheese and virgin olive oil. "Who?"

"Mays Communications," Vic responded and then met her sister's stare. She wondered had her voice given away the odd sensations she'd been feeling for the past two hours since laying eyes on the fine brother with the eyes the color of a tiger, a body that rivaled Dwayne 'The Rock' Johnson, and a soft, yet controlled, deep voice that sounded more seductive than authoritative. And there was something about Lennox that stated no-nonsense, that what he said was what he meant. No more. No less.

"How is Señor Mays? It's been a long time since I've seen him." Victor Morrison asked his youngest daughter.

"It was his son, Lennox," Vic breathed out as an image of Lennox invaded her thoughts. She felt crazy. No man had ever affected her the way he had and she'd just met him!

"I had forgotten about his sons. He's got three of them," he said as he looked up at the waiter and gave his order, followed by Maxi and then Vic. "You know we worked together years ago. He was one of the first minority businesses in Chicago doing telecommunications. When the phone companies deregulated, he was right there as a contractor—and his boys are just like him."

Vic had heard parts of what he'd said, her mind flittering over the sinfully gorgeous man, who fit a pair of jeans better than the Wrangler man and had seemed unaffected by her and her position. She looked up just as Maxi cleared her throat, a wicked smile behind her napkin as she dabbed at the corners of her mouth. "So, what was the hold up with the installation?"

Lennox Mays had been such a surprise to Vic that she hadn't bothered to ask him the whys of the delay. She shrugged her shoulders, averted her eyes then picked up the glass of water in front of her and took a long drink. She knew that Maxi would be staring at her, for this was so unlike her. She was detailed, to a fault, when it came to construction and its varying aspects and she didn't miss a thing. Including the wicked heat pooling at the pit of her stomach, the way her hand had nearly sizzled in his, and the intensity of his gaze.

"Okay, so when do they start?" Maxi asked her eyes trained on her sister. She hadn't seen that look in Vic's eyes—the faraway, almost dreamy stare—since her first school girl crush in high school. Whoever this Lennox Mays is must be some looker. "Vicki, are you okay, girl?"

"Ugh?" Vic held the glass in mid air.

"Are you okay?" she asked again.

She blinked her eyes and noted that both her sister and father were staring at her. "I'm alright—just a little tired, that's all. What did you ask me?"

"When is Mays going to start the installation?"

"Oh. They are supposed to start tomorrow at six."

"In the morning?" Maxi asked as Vic nodded her head up and down. "That's awfully early, Vicki, especially for a Saturday."

"I know, but he didn't object and the sooner we get the basic install completed, the sooner we can move on to the more complicated stuff."

For the remaining dinner, they talked about the current construction projects they were involved in and ones they wanted to pursue. By the time they'd finished, it was close to eleven and Vic was already exhausted from rising too early that day.

She kissed her father then Maxi and climbed into her waiting car. The top down, she waved over her hand over her head as she peeled away from the curb and headed home. As she drove, the music from the car's CD player sent soft tunes out among the warm night air, George Benson sand about love and kisses in the moonlight. Vic glanced up at the half moon overhead.

At the site, she pushed the remote over her visor and watched as the electronic fence opened. She depressed the remote again and was granted her entrance into the secured, underground parking.

Finally inside her unit, Vic removed her sandals and padded barefoot to her bedroom. As she removed her clothes, replacing them with a plum colored short satin chemise, she climbed into bed and thought of just how early six am really was.

"Maybe I should have told him seven."

Chapter Four

The sound of drilling evaded the beautiful dream Vic was having of laying on a white sandy beach, a drink in hand, as the sun tanned her to a beautiful deep bronze with red undertones and large hands kneaded and massaged her shoulders. She rolled over and heard the sound again. She sat up quickly, her ear trained.

What the …?

Vic peered at the digital clock resting on her night stand. She closed her eyes and then opened them again. There was no way that clock read three in the morning! And the incessant sound of the drilling continued. The alarm hadn't sounded and she hadn't heard Little Bit bark, so who in the world could be working. Vic groaned and remembered that Lennox Mays's men were supposed to start work today, but that was at six.

Climbing out of bed, Vic angrily tossed on her robe, shoved her feet into a pair of white bunny slippers, and with Little Bit on her heels, headed to the service elevator. The drilling sound was coming from somewhere directly below her and if it was Mays's crews they should have known that they needed to start in the basement—not on the tenth floor.

Once the doors opened, Vic stopped dead in her tracks when she spied Lennox Mays, in a squatting position, his back to her her—the red shirt he wore stretched across his wide back, a pair of jeans covered his lower half. Large spools of various size wires were placed along the perimeter.

She watched as he worked, his left hand busy stripping several wires, his large arms flexed as he did so. Just as she was about to attempt to head back to her unit undetected, Little Bit rushed over and began yapping, quite loudly at him. She called to the dog just as Lennox jumped to his feet, removing tiny white ear buds from his ears.

Lennox had decided to get an early start on the work, calling two of his best crew members. They had agreed to meet at two that morning, versus the six am start time Victoria Morrison had given him.

He'd been in business with his father a long time and in that time he'd come across plenty of women, but in all his years, he'd never seen one as interesting or as beautiful as Victoria Morrison. From her curvaceous figure to her no-nonsense manner, he was intrigued. He'd never really liked mousy women anyway. He wanted a woman who could hold her own, yet still be a woman—just like his mother and sisters.

Once he'd arrived at his home, he couldn't shake her image from his mind, even going so far as wondering what she liked to do to unwind, what her favorite color was, did she like to shop and could she handle a man telling her what to do.

When he awakened, his first thought was of Victoria Morrison and as he stripped some wiring his mind had just traveled to her. So he was pleasantly surprised to see her standing there.

"Hey pooch," Lennox said as he held out his hand and watched as the miniature dog came to him, sniffed his hand and then began licking it. He picked up the dog and cradled the dog gently to his chest.

"Traitor," Vic whispered under her breath which caught in her throat as she watched him glide over to her. For the second time in less than twenty-four hours, Lennox Mays had the oddest look in his eyes—the golden depths deep and unreadable. Vic wrapped her arms around herself and trained her eyes on his face, the color of crème Brule, his lips full and soft looking. She didn't want to eye him up and down as she had earlier for this man wore a pair of jeans like no man she'd ever laid eyes on. And if what he was sporting in the back and the front was a hint . . . humph. Seriously, she wanted to see Lennox Mays naked.

The closer he got, his eyes traveling lazily up and down, Vic realized she was standing in front of him dressed in her bed clothes.

"Mr. Mays, what are you doing up here?"

"Working, Ms. Morrison." His eyes traveled languidly from the top of her head, her hair tossed about her shoulders, down to the peaks of cleavage, to the toned legs peeking sensuously out from underneath the silk robe. Lennox began rubbing the dog's head to steady his hands when what he really wanted to do was pull this siren to him and sample the lips that were pouting out at him.

"I thought you'd be here at six?" She crossed her arms under her chest, which gave him even more of a glimpse of her full cleavage. The creamy skin begged to be touched, kissed, and suckled.

"We got here at two and we've got half of the basics nearly complete." He continued walking toward her. "I'm here laying wire for the floors above with fiber optics for cable." He stopped in front of her and inhaled the lingering scent of some perfume he couldn't quite place. His sisters and mother were big on fragrances and could identify one with just a whiff. He had never cared before, but now he wished he could identify the wickedly entrancing scent so that he could buy her a lifetime supply. "What are you doing here?" He nodded at her attire, stifling a snort of laughter when he looked down at her feet and saw them encased in a pair of slippers with bunny ears poking east and west.

Vic pulled the robe closer only to realize that the short robe only rose higher as she did so. She watched as his eyes traveled down the front of her body. "I live here," she responded and then headed back to the elevator, the soles of her slippers made padded noises on the concrete. Her mind twirled as she rushed toward the elevators.

Lennox stood there, transfixed as he watched the hem of the robe ride dangerously upward, granting him one wish: a wicked view of her shapely legs and a hint of a full bottom. His eyes were transfixed on the hem as it swished back and forth, then side to side. He swallowed hard and felt his eyes narrow of their own volition. Had the dog not licked his hand, he would have forgotten all about the little pooch.

His eyes rose to meet hers as she spun around and headed back in his direction.

"Can I have my dog?" she held out her hands toward him.

"Sure," he said as he handed over the small dog.

"Thank you."

"No, thank you," he murmured, the view of her dressed in that short gown and matching robe would never, ever escape his mind. And if the outline of her sumptuous body was any hint of what she owned under that flimsy material, then he'd have a hard time ever getting over the simple fact that he wanted to sample this woman's entire body, head to toe, in the most intimate, primal way.

She turned and headed back in the direction she'd come from and he stood and watched her as she did so. In that short time he had made up his mind. Victoria Morrison was going to be his—mind, body and soul.

Chapter Five

For two weeks, Vic interacted with Lennox Mays only when necessary. She had been completely embarrassed to have been standing in front of him dressed in a short gown with nothing underneath. But if he had been interested or aroused, she couldn't tell, for his eyes remained fixed and his emotions steeled. She couldn't read his expressions for he didn't seem to have any. Even when she glimpsed him speaking with his workers, he gave directives and answered questions, but she just didn't see his smooth face show any signs of emotion.

"Vic, Mr. Mays needs to see you." Bobby appeared on the fourth floor where they were finishing up the drywall.

"Where is he?"

"On the roof."

Vic stopped smoothing out the strips and turned to face her foreman. "What is he doing up there? It's not finished."

Bobby shrugged his shoulders, shaking his head and raising his hands at the same time. "Beats me, Boss Lady. But all I know is that he asked for you to join him."

Vic laid down the drywall spatula, wiped her hands on a nearby cloth and then headed to the elevator. She thought of how she'd avoided him and knew that one day she would have to come face to face with the brother who was just too fine to be real and a body that made her want to do things to him, scandalous, wicked things.

Lennox watched the traffic roll along scenic Lake Shore Drive. He enjoyed the view from the top floor and knew that when the job was complete he wouldn't see Vic again. And that was something that he absolutely could not have. Since meeting her he'd wanted to get to know her, to find out what made Victoria Morrison a woman, one that was fiercely independent and well respected in this testosterone laden industry. And she was avoiding him, he knew it. The day he'd seen her in her night clothes had been the last time he'd lay eyes on her up close. She had taken to calling him, sending emails late in the evening, or having her foreman talk to his, but very little personal interaction.

At first he was miffed, thinking he couldn't believe she would purposely avoid him. Then when he thought more about it, he knew that her unintentional display of flesh had caught her short and she was trying to avoid any comment on it. Well, he wouldn't mention it if she didn't, but he wasn't going to have her avoid him another day. Today he planned on changing all that.

Lennox looked up as a late summer breeze whipped slightly around him, bringing a welcomed chill to the air. He was looking forward to the coming autumn—his favorite season. He figured he'd head up to his cabin in Galena come October, which was only two months away, taking the scenic back roads which would allow him to witness the deep reds and yellows of turning leaves.

He heard the construction elevator stop. He knew she'd wonder why he'd come up to the floor that sported exposed iron beams, but he found sitting on the lone concrete patio situated several feet from the elevator gave him peace, especially when he had a lot on his mind, in particular, how to get Victoria to go out with him and into his bed. He had found the unfinished floor the day after Vic's little unintentional show. He shook his head and blew out his breath.

"My God, Mr. Mays, what are you doing up here? I don't allow anyone up here without a harness."

Lennox stood then turned to face her. He noticed that her head was covered by her hard-hat, her upper body covered in a red and black stripped flannel shirt, black jeans covered her lower half and her feet were encased in black boots. He wondered how many work boots she had to match her shirts.

"I really like it up here, Ms. Morrison. Won't you join me?" He said as he sat back down and allowed his feet to hang over the edge. He looked up at her and then patted the area next to him.

Vic looked down at him; his tiger-like eyes stared right at her unblinking. It was as if he was staring right through her. Or was he remembering the last time he saw her? The heat of embarrassment crept up her chest to settle right around her neck. She saw his hand move again followed by his mouth.

"Please sit, Victoria." His deep voice snatched her attention and she did as he requested. "It'll be easier on my neck."

"Okay," she replied and then wondered had she heard him call her Victoria, his voice deep and authoritative. And while no one but Max and her dad ever called her by her full name, the sound of it was melodic and soothing coming from Lennox. "Umm, Mr. Mays what do you need?"

He glanced at her face and then down at her feet as they swung carelessly back and forth. The simple act reminded him of his adolescent days spent day dreaming at the beach, sitting on the rocks with his feet dangling in Lake Michigan. "Please call me Lennox. Mr. Mays is my father."

"Okay, Lennox. What's up?"

He leaned to one side and retrieved a black portfolio from his leather briefcase nearby. He handed it to her.

"Inside you will find a summary of the work completed to date, the work yet to be completed, our approximate completion date and the costs we will bill you. I'd like for you to look over the documents and then sign off on them if it meets your approval. And then when you return the sheets I'd like to take you to dinner. Preferably sooner versus later."

Vic blinked at him. Her mind raced as she tried to ingest all he had said to her including his invitation to dinner. She hadn't been out on a date in over a year and had used, as Maxi said, work as an excuse. But it was easier to just be alone versus trying to get close. Her mind raced then went into overdrive when she felt his hip flush with hers, his long, thick fingers, with the neatly trimmed, clean nails, drummed on his muscular thigh, clad in a pair of tan Dockers.

"Why Ms. Victoria, the look on you face is akin to going to the dentist. Do I revolt you?"

Vic blinked her eyes and looked into his. And while the words had escaped his lips, the emotion didn't reach his eyes. But she did note that his right eyebrow was raised. He was awaiting an answer.

"Umm, Mr. Mays."

Lennox made exaggerated moves, turning his head around to look first to his left then over to his right before looking behind him. He looked down beside him and then looked inside of his briefcase. "I don't see Mr. Mays anywhere. Do you?"

Vic couldn't help the laugh as it bubbled forth. She noted the mirth that shone in his eyes and was caught off guard. The soft look of his eyes gave a boyishness glint to his often stoic expression. He leaned against the iron beam and smiled. She noted the evidence of smile lines framing his face right above his goat tee.

"Lennox, I don't mix business with pleasure."

He sobered.

She watched the stoic expression return. No, she much preferred the less serious Lennox.

"But if you must look like you just lost your puppy, then I guess I could meet you."

"Wow, now I'm a charity case," he replied as he shook his head. "I may have a cup around here so you could deposit a few coins into."

Vic wanted to slap her own self upside her head. She hadn't meant it to come out as if she were doing him a favor. Lord, how was she going to fix this? She placed her hand on his and waited until he looked up.

"Lennox, I didn't mean it like it sounded. Sure, I'd love to have dinner with you. But I just want to warn you that I'm not looking for a relationship. My work keeps me pretty busy and I rarely have time to wash my own hair, much less go out to dinner."

"Fair. I'm not asking you to marry me or have my children." He stood and then looked down at her. "What time shall I pick you up tonight?"

Vic looked up into his eyes which were now a mysterious golden brown. She had been rude and her mother would most definitely had chided her for her behavior. No matter the situation, Elnora didn't tolerate rude behavior.

Lennox held out his hand to her. She placed her hand in his and allowed him to pull her up to stand on her feet, her body an inch from his. He looked down into her upturned face. His hand itched. He wanted to touch her, pull her hair from under her hat and run his fingers through the length, then feel her slide across his body as he kissed her senseless. And he knew if she let him, he was going to do just that.

Vic inhaled deeply and averted her eyes. Looking into his gave her a heady feeling. "How about seven. We can meet."

"No, Victoria, I'll be here at seven to pick you up."

Lennox squatted down, placed the portfolio in her hands, picked up his briefcase followed by his hard hat. He looked up at Victoria standing over him and steeled himself against the wicked image of her femininity pressed against his lips as he gripped her full behind, with her fingers holding onto him as her sweet looking lips called out his name over and again. He shook his head slightly. His mind was made up. Contrary to what he'd just said, Victoria Morrison was not only going to let him love her mind, body and soul; but she was going to marry him and become the mother of his children.

Chapter Six

Victoria looked at the clothes strewn in small piles along the floor. When she heard whimpering, she dropped to her knees and began carefully lifting clothes. Little Bit was lost somewhere in one of the piles.

"Oh, baby, I'm so sorry." Victoria lifted a blouse to find a shivering Little Bit. She gently picked her up, held her to her chest and began to apologize in a soft voice. Little Bit nuzzled her small head under the side of Victoria's chin. "You okay?" She lifted the dog and began inspecting her head. Little Bit began licking the tip of Victoria's nose. "Thank you for forgiving me. You know I didn't mean it." She kissed the dog on the top of her head before placing her on the bed. "Now, you stay up here."

After another hour, Victoria had decided on a black and white abstract print sleeveless dress. On her feet, she added a pair of black patent leather, open toed sandals with three-inch heels. She ended her adornment by dabbing her favorite cologne, Chance, behind her ears and along her breasts. She paused. *Why am I doing this?*

Victoria shook her head and headed out of her room to wait for Lennox to arrive.

Lennox pulled up to the gate and depressed the remote. The electronic gate swung open followed by the overhead door. He pulled his midnight black Infinity into the parking spot he'd used numerous times over the weeks he'd been at the site. Stepping out, he pulled his light-weight blazer from a hanger in the rear of the vehicle, tossed the coat over her shoulder, and then grabbed the bouquet of flowers, a mix of red roses, daisies, lilies, lisianthus, daisy poms, wax flowers and salals. He had liked the bouquet when he spotted them at the neighborhood florist and though it would be a nice touch to their evening out.

He inhaled deeply just as he peered at himself in the reflection of the car window. He'd finally admitted that he had wanted to get to know Victoria on more than just a base level, he wanted to know what she liked and disliked; what made her mad; what she did when it rained and did she mind allowing a man to be a man. He knew that a woman in a man's industry had it hard and often times than not, had to take on a masculine demeanor to get the point across. But Lennox didn't want her to be on top if she didn't want to be. Well, not outside of the bedroom, at least. He knew from watching her that there lay something much deeper inside of her, a possible need to just be a woman. And if he knew people right, he sensed her desire to be just like her sister.

He had met the other side of Morrison Construction one day while going over an addendum to the plans for the building wiring. He watched as Maxine Morrison stepped onto the construction site dressed to kill in a form-fitting, two-piece suit the color of ocean blue. All eyes on deck followed as she headed to where he and Victoria sat going over some additional wiring plans.

And while he could appreciate a good looking woman, it was something about Victoria that had him held captive and no other woman, not even her sister, could compare. Yet, he'd seen the longing in her eyes as she watched her sister head in their direction. The look in Victoria's eyes had not been jealously or envy, but longing. Lennox surmised that Victoria wanted to hang up the tool belt for a fitted skirt. One he'd love to see her in.

Stepping into the elevator, Lennox depressed the button that would take him face to face with the one woman who had caused his blood to boil to volcanic proportions, ready to blow at any time.

Victoria heard the sound of the elevator chime. She glanced at her reflection in the hall mirror one last time and headed toward the door. Hearing the knock, she popped a mint into her mouth, took in a deep breath and then opened the door.

Damn!

Her knees buckled as she eyed him, his curly hair cut neatly, his goat-tee freshly trimmed, his chest covered in a blue, ribbed Johnny collar V-neck polo with short sleeves, his biceps strained against the fabric, his firm, well-developed pectorals made a wicked outline on the cotton material. His lower half was covered in a pair of black slacks and what looked to her to be a pair of Johnston and Murphy black leather fisherman sandals on his feet. Victoria swallowed. Hard.

"Good evening, Victoria." He smiled then leaned on the door frame, his golden eyes absorbed her. "Wow. You look fantastic. I hope I'm not underdressed." He continued to appraise her, his eyes taking a visual tour. When their eyes met, Victoria saw the heated glare, the irises smaller, and the color richer, deeper.

"Oh." He straightened. "These are for you," he said as he handed over the large bouquet.

Victoria inhaled the fragrance of the flowers. "Thank you, Lennox. I love flowers. Roses are my favorites." She stepped back. "Let me go put these in some water then we can head out."

"No rush, our reservations aren't until 7:30." He stepped over the threshold and then stood transfixed as he watched Victoria walk down the hallway, her hips swung deliciously from side to side. The volcano was bubbling.

"I hope you like steak. I made a reservation at Gibson's," he called out as he placed his hands in his pockets; the instant hardness struck him with a vengeance.

He watched as she walked toward him, her shapely legs accentuated by the high-heeled sandals, the hem of the dress played peek-a-boo, rising with each step to give him a glimpse of the toned area right above her knees. His eyes rolled lazily upward, noting her small waist, then the bodice of the dress, which accentuated her full breasts. Her long hair hung about her shoulders.

He licked his lips. Lennox didn't think she understood the raw sensuality she exuded, the absolute magnetism that drew him without effort. He'd been around a lot of women, had had his share, but this was a first. He wanted this woman as many times as she could handle him. And then he knew he'd want her some more.

"I'm ready." She paused to stand in front of him, the intoxicating scent of his cologne threatened to wreck havoc on what little restraint she had. Ever since she'd laid eyes on him, she hadn't been able to shake him—his eyes, his image, the way he fit a pair of jeans. And never in all of her years on earth, had she been so wildly attracted to any man to the point of where she just wanted to strip and let him have his way with her and vice versa.

She nearly jumped out of her skin when she felt his large hand at the small of her back as he opened the door and waited for her to exit. He placed his hand out to her. She looked down and then back into his handsome face. "What?"

"Please, give me your keys."

"Oh," she responded as she fished them from her purse and then placed them in his outstretched hand. Once he locked the door, he handed the keys over and then took her free hand in his.

At the car, he held the passenger door open as she sat and then swung her shapely legs into the car.

As they rode along, they spoke of construction and wiring as the Infinity ate up the road in front of them. And while Lennox was in no hurry, he needed to breathe, to get a little air before he burst into flames. The siren next to him was lighting him up and he was remised to do anything about it right then.

Once at the restaurant, Lennox held the door, ensured she was comfortably seated and even ordered for her when prompted. Victoria had never been doted on by a man. Most assumed since she worked in a male-dominated industry she wanted to be treated as such. That was so far from the truth.

At the end of dinner, Lennox sat back and watched her.

Victoria began to fidget, her fingers touching her hair before smoothing down the bodice of her dress. She looked up at him and noticed he was staring at her.

"What's the matter?"

"Victoria, has anyone ever told you that you are incredibly beautiful?"

She shook her head. She had been told she was cute, attractive even, but never beautiful.

"Then let me be the first," he said, raised his glass of wine, sat up straight and then leaned over the table. "Victoria Morrison, you are an incredibly beautiful woman."

Victoria watched him as he took a sip of the blush wine, his long fingers gripping the stem; his lips barely touched the rim. The heat rode up from the core of her body, skittering across her breasts to settle right under her neck. She dabbed at the slight perspiration at the same time she looked up into Lennox's eyes. The color was the same as when she'd stood in front of him that early morning.

"Thank you, Lennox."

He smiled at her. "What else would you like to do tonight?"

Get naked with you.

Victoria blinked at the thought, glad that he couldn't read her mind. She didn't want Lennox to think she was easy or made it a habit of sleeping with men on the first date, but there was something so interesting, so sensuously sexy and downright raw about the man sitting across from her that all she wanted to do was just feel his naked body on hers, his hands making a wicked path across her entire body, his smooth-looking, full lips attached to hers.

"Any thoughts?"

If you only knew, her mind screamed before she spoke. "I'm game. I don't have anything specific I'd like to do."

He smiled at her, the motion made his eyes lighter. Victoria watched them change colors to a golden tan right before her and decided that she truly loved this color the best.

"How about I show you what most of Chicago hasn't seen?"

"And what's that, Lennox?"

He shook his head and placed his hand out to her. "You game?" Lennox watched as she tentatively placed her hand in his. He turned her hand over and began massaging her palm with the tips of his fingers. For a woman who worked in construction, he found her hands awfully soft, yet firm. An image of her massaging his bare back came into mind. His eyelids lowered.

Victoria saw the shift in his demeanor and wondered where his mind had drifted to in just that short time. When his eyes settled back on hers she noted the seriousness of them, the way they tended to look at her as if he were seeing inside of her.

"Are you, Victoria?"

She had to admit, the way her name slipped past his slightly full lips caused her concentration to skip a beat—it was breathy while being somewhat authoritative and awfully sexy. She nodded her head and allowed him to pull her from her seat to her feet.

"Then, baby, let's blow this pop stand."

Chapter Seven

Victoria stood on the observation deck and peered through the large telescope with her mouth agape. She marveled as the stars overhead twinkled brightly making up the Big Dipper. As a little girl she had visited the Adler Planetarium, stared at the various exhibits showcasing the solar system and stratosphere, but she had never seen the stars or the surrounding planets this close.

"We've been doing some fiber optic work here," Lennox whispered the explanation in her ear as he stood behind her. "So, I have keys to the place."

Victoria shivered. He was so close to her that she could feel the heat emanating from his body, felt the rise of his chest against her back as he inhaled, and smelled the scent of his cologne, one that she came to expect every day that he worked at the site.

"If you train the scope a little to the north, you will be able to see Jupiter," he said as he reached around her and began to reposition the scope. "Tell me what you see," his breath caressed her ear. And she could feel the electric current that popped and fizzled around them, snaking an erotic charge around them.

"Victoria, did I tell you how good you smell?" He let his hands drop to her shoulders. "Please forgive me, but I just have to ..." his voice trailed off as he bent his head and placed a kiss on her neck.

Victoria's head dropped to one side, granting him more access to the sensitive spot along her neck, right under her ear where he was placing small kisses at. She moaned loudly and felt her bud throb.

"Why have you been avoiding me, Victoria?" he asked as he continued nibbling and kissing her neck. "And do not lie and tell me you haven't." His lips left her neck and then he twirled her around to face him.

Victoria stifled the gasp that threatened to bubble forth. The look in his eyes was a mix of plain, hot desire, passion and lust. She watched him and knew that lying to him was not an option she should exercise. Yes, she had been avoiding him, had been trying to excise the way he had made her feel, the wicked images he invoked anytime she laid eyes on him. If she didn't know any better, she would swear that she loved this man on first sight. She liked his quiet strength, his manner, the way he walked, with confidence, not arrogance, and the way he wore a pair of jeans. How could she tell him this? Tell him that ever since she'd laid eyes on him she couldn't shake his voice or his image from her mind?

"Tell me," he said and then dipped his head close to hers as he took her face between his hands, his thumbs stroked across her lips. "Tell me, amore." He placed his lips on hers and plied until she obeyed the silent signal his lips were sending. She opened her lips, allowing his tongue to slide between and taunt hers, lapping and lavishing. His hands fell away from her face to pull her close before wrapping his arms around her, his lips and tongue devouring. Victoria pushed her body even closer, flattening her breasts to his chest, her hands roamed up and down his back, stopping right at the top of his butt.

Neither was able to explain their feelings, so foreign, the deep passion waiting to be sampled and hopefully savored countless times. And they both knew, once would never be enough.

Victoria broke the kiss. "I haven't been avoiding you, Lennox. I've been busy."

He chuckled softly. "You lie, but I will allow you this one time." He kissed her again, this time sampling her lips with small pecks, alternating between licks and kisses, slowly and methodically.

Victoria felt as if she wanted to tear her hair out by the roots. The slight ministrations were causing her mind to race, her pulse to quicken, and the bud between her legs to throb with an acute ache. This man, the one seducing her with his lips, was the one she wanted to cure her heat, for she was about to have a stroke if he didn't. And she surely didn't want him to stop.

"Lennox." His name came out on a long hiss. She needed him. Needed to feel his weight upon her. His mouth all over her. His hard member inside of her. She had never found herself near begging. From just a kiss!

"Yes, Mija," Lennox said as he continued his seduction. He wanted to feel her, minus the clothes, to hold her close to him. As he kissed her again and again, an odd thought entered his mind. He remembered his father saying that once he had laid eyes on Lennox's mother he knew that she was the one. Lennox stilled, pulling his face back slightly—enough to see Victoria's face. Yes, his mind reaffirmed, she is the one.

"Please, Lennox." She tilted her head before resting her forehead on his. Her chest rose heavily up and down while her hands held on to his biceps tightly.

Lennox picked Victoria up off of her feet and instinctively she wrapped her legs around his waist, her arms locked around his broad shoulders. Hearing her shoes fall to the deck floor, he lowered his head and buried his face in the tops of her cleavage as she began to slowly grind round and around on his rock hard member.

Her head hung backward as she felt his fingers slip around her satin panties to find her bud. She bit her bottom lip to keep from screaming aloud as he began to gently coax the bud to life. Shamelessly, she ground her bud against his fingers as her hips twirled.

"That's it, Chica, come for me." He ordered as he held her effortlessly with one arm while his lips and tongue continued to take turns assaulting her cleavage as his fingers continued to ply her supple bud, stoking the fire to a roar.

Victoria's bud throbbed as he flicked his finger across it, pulling the orgasm up and out of her, causing her to push against his hand once, then twice just as the sensation overrode all of her senses and had her hissing out his name just as the wicked emotion rolled over her entire body.

Her chest heaved as her breathing began to return to some semblance of normal. She had never, ever, in her life, experienced anything like what Lennox had just done to her. And if this was just the beginning, she wasn't too sure she could stand the rest.

"I like the way you say my name, Victoria." He licked his fingers then placed a kiss on her lips, allowing her to sample her own essence. He slowly set her on her feet and then looked down into her face and saw the surprised look. Based on her reaction, he wondered had she ever achieved an orgasm by being stroked or ever tasted her own, intoxicating sweetness. And the way she came apart for him. Umm, he couldn't wait to sample more, but he needed to have her say she wanted him and not just on a physical level.

"I better get you home," he said as he straightened her dress, pressing the front of the material with his hands, his fingers lightly grazing her breasts. He glanced at her and almost laughed aloud at the look of incredulity on her face. Yes, he was going to leave her just like that—he wanted to hear her say it.

They rode in silence. The only sounds came from the Bose system playing some Miles Davis. In all her years, there had never been a man who'd tempted her body, stroked her clitoris and then straightened her clothes without so much as a peep. The two she'd had never took the time to make sure she was satisfied. And she knew from the feel of the hefty budge in Lennox's dress slacks that he was just as aroused as she. But he hadn't gone any further. What, was this some vampire mind trick, or some kind of beguiling spell?

She was still without words when she watched him maneuver the Infinity through the gate and then to the underground parking space she had designated for him when working at the building.

Victoria placed her hand in his as he helped her from the car and then led her to the elevator. He stood close, his hip nearly flush with hers, and smiled at her, but he didn't say a word. She even dared glanced in the area of his groin just to see. She saw no signs of an arousal.

At her floor, Lennox held out his hand. Victoria placed hers in his. She smiled ruefully when he pulled her close to his body. "Thank you for a great evening, Victoria. I hope you enjoyed yourself." He kissed her lightly on the lips then released her.

"Umm, yes I did." She looked into his eyes, now the color of burnt gold. They were the same color she had witnessed as he brought her to that magnificent orgasm. And right now she wanted to see him in all his glory, in full nothingness, lying on her, filling her with what she'd felt. She tilted her head to the side as he put his hand out to her again.

"Give me your keys, Victoria."

She rummaged around in her purse; hoping like hell that he was going to come in, begin a new, stoke her like he had at the Planetarium, slide inside of her. The keys appeared, falling to the floor. She watched as Lennox squatted down, that look of lust in his eyes as he slowly rose to stand in front of her. Without taking his eyes from hers, he placed the key in the locks, turned the knob and then stepped back, handing her the keys.

"I'll see you Monday morning, Chica. Buenos's noche." He turned and headed back to the elevator. He watched her watch him as he waited for the contraption to arrive at her floor. Once the doors opened, he waved and then disappeared.

"What the…," Victoria mumbled as she watched him walk away.

She closed the door and stood motionless. Her body was humming, throbbing, screaming all at once. There was just no way that man had done what he did to her and hadn't finished, hadn't even let her at least stroke him with her hands. Her entire body ached with a need, a wanton that she had never felt before and knew that there was only one man who would be able to quiet her body—to satisfy the aching he'd created. She wanted to scream. Instead, she walked slowly down the hallway to her bedroom.

Chapter Eight

Victoria stood still. She trained her ear and then watched as Little Bit jumped from the bed and ran down the hallway, stopping at the door, yapping loudly. Victoria rushed down the hallway. Upon reaching the door, she didn't bother looking through the peep-hole. She knew.

Lennox stepped quickly across the threshold once Victoria opened the door. He shut the door behind him and then grabbed Victoria, pulling her to him; his mouth covered hers in a sensual assault. Her hands pulled at his shirt, pulling the fabric free of its tucked confines. He paused long enough for her to remove the shirt from his body. He resumed his asault; his lips kissed her, beginning at her forehead down to her lips, where he forced her to open hers to accept his tongue. When she groaned, grinding her pelvis against his rock-solid hard-on, he reached behind her and unzipped her dress. When he heard the material meet the floor, he stopped.

"Umph," was all he could muster. Her bare breasts greeted him, the nipples large and dark, peeking up at him, beckoning him closer, calling his name. Or was that Victoria calling his name? He dipped his head, taking her breasts in his hands, and began slowly kissing the heavy mounds. He flicked his tongue across the areola before inhaling one nipple. He pushed the mounds close together and feasted on her nipples, suckling and pulling on the hardened buds until he felt Victoria buckle.

Victoria held on to Lennox's shoulders as he lavished her breasts followed by her nipples. She swore he had been licking and sucking for hours. The loud moans and groans could not be helped as he assaulted her senses, summoned forth the sounds from her, and pulled the heat from her body. And she knew that if he didn't move soon, she was going to pass out from the sheer ecstasy his mouth and tongue was eliciting.

"Please, Lennox. Oh, my, God, please."

"Please what, Mija?" he asked between suckling and licking.

Victoria was wild. She had never asked a man to make love to her, to slide inside of her and take her there, to take her to a place she'd never been before. But this was the man she had to have, she wanted. "Oh, please make love to me. Make me come again."

Lennox lifted his head and met her eyes. The wild lust shone clearly. He picked her up off her feet.

"Where is your bedroom?"

Victoria pointed down the hall.

"Good, that'll be last, mi Corazon."

Lennox thumbed her nipple as he carried her slowly down the hall. He glanced to his left and noticed her home office. He placed her on her feet and then stepped back. His eyes drank of her standing there braless with her feminine mound covered in red satin. He put his hand out to her and then twirled her around. He was about to lose control. She had on a thong.

Lennox turned her around again and then knelt in front of her, his fingers looped in the band of the thong. He pulled the flimsy material down her shapely legs, sniffed the crotch and then placed them in his pants pockets. He grabbed her by her behind and drove his tongue between her feminine folds.

"Lennox," she hissed.

He twirled his tongue round and around, loving the taste, the unique scent of her, the throbbing of her clit as she ground her pelvis against his face, the nectar covering his goat-tee. His hands busily kneaded and filled themselves with her luscious, soft, but firm derrière.

When her body tensed, her nails digging into his shoulders, he knew the second release was on its way. He held her close, refusing to let her go or slow his ministrations until he knew she had not only reached her peak, but had come down enough for him to begin the next wave of his assault.

"Corazon, you come apart beautifully," he said as he rose to his feet. He pushed items from the desk onto the floor and then lifted her, placing her gently on the desk. Stepping back, Lennox removed his slacks followed by his briefs and sandals.

Victoria closed her eyes.

"No, open your eyes. I want you to see what you've done to me."

Victoria opened one eye followed by the other. He stood there and watched her watch him. She started at the curls atop of his head; saw the fire in his dark golden eyes, the smooth goat-tee framing his oval shaped face, the pulse jumping in his neck, the thick cords of muscle on his shoulders. His marvelously sculpted chest was covered in hair that tapered down to a lean waist. His member, larger than anything she'd ever seen, pointed solidly in her direction. She looked at his thighs, the muscles pronounced. When she ended at his large feet, the nails trimmed, she thanked his creator—this man was beautiful from head to toe.

She shivered as he began walking to where she sat on the desk. He reached out with a lone finger and began to trail it across her, starting at her lips, outlining them before letting the finger linger over her right, then left breast. His finger continued its trail, dipping scandalously downward, twirling tufts of hair that covered her feminine folds.

He watched as the desire in her eyes deepened. For a moment, Lennox wondered if he had awakened a sleeping giant. He gasped when she reached out and touched his member, as if she had never touched a penis before. But he almost lost it when she licked her hand and then began to massage him, gently pumping his hard member in and out of her cupped hand, insinuating the primal dance.

Her small hand was soft and warm, and he loved the feel of her. Taking her free hand in his, he began to suck each finger as he made love to her hand. He trained his thoughts on mundane things as a means of holding back the orgasm that threatened to coat her hand.

After what seemed like an eternity, he growled. "Enough."

He pulled her toward the edge of the desk, his member poised at her opening. He raked his hands in her long hair, crushing his mouth to hers as he slid inside of her. Her hips bucked forward, her tunnel tightened around him as he drove in and out of her, slowly at first and then with a fierceness that caused him to forget all time. All he wanted, all he needed was her. As she moved with him, his member felt larger and she accommodated him, squeezing and loving him. They were a perfect fit.

"Come for me again, Victoria." He ordered and then began to slide quickly in and out of her. Her head rolled backward. He bent his head to capture the nipple that bounced up and down with their movements. The moment he pulled the taught offering into his mouth, he felt her squeeze him unmercilessly. He became a machine, her love machine, as her juices mingled with his and her body quivered in a languid orgasm.

"Lennox," she yelled out his name as her body quivered uncontrollably. He held onto her, his hips continued moving; his member stroked in and out of her. He wanted to come, but not before he called forth another orgasm from her.

Her hair was wild as she peered up at him. He pulled her close, held her to his chest, close to his heart, liking the feel of her breasts against him as her chest heaved to and fro.

"My goodness," she whispered. "I've never …" she stammered.

Lennox shook his head. "Corazon, I am not done for the night. There will be little sleeping." He picked her up and headed to her bedroom.

Victoria couldn't believe what she was feeling. This man had just brought her to three glorious orgasms and here he was talking about not being finished. Oh my! And she wanted more.

Lennox placed her on the bed and then watched as she scooted to the center. He climbed onto the bed and covered her body with his, grinding his pelvis into hers. She ground her hips, loving the thick fullness of him. Victoria roamed her hands over his back, felt on his taunt behind, back up to his powerful back then around the front to the hairs on his chest, which were soft and curly.

His hardened member pressed against her bud made her ache again. She opened her legs, inviting him to slide inside. She moaned loudly as he began to slip into her, slowly, her tunnel opening to him, pulling him forward, inch by glorious inch. When he'd been sheathed by her, she wrapped her legs around his waist and groaned. He had filled her!

"That's it. Make love to me, Victoria. Make me come."

Victoria whirled her hips in provocative circles. He placed his hands under her and held on as she proceeded to make him loose control. Like a piston, he drove in and out of her and she matched him, squeezing his member until he felt the knowing sensation at the base of his member. He held her, kissed her, nibbled at her neck, buried his head in her chest as his release plowed forth and saturated her womb.

Her eyes rolled into the back of her head as once more the heady sensation overwhelmed her. And while she considered herself a neophyte in the sex department, if this was what it was all about then she had been missing out on some of the best feelings in life. She thought about the man pulling the feelings, emotions out of her. The fine, sexy Lennox Mays with the eyes of a predatory tiger and the body of a sculpted god.

Lennox rolled them over. Victoria settled her body atop his and almost purred like a cat when he wrapped one arm around her as the other lightly stroked her back.

And true to his word, they didn't sleep that night.

Chapter Nine

"Wow!" Maxi gleamed as she stepped into the office. "Those are beautiful flowers. Okay, what's going on? The grapevine has it that you've been leaving on time the past three weeks." Maxi lightly touched the profusion of lilies and greenery. She eyed her sister as she walked over to the couch, sat down and then patted the empty spot next to her.

Victoria laughed as she rose from the seat behind her desk and joined her sister.

"And word also has it that that fine assed Lennox Mays leaves shortly thereafter. Aren't they almost done?" She patted her sister's hand.

"They've one more week. And once the building is complete Lennox's crew will return to make sure there are no issues with connections."

"Oh, we've gone from Mr. Mays to Lennox." Maxi tilted her head to one side. "My baby sister is in love."

Victoria blushed at the thought of it all. She found herself looking forward to seeing him each day. And for the three past weeks they'd spent countless hours together, talking and getting to know each other mind, body and soul. When she awoke in his arms this morning, she looked into the face of the man who had unselfishly given his body and mind to her, calling forth every sensation she owned, and then some, she knew she had fallen in love.

"Max, he is sooo…" her voice trailed off. She had so much to tell and didn't know where to begin. She hadn't intended on this being a surprise for Maxine, she just had been so wrapped up in Morrison Construction during the day, and the arms of Lennox Mays at night.

"Has my sister finally found the right one? I mean, that Scott dude was wacked. He hadn't a clue as to what women like us really need. Women who have chosen to make a way in a man's world."

"Lennox truly understands me Max. And I've fallen. Hard."

"This calls for a celebration. Dad needs to meet this Lennox Mays. Bring him to dinner tomorrow."

"Let me check with Lennox and I'll call you later."

For the next two hours, Victoria confided in her sister, with them ending their impromptu meeting when Lennox arrived to have lunch with Victoria.

Victoria and Maxi watched as he walked into the office. Maxi pinched Victoria lightly on the arm as she eyed the man who had put the light in her the sister's eyes.

Lennox kissed Victoria lightly on the lips before moving over to place several bags on top of the table in the corner of her office. "I hope you're hungry, mi Corazon. I brought lunch." He smiled at Maxi. "Hey, Maxine, it's good to see you again. If I had known you were going to be here I'da bought you a sandwich. But you can have half of mine if you'd like."

Max shook her head. "No, I have a meeting with a potential client. I'll catch up with you two later." She rose from the couch. "Vic, call me later okay." She headed to the door. "Bye yall."

Victoria waved and waited until the door shut. She walked over and locked it, a wicked smile spread across her face as Lennox walked over to her. He took her hands and placed them above her head, his lips capturing hers, his tongue mating with hers, exploring her mouth.

She moaned as the heated sensations started at the tips of her toes and rose slowly, marking each nerve ending in her body. Lennox released her hands and crushed his body to hers as she wrapped her arms around him, the feel of his member, which was hard as steel, pressed against her. Never, she thought, in a million years would she ever get enough of this man, of his body.

"I'd love desert before lunch," Lennox whispered. He began to walk backward, heading toward the couch, taking Victoria with him. "Be my desert."

Victoria fell onto the couch. She watched as Lennox walk over to the windows and shut the blinds. He began to remove his clothes as he walked back toward her. She licked her lips absently when he'd shed the last article. Standing before her, his hard member jutted out toward her, his sculpted body called to her, ordered her. She slid from the couch and onto the floor, taking his member in her hand before licking the tip. She felt his fingers in her hair, loosening it from the scrunch to allow the tresses to fall over her shoulders as she took the hardened member into her mouth, her tongue and lips working in concert. She found the sounds he made pleasurable and wildly erotic as he told her what he was going to do to her for being so good.

Releasing him with a pop, she stood and shed her work clothes.

"Victoria, where are your bra and panties?"

"Umm, at home." She slid her naked body up and down his. "Are you disappointed?"

"No," he responded as he bent to capture a nipple between his lips. "I love it. I love you, mi Corazon." He paused, looking up into her eyes. He had wanted to tell her the day he laid eyes on her, but knew that a declaration of that magnitude would possibly spook her. But each time he had been with her, in and out of the bed, he found himself deeper in love with her. And once the families met, he had every intention of asking her father's permission to propose marriage.

"Are you okay, with that, Victoria?" He straightened. Taking her face gently in his hands he continued. "I knew that I wanted to you in my bed and no one else's the moment you called me the Telephone Man and the night I saw you dressed in that little wisp of nothing." They shared a laugh. "And I fell in love with you that day on the roof top."

Victoria looked in his eyes. In the time she'd gotten to know him she found that his emotions shone through his eyes. When he was irritated they changed to a serious flat gold. When he was aroused, they became a deep golden blaze, with the specks of green becoming more pronounced. And when he was satisfied, they reminded her of a lion. Right now, her Telephone Man turned lion was satisfied. And while she was somewhat inexperienced at matters of the heart, she knew herself well enough to know that what she was facing was a man she would rather not live the rest of life without.

She rose on the tips of her toes and kissed him lightly on the lips. "I love you, Lennox."

He tilted his head to one side. "Say it again."

"Lennox Mays, I love you so much."

He pulled her into his arms and held her. Victoria could feel the rapid beating of his heart close to her own and realized that her declaration had truly touched him. This man had placed his heart and soul in her hands—had awakened every inch of her, including her heart.

Her head rose just as his lips began its sensual assault, one that Victoria had come to expect, want and need. She had never been so turned on by lips, but Lennox's full, soft lips touching hers and all points east, west, north and south always seemed to send her senses on a tailspin.

"You will not regret a day with me, Mija." He continued to kiss her, raining across her face, then down the center of her chest, pausing to kiss the spot of skin that covered her heart. She held his head to her bosom, the rapid beating of her pulse pronounced.

"I need to quench my thirst for you, Mija. Can I?"

Without waiting for a response, Lennox lowered to the floor and pulled her mound close to his face. He pressed his nose into her feminine folds, inhaled deeply and then flicked his tongue across her bud.

Victoria shuddered and held on for the satisfying ride she knew would leave her satiated while at the same time wanting more.

And as if this was her first time, her body reacted with a vengeance, her bud throbbed. She threw her head back and held onto Lennox as the climax rolled over her. Without question, this man was it and if she was wrong, then Lord, she'd check herself into the closest convent.

Chapter Ten

Victoria absently responded to the incoming call on her cell. She hadn't bothered to look at the caller id.

"Hey there sexy," the voice stated.

She looked at the caller id and frowned. It was Scott.

"Have you reconsidered my offer to take you to the BCU dinner?"

"No, Scott I have not. I told you, I have a date."

"Truly you don't think that playboy Lennox is right for you."

How did he know about Lennox? She wondered. She had requested Lennox escort her and he agreed. She frowned at what Scott had just said, thinking that he had gone too far.

"I hear he's quite the lady's man, Vic. You can do better. I mean, I know I messed up. Susanna was just something to do."

"Yeah, right, Scott. Do you remember telling me it was my fault you slept with her. That you just happened to fall into her vagina?" She shook her head. Why was she entertaining this nut case? But she had to admit, it was going to be something to see his expression when she walked into that event with her arm on Lennox's. "Scott, I've got to go. I'm really busy. And do me a favor, honor my wishes and don't call me again."

"I can't do that Vic. I care deeply for you and I won't see you make the biggest mistake of your life and get tangled up with the likes of that Mays dude."

"That's not your business. Please just leave me alone..." she began as she looked around to see Lennox standing feet away, his eyes the shade of gold bullion. She wondered how long he'd been there and had he overhead the one-sided conversation. She got her answer when he stalked over to where she was standing. He held out his hand for her cell. Victoria shook her head and mouthed "I got this."

Lennox folded his arms over his massive chest. Victoria had told him about that Scott and he hadn't believed the man tried that simple crap of deflection and thought it would work on Victoria.

"Scott, I've got to go. Stop calling me." She disconnected the call and placed her cell in its pouch connected to her hip. The last thing she wanted to do was have a conversation with Lennox about a has-been.

"Do I need to call Scott?" He asked.

Victoria saw the angry look plastered on his handsome face and noted the gold fury swirling in his eyes. She wasn't pleased.

"I took care of it." She responded and then returned to measuring several pieces of dour rock.

"Apparently not, Victoria. If you had he would not be calling you."

"I don't want to talk about it, Lennox." She changed the subject. "What time are you coming by, tonight?"

"Why don't you have Scott come by?" He replied and then turned quickly, leaving her alone.

She opened her mouth to reply. No words came out. She didn't need him to interfere—didn't need him to ride in on the white horse. Or did she? In the time they had been dating, she had never seen Lennox angry and thinking about the raging storm in his eyes she knew she didn't want to see it again. He looked possessed.

"That wasn't too great, Boss Lady," Bobby said as he appeared. "I'd be angry, too."

"Look, I can handle Scott and Lennox."

"Yeah, but a man needs to protect what's his. You have to let a man be a man, Vic."

"I do?"

She watched as Bobby shook his head. "Yes you do. And I can't blame you. In business you take no prisoners. But this is …." He swept his hands outward. "In matters of the heart, a brother like him needs to be king of the castle. He's good, Vic. He doesn't care what you do for a living—he's secure in that. You have to make sure he's secure in your heart." He sat on the construction horse and pointed toward the area Lennox had just vacated. "Look, it doesn't make you weak or lessen your effectiveness as a boss if you show a little emotion. It just shows that you are a woman, a good looking one at that, with real feelings. Got it, Queen?"

"Wow. That bad?"

"No, not too bad. But Scott is only angry because his plan backfired on him. Most women when cheated upon blame themselves initially. You on the other hand never fell for the garbage."

She looked at her foreman with wide eyes. "How in the heck do you know all of this?"

"Scott's people. He had wanted to join this company with his—he having some cash flow problems—and when you didn't respond to his charms as fast as the other women had he thought he'd up the ante. Shoot, knowing Scott, he figured yall would be married by now and he'd be head of Morrison Construction."

Victoria shook her head. To think, she had considered, but never really thought they would marry. There had been something in the corner of her mind that just didn't see her with Scott permanently. But with Lennox, all she wanted was forever with him. She was in love with him and was remised to do anything other than love him. And then here she was allowing Scott's silliness to interfere. Oh no, what have I done?

"Did you see where Lennox went?" She removed her tool belt.

"He left." Bobby said. "If you like, I can ask some of his crew where he went. They're on fourteen stringing wire."

"No, I'll call him on his cell." She pulled her cell from its pouch and dialed his cell. She listened as the voice mail came on. She left a message. Sighing, she reluctantly returned to measuring and then cutting the dour rock for the floors. "Thanks Bobby." She turned her back on him, not wanting him to see the tear that escaped her right eye. They had never fought because neither one of them believed in arguing. They had agreed to disagree, but anger had never been a part of their relationship.

At the end of her day, Victoria dragged to her condo. Greeted at the door by Little Bit, she picked up the dog and cradled her close. "Oh, I done messed up, big time."

Several hours and countless checks of her cell and the caller id of her land-based phone, she still hadn't heard from Lennox. The event was tomorrow night. And regardless, she had to attend.

Victoria grabbed her evening purse and wrap. She checked her image in the mirror, having used a little extra concealer under her eyes to hide the slight bags from lack of sleep and crying. She knew she had it bad—she was deeply in love with Lennox and was angry that she allowed her inability to allow him to protect her to interfere.

Stepping out of the condo, she turned and was face to face with Lennox.

"I'm so sorry, will you please forgive me," they both said simultaneously, smiling somewhat sheepishly as their eyes met.

Victoria thought about what Bobby had said, taking it to heart and knowing that she should have allowed Lennox to get Scott to move on. A part of her wanted to show that she could take care of herself, but the other part, the ultra feminine part of her, wanted Lennox on the white horse. The warring emotions had confused her until Bobby had set her straight. Now, standing before him she realized that she should have handed over the cell phone and allowed Lennox to protect what he'd come to possess: Her.

Lennox looked at Victoria and thought of how angry he had been. Anger was a foreign emotion to him so when he'd felt it the other day it had surprised him. He always attempted to still his emotions, made sure that he was in control. But when it came to Victoria he didn't know the word—she brought out all the emotions and feeling he had prided himself in containing. And when he'd figured that her ex wouldn't get the hint he had wanted to find this Scott character and re-arrange a few things.

He placed his arms out toward her and watched as she walked into them and wrapped her arms around his neck, her lips upon his.

"I don't ever want to fight with you again," Victoria said between kisses.

"I've been so miserable. I should have given you the phone."

"And I should have just trusted that you could handle the situation." He returned the kisses and groaned loudly as the kisses intensified.

Victoria took his hands wrapped around her waist and moved them up to her breasts. And while in the back of her mind she knew that the BCU event was in one hour, what she needed and wanted was right in her arms.

She reached around her back and unzipped her dress, allowing the fabric to pool at her feet. Dressed only in a bra and thong panty, Victoria slid her body up and down his and was rewarded by the feel of his hardness against her.

Lennox grasped her hips; the sensation of her grinding hers into hers was taking him to the edge. She shook her head and moved his hands to her taut behind, her feminine mound ground around and around as he artfully plied and massaged her.

"I want you, Victoria."

She responded by removing the jacket to his tuxedo, followed by his dress shirt. She loved the view of his sculpted chest and the soft hairs that surround his pectorals and nipples. Reaching out, Victoria raked her hands through his chest hairs. Her hands lowered to unbuckle his belt, followed by unbuttoning then unzipping his pants. She watched as Lennox kicked his shoes off, pulled his socks off with his feet and then kicked his pants to the corner of the hallway. She was relieved that she was the only one living in the building.

Victoria removed her bra and thong, allowing the articles to join her dress on the floor.

Without warning, Lennox lifted her, his hardness poised at her entrance. She saw the emotion, felt it in her own heart, the love and passion they elicited from each other. She never wanted to be without him again.

"Now, Lennox," she demanded and was rewarded when he entered her slowly, allowing her tightness to pull him in, cover him, sheath him. Once at the hilt, they moved in unison, their bodies joined as one, fluid and commanding. He was hers. She was his.

Victoria closed her eyes. The sensation started without warning, sliding up her toes, making her hips crash against his as he slid in and out of her, his member growing with each magnificent stroke. The orgasm started slowly, unlike any she'd experienced with him. It was almost as if her body had wanted to prolong the sweet sensation, to drag it out into eternity.

"No, Chica, look at me," he stated and then began to move quicker, pulling the sensation from her, loving the feel of her gripping him possessively, the sounds and scents of their lovemaking filled the hallway. It was an elixir—a balm to his entire being.

"Lennox," she mouthed his name over and over, her legs tighter around his waist as her core surrounded him in a vice. He held on to her and watched as her face was a beautiful mask of desire and temporary satiation.

He held her to him and allowed her to come down before he reached his own release.

"Hold on, baby." He moved in and out of her, his body sending the signal to hers that only she could pull this out of him; could make him loose control.

Lennox knew that he would never get enough and that his decision was the right one for him. He just hoped that Victoria felt the same.

Chapter Eleven

"Papa, I need to talk to you," Lennox stated as he walked into his father's office and took the seat across from his desk. He looked at his father and was glad to see him back and working following his back injury. He had returned to work a week ago.

"Are you okay?" Manuel Mays looked up at his oldest son and smiled. And while he loved all of his children, this one was most like him in temperament and mannerisms.

Lennox picked up the paperweight from his desk and glanced at it. He and his father had never really discussed matters of the heart even though he had been the one to educate him and his brother on sex. He stifled a chuckle remembering how his father had pulled each of them into the garage and gave them a crash course in Sex 101. At the time, Lennox recalled, he didn't know which one of them was the most nervous.

"I'm well, Papa." He looked into his father's eyes and then blurted out: "I want to get married."

Manuel made a tent of his fingers, resting them on his chest and then leaned back in his chair. "You want to marry Victor Morrison's daughter." Came the statement.

Lennox's eyes widened. Though they had been dating for just a little over a month and hadn't been sneaking around, he hadn't told any of his family who he had been dating. He had wanted to invite Victoria to the upcoming family picnic for Labor Day and introduce her then. He watched as his father nodded his head and laughed.

"We all know. The construction industry may be large, but among the minority community it is small. Plus I heard you and Victoria made quite a couple at the BCU event last week."

Lennox smiled at that memory. After they had made intense love in Victoria's hallway, they had dressed and attended the black-tie event together. And when Scott approached, Lennox had stepped forward and asked the man one question without batting an eye: "How lucky do you feel tonight?" He had watched as Scott's eyes widened, his Adam's apple bobbed up and down from the hard swallowing. Once Scott averted his eyes, he stepped back and left without a word.

The sound of his father's movement brought his attention back to the present. Manuel rose from the chair and walked around to stand over his son. He placed his hand on Lennox's shoulder. "Do you love her?"

Lennox nodded his head. "With everything I have, Papa."

"Does she feel the same about you?"

"Yes."

"Well, it is time to bring the families together. When will you ask Victor for her hand?"

"We are supposed to go to dinner tomorrow night. I thought of calling him and possibly meeting before that."

"Does Victoria know this?"

Lennox shook his head no. He wanted to surprise her. "I'm praying she won't turn me down."

"You have my blessings. Come by tonight and tell your mother."

Lennox rose from the seat and was embraced by his father. "Gracias Papa. I'll see you later."

Manuel watched as his son walked out of his office. The marriage of Morrison and Mays would be a great one. He picked up the phone.

"Momma, we have another son ready to get married."

"Daddy, you be nice to Lennox." Victoria chided into the phone as she finished dressing for dinner. "I don't want any cuteness out of you tonight." She thought of when he'd met Scott. He hadn't cared for him—that she could see in the way he had provided one word responses to Scott's questions.

"Sweet-P, I mean no harm. I just want to make sure this man is treating my baby girl right."

Victoria stilled as she sat on the edge of her bed, her knees buckling at the thought of last night, when Lennox had treated her to a night of beauty. She had been surprised when she arrived home after an unusually stress-filled day to find Lennox had cooked, her table set and her whirlpool tub filled with scented oils. He'd even placed a ribbon around Little Bit's neck. By the end of the night, Lennox had pampered her from head to toe and she had fallen asleep nestled safely in his arms. Oh, he had treated her right—she knew she could get used to coming home to him every day and lying in his arms, making love to him every night. Could she do forever? She wondered. The sound of her father calling her name snapped her out of her revere.

"What did you say, daddy?"

"I said I'll try and be nice," she heard him say.

"Okay, Daddy, I mean it. Best behavior. I'll see you in a couple of hours."

Lennox held open the door and watched as Victoria walked in ahead of him. They had been out plenty of times over the past month and he'd seen her in various stages of dress, and undressed, but the dress she wore tonight called out to him. Once he had arrived at her door, he had wanted to slide his hands all over the silk fabric, feeling her curves through the material and then take her right there, dress and all.

"Baby, all eyes are on you in that dress." He whispered in her ear. Upon feeling her shiver, he smiled. Yeah, he thought, the brothers may be looking but she was going home with him.

Lennox looked up just as Victor Morrison's face came into view. His nerves had never surfaced like they had at the sight of the man who'd earlier granted him his blessing to marry his youngest daughter. His thoughts went to their earlier meeting where Mr. Morrison had grilled him as to how much did he love Victoria, was he comfortable with her working in the construction industry, would he love her until the day he breathed his last breath. Lennox had assured Mr. Morrison that he would do all of the above and then some. He had thought long and hard after speaking with his mother and knew that while Victoria may want to hang up the tool belt, he'd stand by her and allow it to be her decision. He no more wanted to control her than he wanted her out of his life.

"Mr. Morrison, it's a pleasure."

"Same here, son." Victor Morrison rose, clasping his hand in Lennox's just before he pulled him into bear-type embrace. Victoria raised her eyebrows and glanced over at her sister. Maxine shrugged her shoulders.

"How's your father? We haven't talked in a while."

"He's good. Getting prepared to do what you did and retire."

"I'll have to call him and introduce him to the great world of retirement." Victor released Lennox's hand. "So, how's the rest of your family? Your mother?"

Victoria sat next to Lennox and watched and he and her father spoke like old friends. If she didn't know any better, she'd swear they'd met before.

At the end of dinner, Lennox and Victoria headed to Lennox's home.

"Come here, Mi Corazon." Lennox took her hand in his and led her to deck located at the rear of the house. Once there he looked up into the sky and watched as the clouds parted to reveal a full moon. Picking up a remote from a nearby cabinet he depressed a button. He smiled at Victoria when a song by Heatwave floated out of the speakers.

"Dance with me." He pulled her close once she nodded yes. They danced to the smooth song Lennox singing along, his deep baritone surprisingly joined he falsetto of Johnny Wilder as he sang about the woman of his desire being the star of his story.

His hands ran lightly up the back of her dress, liking the feel of the material. He smiled when she leaned closer, placing her head on his shoulder as they swayed to sultry tune. "You are truly beautiful, Victoria. And I know that you love me. But what I need to know is that do you love me enough to marry me?"

Victoria paused. Had she heard him right? Did this dream of a man just ask her to marry him?

"I asked your father for your hand in marriage and after a long grilling he agreed to let me ask you to marry me. And I spoke to my mom and she said she can't wait to meet you. Now, all I need to do ..."

She watched as Lennox stopped dancing, knelt on one knee and took her left hand in his.

"Victoria Morrison, will you make me an eternally happy man and marry me?"

She nodded. "Yes, Lennox, I'll marry you," she responded as a lone tear escaped and rolled down her cheek. She had never been so in love before. And the one thing she absolutely loved about her sexy Telephone Man was that no matter, she knew he would never try to change her.

Built To Last
By
Edwina Martin-Arnold

Other Titles by Edwina Martin Arnold
Soldier Boys
Chocolate Friday
House Guest
Jolie's Surrender
Eve's Prescription

Chapter One

Sunrise approached as Jackson Jack slipped into the house in South Seattle where he was remodeling the kitchen. Dawn slid in with him, making him smile as he watched the light highlight the cream walls and walnut colored wood floor with an amber brilliance. Shaking off the chill of the brisk air, Jackson shut the front door and began making his way to the kitchen through the hallway of the small house. Late August and it was already cold in Seattle. If the city wasn't so beautiful, Jackson swore he'd move.

The bathroom door opened as he passed, startling him, and he stopped in his tracks. He only had seconds to appreciate the lush nakedness of the woman who walked right into him, wetting his white tee, and jangling his tool belt. But what he'd seen was a chocolate treat, delectable enough to make his stomach want to growl, and smelling so sweet he swore his tooth began to ache.

The woman shrieked like he was Jason or Mike Myers and her long hair, held in a loose ponytail, bounced as she fell back. Automatically, his hands flew out to her shoulders to steady her. Smooth warm skin greeted his rough fingers.

Seconds later, he realized he'd made a huge mistake! A knee to his groin had him doubling up and stumbling backwards while he gasped for breath. The yelling continued, disturbing the quiet morning air as fists rained down on his head. If he wasn't suffering so, he would have truly appreciated that such a slender woman could generate so much force, and that her full breasts jiggled very near his face. A part of him was disappointed when she eventually wore herself out and stopped. Leaning against the wall, still hunched over, he watched the cutest bubble butt run away and disappear into the small master bedroom with a loud slam. The decisive click of the lock being turned was loud. Like that flimsy thing could keep him out if he really wanted in the bedroom.

Good Lord, he thought as he struggled to stand straight. Slowly, he made his way out the house. It felt like it took a half an hour to reach his Chevy Silverado where he gingerly stepped into the passenger seat and sat down heavily. He took deep breaths, and as the pain receded, he realized he probably knew who the woman was. He'd been told she was a spitfire and by God her family members who had warned him were right.

He wasn't surprised when he heard the sirens. In fact, he didn't flinch when the police car skid to a halt at an angle in front of his truck. He just sat there, wondering how long it would take to clear this mess up. If he had to go to jail, somebody was going to pay extra. He had other jobs waiting and this one would have been done in a day or two if it hadn't been for the hellion. Speaking of the devil, she came bursting out of the house fully clothed in black, silky looking, designer sweats and fancy tennis shoes that looked like they'd fall apart in the rain. Her arms were waving and she screeched, "That's him, that's the rapist!" as she headed straight for him, looking like she wanted to us her fists again. Those he could handle. It was her knees he wanted desperately to avoid.

The officers looked at him, sitting there with the passenger door open and one drew his gun. Jackson sat up straighter, wondering if he should have left. No, he hadn't done anything wrong, and he wasn't one to run at the first hint of trouble.

Hands held up, Jackson said, "Officers I don't know what's up with the crazy woman, but I can assure you, and prove, that I'm supposed to be here."

Mia Walsh felt justified as the officers approached the pervert. How dare he break in her house and assault her! She rubbed her sore knuckles as anxiety and anger coursed through her.

One of the officers approached her. "Are you the owner of this house, ma'am?"

"Yes, uh no," she stumbled over the answer. "My parents own the house. Why do you ask? Why isn't he in handcuffs?"

"Do you have a cell phone handy?"

Mia pulled one out of her sweats.

"Can you call your parents?"

"Yes," Mia answered, looking at the man as if he were crazy, then dialed the number, waited, hung up, dialed another number, waited, and then hung up. "I got their voicemails."

The officer left, then came back to her after speaking with the pervert.

"Do you have a brother, ma'am?"

She nodded.

He pointed to the phone in her hand. "Please call."

She did. Mark answered on the first ring. She'd barely greeted him when the officer was motioning for the phone. She gave it to him. The man turned his back and began walking away as he talked. Mia could hear mumbles, but couldn't distinguish what was being said. After a couple of minutes, the officer went to the pervert and seemed to be talking to him and her brother. Then, he handed her phone to the rapist!

Several minutes later, the police let the pervert drive away. What the hell? Mia uncrossed her arms and stomped off the porch. Both officers approached and before she could say a word, the female thrust the cell at her and said, "You need to talk to your brother, ma'am. The gentleman had every right to be here."

"What?" she yelled.

"Your sibling can explain. Take the phone please."

She did and watched a little stunned as the officers left. "Mark, what's going on?" she said as soon as she put the cell to her ear.

"You, being a drama queen, again. Why didn't you let us know you were coming home?"

"Since when do I have to notify you that I'm coming to Seattle? You're my brother, not my keeper."

"A damn keeper is what your spoiled butt needs. Are you going to be a professional do nothing forever? I can't believe you let mom and dad foot your bills all the way through college and you've done nothing with the degree. No, you had to go play in New York under the pretense of getting more education."

Mia interrupted, "Mark, I paid my own way through law school."

"That's not the point! When are you going to work, be responsible, and contribute to society like the rest of us?"

Fury flashed through her followed closely by panic. God, I can't believe I didn't pass the damn bar! If her brother knew the whole truth, he'd have field day. Pushing the thought to the side, she focused on what her high and mighty brother was saying now.

"If you'd let someone know what you were up to, this mess could have been avoided. I can't believe you called the police on J..."

"You know him. He's was in the house and…"

Her brother made a strange noise, cutting her off. She could imagine the contemptuous look on his face when he said, "Of course he was there! Did you look around? Didn't you notice the kitchen is torn apart?"

"Yes, but…"

"He's has a small construction company, Mia. He's remodeling. Technically, he had more of a right to be there than you."

Mia was silent as the words sunk in. Then she muttered, "Oh."

"Yes, little sister, who creates chaos wherever she goes."

She was tired of Mark. "Shut up, please. I'll be out of the house in thirty minutes. Tell the worker he can come back then." She pushed the off button so hard, her thumb hurt.

Two hours later, Jackson approached the house again. Mark had called and promised his sister would be gone in an hour, but he was still cautious. He'd never been accused of being a rapist and he for damn sure didn't like it. This time he rang the doorbell twice before using his key to enter.

He yelled, "Hello," loudly as he paused in the doorway to see if someone answered. Only normal house sounds greeted him, so he went to the kitchen, thankful there were no hellcats rushing around naked, calling him names, questioning his character.

He'd only meet the woman briefly, but he'd decided that he wanted no part of her, no matter how good those parts looked in her birthday suit. He'd met her kind before. Stylish, refined, beautiful, supposedly classy, all of those characteristics were just fine by him. It was the spoiled attitude that usually came along with her type that bothered him.

Shaking his head, he reflected on how his knowledge was first hand. The Sophisticated Lady who had gotten to him had been a Harvard graduate who'd come to Seattle to work in the Technology industry. She'd bought a four bedroom house that she called a bungalow, and he was hired to remodel it.

At first, he thought it was cute that she acted like she was so much above the Seattle hicks. One of her favorite subjects was her family's blue-blood history and how many mucky-mucks she knew so well in her short life of twenty-five years. He really didn't care because she acted like the sun rose and set on his black butt.

The whole sordid affair lasted about a year, until she got a job offer for a zillion dollars from some company in L.A. Suddenly, he was demoted to bumpkin and his princess flew the coop with barely a kiss on his cheek. No, he knew her type and he much more preferred the down to earth, real women like his mother and the legendary soul singer, Patti LaBelle. His mother had owned a small restaurant that specialized in Philadelphia style Cheese Steaks up until her death of a heart attack five years ago. Ms. Patti, as he called her, came from the city of brotherly love and every time she'd come to Seattle, she dropped by the restaurant or had his mother deliver food to the hotel.

Between the two women, he knew what a true lady was about. He learned as he'd watched Labelle and his mom discuss everything from recipes to the best cleaner to disinfect the house with. Real women encouraged comfort, made people feel at home, and left a certain warmness in the heart that he couldn't explain if his life depended on it. He just knew it when it was there. His mother displayed it countless times with the patrons of the restaurant, and he'd witnessed it in Ms. Patti's equal treatment of all those around her. His highfaluting, ex-girlfriend and Mark's sister were definitely lacking in the real department. If he never saw them again, it would be too soon.

Jackson ran his hand over the fine wood of the cabinets he was about to install, reflecting that the grain was much truer than Mia. He believed that's what her brother had called her when they'd spoken on the phone.

He loved wood and had since he'd first really touched it in an eighth grade shop class in middle school. His teacher had been great, exposing his students to just about every type imaginable, explaining the special properties of each and telling them why he thought wood was the greatest creation on earth. Jackson agreed and knew when he was older he'd do some occupation where he could touch it every day.

He moved the cabinet around, checking it out thoroughly and admiring longer than he probably should have. Cherry wood. He remembered how he'd talked the Walshs into using it. Although once they saw it, it was an easy sell.

Strangely, the thought made Mia pop into his head again. Hell, the woman was certainly distinctive and memorable if nothing else. He forced his thoughts back to the wood to push images of the irritating woman out of his mind.

The woods color reminded him of her supple skin. "Dammit," he muttered when he realized he was doing it once more. Hefting up the cabinet, he prepared to install it, vowing not to think of Mia Walsh again.

Chapter Two

Thirty minutes after Mia left her families' rental property, she was letting herself into her childhood home after paying the taxi driver. Her parents, Mathew and Marie, weren't there and the house was cold as if the heat had been off a long time. She'd looked in the garage and both of their cars were there. Where were they?. She walked through the house. It was spotless. The kitchen was clean and orderly with silver pots that twinkled from their place above the island. The ceramic floor shined, not a piece of dirt to be found. It was so strange; Mia thought as she wandered down the silent hallway and glanced into her parents' bedroom. The bed was made and nothing was out of place.

Mia jumped when the phone rang. She rushed back to the kitchen to grab the receiver. The woman on the other end was very polite and official-sounding when she assumed she was her mother after Mia said, "Hello." Before she could correct her, the woman began mentioning things like tissue sample, test results, and chemotherapy.

Mia's heart stopped.

All thoughts crumbled like ashes in the wind. She sat on the hard kitchen floor that suddenly seemed to stretch out for miles, contour oddly warped. Her throat dried up and she swallowed desperately to avoid the cough she felt building. Pressing the phone to her ear, she listened carefully, hoping that her brother or some other prankster would jump from the walls yelling that this was some weird twisted joke.

The voice continued, very matter of factly, as the woman explained that she needed to change her mother's appointment with the oncologist. In a voice that sounded strangely hollow, Mia told the woman who she was and guaranteed that she'd have her mother call as soon as possible. Then she finessed more information out of the woman to find herself staring at the floor, eyes wide and hurting. Thyroid cancer. Mia didn't know how long she sat, phone pressed to her ear long after the woman hung up.

When she stood, she stumbled, legs stiff and uncooperative. She dropped the cordless and the batteries tumbled from the back. Her fingers felt thick as she struggled to fix the phone, then she dialed her brother's number. The time between each of the three rings stretched like an eternity.

"Mark, why didn't someone tell me? Where are they?" She didn't realize she was crying until she heard her own broken voice.

Silence, she would kill her brother if he played games now. He sighed, before saying, "Alaska. They boarded a cruise a few days ago. With all that mom's been through, they wanted some time away."

She was scared to ask, but had to know, "Is…is she alright?"

"She's had the surgery, came through chemo great, and last report was that's it's all gone. The call's just routine follow-up. Mom is fine." Her brother almost sounded compassionate, which made her cry harder. "Hush, Mia. She's okay."

Squeezing her eyes tight, she said, "When will...they be back?"

"September first."

A week! She couldn't see her mother for a whole week.

"Mia, are you alright? I can come over there."

Mia smiled, remembering how close they were as children. "No, Mark, I'm okay. Just shocked. I'll be fine."

After she hung up, Mia drifted into the living room and ended up lying on the couch. She didn't recall falling asleep, but she woke up disoriented. Weak sunlight from the skylight warmed her face and made her squint when her eyes opened. Shards of light patterned her skin and the sofa as she sat up and rubbed her aching face. She felt weighted down and heavy as she moved her neck experimentally. Her flesh steamed underneath the sweats she wore.

Running her hands through her long hair, she pushed from the couch, determined to do something so she wouldn't go crazy. She called her three best friends, all of whom still lived in Seattle. One of them could meet her at a bar and grill up the street. Another was available for a lunch the following day. The third, she couldn't reach. Mia changed into jeans and a mock tee with a vee neckline. Grabbing her black leather coat and purse, she hopped into her mother's Mercedes and drove to the spot.

After going inside, Mia didn't see her friend and settled on a stool at the bar. She looked around, acknowledging that the place oozed with stylishly dull décor with its shiny wooden bar and deep mini chandlers hanging from the ceiling just above the patrons and the bartenders' heads. Light jazz played in the background, not loud enough to interfere with the quiet conversations of the happy hour crowd, which consisted of mostly men and women dressed in business attire. Mia didn't really care if she was out of place in her casual clothing. She just wished her friend would hurry up. She ordered a Mojito and sat back to wait. Soon another Mojito arrived.

"Complements of the gentleman over there," the bartender explained.

Mia followed the finger to an attractive man waving from a table where he sat with three other men. She turned to the bartender, ready to refuse the drink when the man appeared at her elbow.

Mia had to look a long way up to reach his face. He was about six foot six of gorgeous male in a dark gray suit and red tie. Male attention was nothing new to her and she enjoyed harmless flirtation as much as anyone. However, she just wasn't interested and, to her surprise, she found herself comparing Mr. Suit and Tie to the handyman she'd ran into literally earlier. He'd been tall, too, but not as tall as this man, probably only six two or three, and although, this man's skin was clear, the handyman's had been smoother, more handsomely sharp. His complexion was darker as well, coal-black, just how Mia preferred her men. Not that she preferred the handyman. When she'd last looked at him, right before he pulled off after the officer had released him, he'd smiled, revealing devilish dimples and laughing eyes that made her want to throw something at him.

Before Mr. Suit and Tie could speak some corny pick-up line, Mia's eyebrow arched to slayer level. "Unless I can blindfold, handcuff, and have my way with you with a few large objects, don't bother." The man's eyes widened and she handed him the drink he'd sent her. Then she showed him her back and sipped the Mojito. It felt good going down her throat.

"Geez, I can see, old maid, in your future."

"Angela Lewis!" Mia jumped up. She hadn't seen her friend in over a year, and she had to stretch up to hug her because Angela was just about as tall as the handyman. Afterwards, she stepped back and said, "You look great." Angela wore a skirt that had a high thigh exposing slit, and her bone-straight hair flowed down her back with just a hint of salon clinging to it, revealing that it was freshly permed. Mia didn't doubt that every male eye had graced her friend's form at least once the minute she entered the room. Her looks and style certainly didn't hurt her occupation as a clothes buyer for Nordstrom.

"Girl, what's wrong with you? That brother was fine," her friend said.

"Not in the mood. I've had enough of men today." Also, she didn't want to be bothered because she was still upset about her mother. However, she didn't want to share that with her friend yet. There would be plenty of time for that. Right now she wanted to laugh and forget for a while, and Angela was always great company.

"Is such a thing possible? I could toy with men twenty-four seven." Angela teased, hugging her again. They both sat at the bar and Angela sipped her drink. She laughed when Mia's brow crinkled, then told the bartender, "That's good. I'll have one of those, whatever it is."

"Ang you haven't changed. We're in our late twenties now. Don't you think it's time you stopped dipping into my food and drinks?"

"Nope. It always taste better coming from your glass or plate."

"You're lucky I love you, girl and put up with your irritating butt."

Her friend just laughed, then said, "So why are you growling at men? Has your time in New York soured you on brothas?"

"No." Her head moved from side to side. "Believe me, it wasn't New York. It's the ones right here in Seattle."

"Damn, Mia. How long have you been home? I got the impression you'd just arrived. How come you're just now contacting me?"

"I got in last night." Mia went on to explain her morning.

Her friend was doubled over with laughter by the time she finished.

"You almost had him arrested?"

"From my point of view at the time, it was justified, Angela."

"Yeah, right, that's what you get for trying to sneak home. Do you know the poor man's name, or do you like to just call him the handyman?"

"No, I did not catch his name."

"Didn't you ask your brother?"

"Why would I ask him that? I don't plan on ever seeing the man again, so I sure don't care what his name is!"

"Whoa. Calm down, sista. It's just if you're going to repeat this story, you'd sound a little less haughty if you knew the man's name and didn't refer to him by his occupation." There was still a lot of laughter behind her friend's words.

Mia ordered another two Mojitos for them, and then she sniffed. "Haughty? Are you trying to say I'm arrogant? I never sound that way."

Her friend burst out with laughter again. "If you don't believe me, go ask the brother you just about castrated when I first got here."

"Be quiet, Ang, before I attempt to do something similar with your tongue."

"You're just mad because you know I'm right."

Mia tried to make an angry face, but she melted into chuckles. "You know what? You're right, Ang. I was horrible and now I'm actually a little embarrassed." She had to admit that ever since she'd found out about her mother, the whole incident with the handyman seemed trivial. "I suppose if I ever see the man again, I'll have to apologize."

"It would be the civilized thing to do."

Their laughing spree was interpreted by two more suits. Angela got rid of the men this time. When she turned back to her friend, she said, "Mia, what's wrong? Why do you look so sad?"

Mia quickly smiled. "Nothing's wrong." She sipped her drink.

"Don't lie to me, girl. The look on your face just a moment ago seemed like someone was a walking on your grave."

Mia felt her face fall. "Horrible choice of words, Angela." She rubbed her cheeks vigorously before saying, "I just found out my mom's been battling cancer. No wait," she said when her friend was about to interrupt. "According to my brother, she's going to be fine. It's just the whole shock of it all that I'm still struggling with."

"Girl, I am so sorry." Angela leaned over and hugged her deeply. "You're mom is so terrific, I hate to think of her hurting in any way."

"Me too." Mia quickly wiped her eyes. She explained how her parents were out of town. "I was going crazy in the house. Thanks for meeting me."

"Anytime, honey. You know I'm always here for you to talk too, just like you've always been there for me."

"Okay, enough sad talk," Mia announced. "Fill me in on all the gossip."

"All right, girl. Did you hear about…" For the next two hours, she and Angela talked and laughed until their sides hurt. By the time Mia left, she felt much less restless, that is until she laid her head on the pillow in her childhood room.

Being with her friend had helped her down play all her troubles. She didn't think about her life plan, she didn't dwell on her embarrassing encounter, and she didn't stress over her mother. All had been relegated to the background for a while and she thoroughly enjoyed Angela. She'd missed her, as well as her other friends. She'd always kept in touch with emails, text messages, and even post-cards, but nothing was like actually getting together with her girls.

She tried to think of something, anything to keep the melancholy at bay. The small scar underneath her ribcage itched and she absently scratched it. Then she lifted up the cover and tried to see the keloid tissue in the darkness. She couldn't make it out, but it didn't stop her mind from drifting over what the scar represented.

The twisted tissue meant complete financial freedom. The end result of an accident when she was seven. Whoever thought money was the answer to all one's problems was sorely mistaken. Having money didn't stop her from having increasingly worse anxiety attacks her last semester of law school. She'd almost went to the hospital after the one she suffered at the end of the bar exam. Several of her classmates were taking the test as well and one of them had to escort her back to her hotel room. She hadn't had an attack since then although she came close when she got the results and saw she'd failed.

Closing her eyes, Mia whispered, "Don't dwell on that now." She tried meditation to make herself sleepy. Humming softly, she focused on making her mind blank. It worked for a while, but then another vision slipped into her head like shadows at dusk, dark chocolate skin, impish grin, and a firm body. She realized the handyman was very solid when he pulled her to him. She now understood he was probably trying to prevent her from falling. Amazing how her panic didn't stop her from acknowledging how attractive the man was. Strange, she thought as she yawned and closed her eyes. Perhaps thinking of the man made her sleepy. She didn't want to analyze that thought and luckily she didn't have to because next thing she knew daylight was streaming through the cracks in the blinds.

That afternoon, Mia pulled up to the Star Crossed café with a small yawn. Although she wanted to see her friend, Jasmine Bishop, she was exhausted and feared she might not be the best company.

"Hey, girl, I'm sorry." Mia recognized the breathless voice as Jasmine's.

"What's up?" she sipped the water the waitress had placed in front of her.

"I have to ask for a rain check. Reggie just got called to the station. I guess a fire fighter got sick and had to go home. He's covering and he was my babysitter. I'd come with the baby, but he's been sneezing, no temperature, just the sniffles."

Mia was actually relieved. She wanted to see her friend and the baby when she had more energy. "That's okay, I understand. Call later and we'll set something up." When the waitress came back, Mia changed her order, making it to go.

Service was amazingly fast and she was grabbing the bag when she heard a familiar voice talking loudly. She looked around and sure enough, her eyes found Mark, her brother. He sat at the far end of the restaurant with another person she couldn't see because whoever it was sat with his back to her. She crossed the small, but crowded floor and Mark didn't even look in her direction. She stopped right in front of him and he was so engrossed in his conversation, he ignored her, or maybe he thought she was just the waitress.

Going for shock value, she bent and hugged him, scratching her cheek on the collar of the dark green suit he wore, before saying, "Big brother, it's so good to see you." Mark jumped a little, then relaxed and hugged her back when he realized who it was.

The person sitting with him chuckled and Mia turned and ended up gasping herself. Her brother was sitting with the handyman.

"Excuse me?" she had to say to her brother when she realized she'd missed what he'd said.

Mark shook his head while running his hands down his white shirt and red tie, a clear sign of annoyance. "I said, just like drinking, you shouldn't lie before midday. It's bad for you."

Mia pointed to her brother's, near empty, beer glass. "I guess you would know, Mark." She flashed a fake smile at her sibling, then nodded at the handyman before saying, "What are you doing on the south end, Mark? Slumming?"

"Don't you think that question's more appropriate for you?" Her brother's voice had all the warmth of an iceberg.

Rather than answer Mark's question, she turned to his companion. He was much more pleasant to look at than her brother. With a real smile on her face, she offered her hand and said, "Hello, I'm Mia Walsh. I don't think we exchanged names the first time we met."

Putting his fork down, playful eyes dancing, and smiling wide, the man stood and her eyes drank in his Levis and red nylon t-shirt as he took her hand into his large one. The vibrant color was very appealing against his complexion, and his work roughed skin felt oddly pleasant against her flesh. "No, I don't believe we did. My name is Jackson Jack. Feel free to call me Jack." He released her hand and sat back down.

Jackson Jack, Mia liked his name. It conjured up images of lumbermen, axes, big trees, and sweaty, hard working, heavily muscled males. The name suited him quite well.

"So now that I know you're name, I believe I owe you something," Mia paused. "I'm truly sorry for my actions earlier. I should have let someone know I was coming home, been in the loop, and all of that…drama could have been avoided."

Impossibly, the grin grew wider. "Apology accepted. It's nothing but a funny antidote now. Are you here for lunch? Would you care to join us?"

Her brother snorted and they both looked in his direction.

"I should say yes to your gracious offer just to torture Mark." She lifted up the sack she held in her hand. "However, I already have mine to go." She smiled sweetly at Mark.

He must have been feeling guilty because he said, "Mom and dad get in around six on Thursday. I take the bus into work, so you can pick me up at 5:30 and we can go out to the dock together to get them. I know they'd both be happy to see you."

"Thanks." Mia was surprised and didn't know what else to say for a brief moment. "Text me the address to your job, and I'll be there at 5:30 sharp. Well, I'll leave you two to enjoy the rest of your lunch." With a slight bow and a smile, she turned and left.

Chapter Three

Both men watched her walk away, one with irritation in his eyes and the other admiration.

"Your sister is quite a woman," Jackson commented.

His friend guffawed. "Unless you're a fan of Shakespeare, I'd leave her alone."

"What?" Jackson stopped watching Mia's graceful stride to look at Mark.

"Taming of the Shrew. I love my sister, but it's going to take a special person to be with her. To say she's spoiled is an understatement." Mark chuckled. "But you already know that from your run in with her."

Yes, Jackson thought, he did know, but self absorbed women didn't usually apologize so sincerely. The realization made him pause even more.

Both their heads turned as the waitress approached. Her shaved head, dark skin, and large earring made her striking. She'd been very attentive to their table and Jackson liked her smile as she approached. "Can I wrap that up?" she asked pointing to Mark's half full plate.

"Yes, that would be great, Taneka." Mark answered, leaning to read the nametag pinned to her chest.

"I see you've cleaned your plate."

Jackson returned her smile, nodding slightly.

"Would you like something else? Coffee, tea…"

Jackson saw his friend's eyebrows lift as he chuckled into his hand.

With a straight face, he answered, "Some more water would be terrific."

"For you anything." The audacious woman winked at him, twisting to sashay away. He made sure he gave the obligatory leer when she turned, obviously to see if he was looking.

He laughed as Mark teased him, but his heart really wasn't in it. He enjoyed the little interlude, but visions of the spunky woman who had just stood before him, sparring with her brother filled his head. Mia Walsh was femininity itself and far more interesting than the waitress, he decided. Today, her thick hair had been pulled back from her round face and it cascaded from the top of her head into a halo of waves and curls. The color reminded him of fall leaves showing all their glory on a beautiful September day, amber, brown, black, and blond all fought for dominance amongst the waves.

Jackson couldn't help recalling other things as well. He'd resisted the urge to openly stare at the hint of cleavage in the neckline of Mia's cream colored blouse. However, all it took was a glance for it to be seared into his memory.

"Here you go, sugar." Taneka's voice rudely disrupted his musings. His water glass was full and she was handing a bag to Mark, but looking at him. When she left, he endured Mark's teasing. It was much better than telling the truth. Despite knowing that Mia was high maintenance and something substantial would be difficult, he was attracted. Truth be told, he'd take his friend's sister any day over the cute, flirty waitress.

5:30 on Thursday, Mia pulled up to her brother's office building in downtown Seattle in her mother's Mercedes. Retrieving her cell from the passenger's seat, she dialed Mark's number. "I'm here," she said when he answered.

"Be right out," was his terse reply.

Leaning back into the plush black leather, Mia relished in the warmth of the seat heaters. Light jazz flowed from the speakers and she must have catnapped because harsh banging on the window where her head lay startled her awake.

"Damn you, Mark," she whispered as she unlocked the door.

He got in the car fussing. "Do you realize you're double parked?"

Mia looked around, seeing that there was a car in front of her that couldn't pass. She shrugged her shoulders. "Why'd you take so long to come out? There wouldn't be a problem if you moved quicker."

"That's classic Mia, always someone else's fault."

Ouch. She rolled her eyes. "No, just your fault Mark." She smiled at her brother's annoyed face as she pulled into the heavy traffic. Luckily, they didn't have far to go. She told herself not to argue with her knuckle- head brother, but she opened her mouth anyway.

"What is up with you, Mark? Why are you always on me? I don't deserve the crap you're always dishing my way?" She could feel her brother's glare, yet she still glanced over to confirm it.

"Stop with the sweet and innocent act, Mia. Your actions merit how I treat you and so much more. You run off to New York and play while going to school on the side. Pop in and out of Seattle without notice to anyone, even though you stay in houses that you don't own." Mark was turned in the seat, facing her now. "You know you're mom's favorite, and the fact is you weren't here when she need you."

Mia slammed on the brakes at the stop sign she'd just pulled up to. "Now I know you're crazy! Mom and dad both love us the same and need us the same. If I had known what was happening, nothing would have kept me from mom's side."

A noise that could only be described as disgust exploded from Mark's mouth before he said, "Really? The queen of selfishness would have put someone else above herself? I doubt it!"

She wanted to yell, shut the hell up, Mark. Instead, she took a deep breath and said, "Don't be scared to tell me how you really feel."

Traffic around the pier was heavy. Mia inched her way forward as she and her brother lapsed into silence.

Mia managed to park in one of the designated areas and the two of them followed the crowd to where the vacationers were going to come out. Her brother's phone rang and he answered. A smile lit up his whole face as he said, "Great Pop. We will see you soon." Without looking in her direction, he put his phone back in his pocket.

Mia stood on her tiptoes, trying to see above the crowd. She resisted the urge to jump up and down when she saw her parents coming, her eyes drinking in her mother. She looked relax and happy as she pulled her small suitcase behind her while holding her father's arm. She was thinner, yes, and her beautifully thick and long hair was now short, lying against her head in soft curls, giving her a sort of elfin look with her pointed chin. However, she seemed to glow with health. Her skin was smooth and there was a bounce in her step.

When her mother's gaze reached her, she saw the surprise and at that minute knew Mark hadn't told them of her presence. Her mother's smile covered her whole face as she nudged her husband and pointed with her chin in their direction.

"What a wonderful surprise!" her father said before engulfing her in his arms. At six foot four, he was a big man, still handsome with flecks of gray in his hair and a small belly he called his, grown man weight.

"My baby girl." He rocked her back and forth and Mia was thrilled. Being in her father's arms warmed her like a heat vent. During her childhood, they'd lived all the daughter-father stereotypes. On the few hot summer days in Seattle, he'd manage somehow to come home from work early to take her and Mark to the park. It was a short walk from their house and she'd always ride on her father's shoulders, feeling like a queen on her chariot, ruling over her favorite subject, Mark, who walked alongside far below. He'd taught her to skateboard, ride a bike, and coached her soccer team until high school. From the moment she was born, she was daddy's little girl, and as far as Mia was concerned, there was very little her father could do wrong.

Presently, he released her before grabbing her brother in a bear hug. A chill that had nothing to do with the weather went through Mia when her mother's thin arms surrounded her. "Oh, you're skinny, Mia. Don't they have food in New York?" Her mother leaned back and looked at her. "However, you're still my beautiful daughter." Her mother touched her face, reading her as no one else could. "You know don't you." It was more of a statement than a question. "Don't blame the others. It was me who didn't want you to be told. I…I just didn't want you to know."

"It's fine, momma." She hugged her again, breathing in the baby powder and vanilla scent that flung her back to childhood when the world was amazingly simply and her parents had the ability to make everything better. "I'm just so happy you and poppa are home."

She leaned back and looked in her mother's eyes. Marie Walsh met the look and nodded, giving her the confirmation that she needed. Relief flooded through her. All the words telling her that her mother was healthy were nothing compared to the nod and the look her mother gave her that said everything is okay.

Two days later, her father reached the half-century mark, and he proudly wore the shirt that Mia had presented him with the day before that told everyone, It's Nifty to be Fifty!

"Sixty is middle aged. I'm not a senior citizen!" Her father's voice boomed through the house that morning, followed by the low and high laughter of her mother and Mark. Mia rolled over in bed and saw it was eight. Going down the hall in her robe, she realized the house was already abuzz with life. The kitchen radio played loud and her mother's ambitious alto and her father's deep bass joined in, accompanying and, at times, drowning out the recorded voice. Her brother's teasing tone and laughter rose with the joyful clang of pots and pans. Mia was smiling as she entered the fray in the kitchen and managed to pour herself a cup of coffee without getting in anyone's way.

"Good morning, sleepyhead," Mark greeted her as he poured juice.

She nodded and rubbed her brother's back before saying, "Morning, Mark." From his expression, she could tell he was surprised she didn't have some smart remark. She couldn't dredge it up. She was just happy to be with her family although a part of her filled with sadness. She couldn't help thinking, was this how it was with her parents and brother? Did they scratch off her absence like scar tissue or dead skin? But what did she expect? Time to stop because she'd left?

Staring into the coffee provided no answers whatsoever. Looking up into the deep brown pools of her mother's eyes threatened to throw her further into a depression. "Are you gonna help us, love, or keep pretending you're a woman of luxury?" Her mother popped her lightly on the thigh with a towel as she said the words.

"Yeah, mom, get her!" Mark laughed.

Mia could help but laugh. "I didn't think you guys needed my help. Everything looks like it's going wonderfully."

"No, we don't need you. We just like your company." Her father teased.

"But since you're here…" He handed her a carton.

Mia took the eggs and put the coffee cup on the counter. The four of them slipped easily into a rhythm as they made a very hearty breakfast together. It was whole lot like old times sliced with new as they laughed while nudging each other with soft-edged critiques of cooking techniques and styles. Mia did elbow Mark when she stumbled, and she tried to pretend it was intentional, but no one was fooled. The amazing thing was that they managed to eat all of the pancakes, eggs, bacon, toast, waffles, ham, and sausage they prepared. Afterwards, her parents staggered towards the bedroom to take a nap they claimed. They were having a small birthday party later and both stated they needed rest before the event. The two didn't look all that tired to Mia, but she didn't want to think about what else they may be doing in the privacy of their bedroom.

As she walked her, mother said, "Knock on the door in two and a half hours, so I'll have time to cook."

"How about I cook," Mia blurted. Her whole family looked at her. I picked up a few skills in New York. It would be an honor to cook for my father on his birthday."

Her mother smiled big. "Yes, baby, we would love to have you do it."

"Great." Mia nodded.

She and Mark fell into a silence as they performed the routine they had perfected in childhood. There was really nothing to discuss as they soaped up dishes, washed counters, and dried utensils, and put away spices. A grunt here, a nod there was all the communication they needed. By the end, Mia decided it was sort of nice not arguing with her brother. It was so nice, she asked Mark to go to the store for her. After a few good-natured gripes, he agreed.

Chapter Four

Jackson stood to the side of the crowd, trying not to ease drop, and denying the fact that he was more than a little amazed. He didn't know if it was wishful thinking or was it really possible that the woman looked even better than the last time he saw her. Her clothes were casual, blue knit pants and a matching top, yet she was a radiant gemstone amongst them, chatting and shining her brilliance on all in the room. As he watched her interact with others, he had thoughts that had no place being in his head at her father's birthday party. He closed his eyes briefly and the after-image felt like it was burning his lids. Wine-red lips, hair loose but tucked behind her ears, exposing high cheekbones and slightly almonds eyes, and the slope of her elegant breasts under her top. He fought the reaction that was trying to escape his belly to travel lower to other regions. Territory that would reveal too much of what he was thinking. He breathed deeply and slowly.

Soon everything was ready and they were being guided into the dining room where Mia adjusted something on the wall until soft jazz played. Mr. Walsh rubbed his hands together as he sat at the table. "This looks absolutely wonderful, Mia, and such a surprise, I never thought I'd be eating a meal my daughter prepared mostly by herself." He watched Mia smile as her mother who was sitting beside her gave her a hug.

"Is it as delicious as it smells, baby girl?" her father asked.

"I sure hope so with all these people here," Mia answered.

"I suppose we'll just have to risk our lives and see," her brother quipped. "I'll take the hit and volunteer." Mark reached for the catfish with a fork until his father's booming voice stopped him.

"Hey! It's my birthday. Back off, son!"

While everyone laughed, Jackson watched the exchange with keen interest. He already knew that he enjoyed the Walsh family, and the addition of Mia only made the whole dynamic more enthralling.

Mr. Walsh cleared his throat. When he had everyone's attention, he said, "Before I dig into this beautiful display, I feel compelled to say a few words." He glanced at everyone present, then let his gaze shift between Mia and Mark. "It feels so magnificent to have both of my children with us today. It's been a long time and I'm appreciative that they are here and everyone is healthy."

Once the applause died down, Mr. Walsh looked at his wife, his eyes bright with love. He grabbed her hand and brought it to his lips. "To my wife, all I can say is thank-you! For your love, your support…and everything else." Mr. Walsh raised his glass and all of them followed suit. As he watched Mia sip, he could have sworn her eyes were misty.

Soon everyone was eating and the meal more than lived up to its aroma. Mia was not a shy eater. She tasted each dish as if she hadn't prepared it and she tore into the catfish with gusto. Her lips glistened and her tongue journeyed across them often in what he assumed was an effort to enjoy every morsel.

"There's hope for you, Mia," Mark's teasing voice rose above the chatter. "You may just yet get married since you can cook like this."

Mia actually seemed to blush. Then she laughed and the delicate color moved like a wave under her smooth skin. He wanted to follow its path with his fingertips, no with his lips.

People were just finishing up when Mark announced, "I'll get the cake." The full sheet dessert was half vanilla, half chocolate because that's how Mr. Walsh wanted it.

"Why doesn't it say happy birthday?" Mark's girlfriend asked.

His friend chuckled. "Because daddy didn't want it to, sweetheart. Just put some flowers on it, he insisted."

The cake was a masterpiece with large white lilies on the brown frosting and red roses on the frosting. He watched Mia watching her parents and suddenly a strange look came over her face. Jackson couldn't interrupt it, but it wasn't happiness that crinkled her brow. As soon as the cake was cut, she excused herself and Jackson watched her slip out the sliding back door. Five minutes passed, then ten. Jackson put the last bite of cake in his mouth and stood up.

"Dinner was excellent." He could tell she was startled as he said the words coming up from behind her as she stood at the far end of the deck railing. Looking over her shoulder briefly, their eyes met before she returned to looking at whatever only she could see in the inky black of the dark night.

"Thanks," was her brief reply. Without looking at him, she said, "Did my mother send you again? They just cut the cake. I know it can't be time to open the presents?"

"No, everyone is still eating." He moved to lean his forearms on the wood beside her, leaving a respectable distance of two feet between them.

"So." She glanced sideways at him, not quite turning her head. "What brings you out here?"

He smiled and decided honesty was the best policy. "You."

She looked at him a little too seriously for his taste. "Really?"

It had rained earlier and the air was chilly. He saw a shiver pass through her body and she crossed then rubbed her arms. He wished he had a coat to give or even better yet, he could warm her with his body. He turned, facing her profile and asked, "Tell me where to find it and I can go and get you a jacket."

She looked at him. "That's very sweet, but I'll be fine."

Now it was his turn to say, "Really?"

Her eyes remained on him, however, her head tilted to one side.

He answered the unspoken question, "A look flashed through your eyes. Maybe I'm wrong, but I sense sadness."

She turned back to the night, and he didn't really expect a response.

"You're very perceptive."

He nodded. "I can be."

There was silence after that and he wondered if he should go back inside, let her brood in peace.

"Logically, I know my mother is okay. Emotionally, I'm still struggling with the fact that…that she was so ill and I didn't know."

Jackson immediately knew what she was talking about. Mark wasn't one to share his feeling much, however, before his mother surgery he'd confided in Jackson.

She put her head down. "I don't ever want that to happen again and, and for the life of me, I try not to let it bother me, but it does. Mark knew and I had no clue. What does that say about me?"

She looked at him briefly, then put her head back down. "Sorry, I know you probably don't want to hear this."

"No, you have my attention and I'm interested in whatever you have to say although I may not have the answers. I can only suggest that you ask your mother."

She nodded, and then a slight smile graced her lips. "I have your attention?"

"Yes, from first time I saw you." He kept his eyes on her face so she wouldn't get too much of the wrong impression. "You made…quite an impact, for lack of a better word. I have to admit that I'm still reeling."

"I don't quite know what I'm supposed to say to that, Jackson."

He liked how his name rolled off her lips. "Nothing, I just want you to know, Mia."

Her smile was more than a tad bit mischievous. "Did I give you permission to use my first name, Jackson Jack?"

"No, you didn't." He scooted a little closer to her. "Would you like me to stop?"

She didn't answer him. After a moment of silence, his fingers rubbed against the deck railing as he began speaking, "This is a lovely piece of timber. Do you know what type it is?"

Her head shook.

"Cedar heartwood. I know it's hard to tell at night but it's a beautiful brownish red color in the light."

"I know. I've admired it during the day. It's new. Did you remodel the deck?"

"Yes ma'am, I did."

"You did a great job."

He nodded before saying, "It was a lot easier because of this wood. It's renowned for its anti-decaying properties. I won't bore you with the details, but the basic idea is that it has natural agents that kill fungi which rot wood. It's not only gorgeous, it's very efficient."

His eyes lifted from the railing to meet hers. She seemed to be interested in what he was saying. "A lot like what you demonstrated today. Beautiful and very capable. The meal was fantastic."

"Thank-you." Her head dipped before she looked up at him with a slight grin. "I suppose you can call me by my first name."

"Oh, talking about wood gave me the privilege?"

"Of course not. Your compliments won you the honor."

"How about the honor of a date?" He was going with the flow and the words just flew out of his mouth. He far from regretted the question.

"A date? What do you have in mind?"

He shrugged and moved a little closer to her. "Dinner and a movie, or dancing. Whatever the lady prefers."

She didn't move even though they now stood shoulder to shoulder. "How about we start with dinner?"

"Sounds good," he agreed.

Suddenly, the door opened and they both turned. Mark stuck his head out. "It's freezing out here. What are you two doing?"

Mia sighed heavily, but she was smiling good-naturedly when she attempted to answer. Her brother cut her off. "Mom says get your butt in here so pops can open the presents."

"Yes sir," his sister responded.

Jackson stepped to the side. "After you, my dear."

She laughed, then asked, head to the side, "How old are you, Jackson?"

"Thirty-one. How about you?"

"Twenty-seven," she answered.

"Well, now that we've got that out of the way, can I escort you back into the house?"

With a smile on her face, Mia let him.

Three days later, Jackson was back at the Walsh house ringing the doorbell. The woman who had invaded his dreams the last couple of nights answered the door and her hair was slightly wet. Jackson's knees almost buckled. Loose wild curls exploded around her face in vibrant shades of auburn and brown as brilliant as any sunset. A black dress with spaghetti straps and a hide and seek lace hem fell to just below her knees adding to the vision. Her red painted toes peeked at him from the strappy high-heeled shoes she wore. Good Lord, he wanted to take the big one in his mouth and see if it tasted as delicious as it looked.

"You look very nice," she said as she stepped out and closed the door. Seeing her attire, he was glad he added a red tie to the black slacks and white shirt he'd chosen for the evening.

"Shouldn't I say hi to your parents?" he asked still standing on the porch as she headed down the steps.

"They're gone," she answered over her shoulder.

He walked up to her and took the coat she carried and held it so she could slip her arms inside.

"Thanks," she uttered.

When her back was turned, he couldn't help bending down and breathing deeply. He'd always been a scent oriented person, and it was more complex than just body odor. Whenever a woman he was interested in smelled good, it was icing on the cake. Especially when he couldn't immediately identify the source. Was it perfume, body oil, or deodorant?

The scent wafting of Mia was delectable. It contained the freshness of rain combined with some sort of fruit- honey, lemon, with just a hint of vanilla. It was trapped in between the nape of her neck and the moist tendrils that lay down her neck like delicate tree limbs. Jackson knew the scent would haunt him the rest of the evening. He wondered if he'd get a chance to see if the rest of her smelled as good.

The woman sure did like to eat. Mia reached over and stole of piece of his filet mignon that he'd just cut into a neat square. He envisioned the aromatic juices flooding her tongue as she grinned in pure delight. He cut another piece and offered it to her from his fork. Grasping his hand, she brought it to her lips. He was mesmerized by the warmth of her fingers and by the sight of the meat disappearing behind luscious lips.

"Um, delicious," she murmured. "Would you like a bite of my Chicken Marsala?" she asked innocently.

He nodded slowly. She put some on her fork and extended it towards him, deepening the cleavage of her dress. He tried not to stare, but he did glance before focusing on her face. Wine, peppers, oregano, and chicken mixed together to thrill his mouth.

"Very good." He smiled. "But I prefer my steak." He cut himself a large piece.

Her eyes grinned just as much as her mouth. The look was adorable.

"I prefer both, I think." She laughed. "You're discovering my well kept secret. I'm a piglet."

"I wouldn't say you're a pig. You just enjoy your food." He looked right in her eyes. "I like woman with healthy appetites in all areas."

"Oh yeah?" She sipped her merlot. "I have a hearty appetite for something else." She raised her eyebrows. "Would you like to join me?"

He had to close his mouth quickly to prevent himself from shouting, Yes! His mother hadn't raised a fool. "I suppose that depends on the activity."

She laughed. "Exercise. From the looks of your body, I don't think it's a new concept to you." He liked that she'd noticed. "Would like to go running tomorrow?"

"Mia, we live in Seattle. Chances of rain are probably a hundred percent based on how the weather's been lately."

"What's a little water? Wear sweats."

He frowned.

"Come on, Jackson. You're a man's man, aren't you? You won't melt in the rain. Or if you do, it would be fun to see," she teased.

"Can't we run on a treadmill? I'll meet you at any gym. Just name the place."

"No, I'm not letting you off the hook that easy. Fresh air is good, invigorates the soul." She leaned towards him. "Come on, Jackson. Don't be a wimp."

"A wimp! You know those are fighting words?"

Her grin grew wider.

"Ahh what the hell. Okay. I'll go running."

She clapped her hands together. "Good."

"If I can get a goodnight kiss later," he continued.

"Jackson! Are you attempting to blackmail me?" She leaned on the table.

"Of course not. I would never do that. I prefer to call it compromise. We both get what we want."

"And all you want is a kiss?" Leaning back now, she crossed her arms.

"That's right, just a little peck right here." His forefinger touched his mouth.

She burst out laughing. "You know what? You're nothing but a hot mess."

"So you think I'm hot, huh?"

"Jackson, what am I going to do with you?"

He chuckled deeply. "I have a few suggestions."

Chapter Five

Damn it! Why the hell did I agree to this! The thought went through his head for the hundredth time as he struggled to keep up with the jogging Mia. The open-mouth kiss at her parents' door had been absolutely wonderful, but he wasn't sure if it was worth this. Well, maybe it was worth it, he smiled inwardly as he recalled the press of her tongue. His feet slogged over wet pavement and dirt as the two of them made their way around Greenlake park. A light drizzle misted his face and actually made him feel much better as he ran in black sweat pants and a matching, hooded, pullover jacket.

Mia turned her head. "Come on, Jackson. It's only a few miles and we are halfway done I'm sure." She slowed up to run beside him, and to his irritation, she wasn't even breathing heavy. Part of him wished she'd return to her position slightly in front of him. It had been just enough for him to admire her round backside and firm, tone legs as she ran in red running shorts and a hoody which covered her head and looked similar to his.

Jackson considered himself to be in pretty good shape. He lifted weights religiously three times a week, and he got plenty of exercise in the work he did. However, he didn't get much cardio, and the way he felt right now, he was sure he didn't need it.

Mia must have decided that talking his ear off was the way to get him through it. "This is my favorite park in Seattle. I love the water from the lake and all the green from the trees and grass. It's so beautiful, don't you think?"

She looked at him sideways and he nodded.

"It's such a surprise, this gorgeous facility in the middle of such a dense urban area. Kind of like a mini Central park." Mia chuckled, apparently amused at her own analogy. Then she asked, "Would you agree, Jackson?"

He had been to Central park once. He'd played on a traveling basketball team as a teenager and they had participated in a tournament in New York city. Struggling to speak clearly, he said, "The only real similarity I see between the two is that they are both parks. Greenlake pales in comparison to Central park."

She nudged his shoulder. "Oh, where's your imagination, Jackson?"

His side was beginning to hurt. He pressed a palm to it as he answered, "I believe I lost it about a mile ago."

She laughed loudly, then lifted her face to the light drops. "You have to admit that some of this feels good. There is just enough moisture to keep us cool." She threw the hood of her jacket back, releasing a riot of curls. "That feels wonderful."

Jackson stumbled slightly, then turned away. If he kept watching her, he was going to fall on his face and embarrasses the hell out of himself. He focused on his breathing as she began chattering away about something or other. What seemed like an eternity later, she gradually slowed to a walk.

"Congratulations, Jackson, you did it."

He tried to smile, but he feared it was more of a grimace.

Turning to face him fully, she said, "Let's stretch." She bent to touch her toes and he sorely wished she was turned away from him. He wiggled his legs and extended his arms before settling on the nearby bench. He was close to deciding that he wasn't going to move for the rest of his life.

She laughed when she saw him. "Are you sure you don't want to stretch a bit more?"

"Quite sure. I did the darn run and I've decided that's enough. I want to sit."

With a look of pure amusement that was very endearing, she said, "Okay," and continued her routine.

After a time, she flipped her hood back up, covering her joyous hair and sat beside him on the bench. They were quiet for a time until she spoke, "I'm thinking about buying a house here. Can you help me?"

The request surprised him. Wasn't she just visiting? Then he began to wonder how in the world did she support herself? Never shy, he asked, "What line of work are you in?"

He got the sideways look again. "My dear brother hasn't gossiped about me?"

He turned right which was towards her, putting half his leg on the bench. "To that extent, no, and even if he had, I like to get my information straight from the source."

"I see."

That was all she said as he continued to stare at her. He'd pretty much given up on an answer when she finally began talking.

"I'm independently wealth."

Not the answer he expected and he didn't know quite how to respond. He ended up saying, "So I guess you can afford a house."

She giggled and nodded. Looking him in eyes, she said, "I was seven and minding my own business, riding my bike on the sidewalk by my house. I don't actually remember getting hit. I just remember waking up in the hospital to a bunch of white faces and panicking. I was in the hospital for a very long time, and I was stuck in the bed at home even longer. Missed tons of school and I couldn't wait to get back. I spent a lot of time doodling pictures. It kept me sane."

She lowered her head and was silent for a moment before continuing. "To make a long story short, it was a drunk driving after afternoon binge that hit me, but he was well insured and I lost a kidney. The money went into a trust. Shortly after I finished college, I received it. Then I went to law school."

"So, you're a big time New York attorney now."

"Nope." She looked out into the trees. "You will be the first person I've told. I…I didn't pass the bar."

The words came out as a whisper and immediately after she said them, her head went down.

"Mia." She ignored him. "Mia." He touched her shoulder. "It's okay if you didn't pass. Just take the test again."

The sound she made was somewhere in between a laugh and a snort. She looked at him with misty eyes. "You don't get it Jackson. I don't fail at anything."

"What? You're not human? You sure look like a beautiful human to me!"

She laughed.

"You're parents don't strike me as the type to have unreasonable expectation. They'd probably tell you what I just said. Take the damn thing again!"

She nodded. "You're most likely right, but like I said, every real goal I've set out for myself I have accomplished." She looked into his eyes. "I don't know what it is about you Jackson, but you're easy to talk too."

"Thank-you, Mia. I'm glad you feel that way." He was silent after that because he sensed there was something she wanted to say."

He was right because soon she began talking. "My last semester of law school I began having panic attacks. After I got the test result, I decided I needed a break and that's why I really came home." She looked in his eyes and smiled sadly. "I need to figure some things out."

"How's it going? The figure things out part?"

She shrugged. "About the only thing I know is that I love to paint and I don't want to take the bar again."

"Then it sounds like you're making progress to me."

"Yeah." She guffawed. "Do you think my brother, Mark, would see it that way?"

"Forget Mark. How you feel about yourself is the most important thing."

She nodded. "I know you're right." She looked at him with the most genuine smile. "Thanks for listening."

"Anytime."

She turned to look out at the park again and when she didn't speak for a time, Jackson said, "How do you want me to help with the house?" He was tempted to grab the hand that sat on the bench next to him. "I know a couple of really good agents I could recommend if you'd like. I can also view properties with you as well, check them out and let you know if I think they're sound."

"Yes," she said. "I want you to do all of it. I'm not sure if I want to stay in Seattle permanently, but I don't want to be in New York. I have so many connections here and I need my own space."

I want to be one of those connections. The thought hit Jackson's conscious so strongly, he was momentarily stunned. On the surface, everything about her screamed she was the type of woman he wanted to avoid. However, that initial layer was slowly being peeled away, and the woman underneath was drawing him in like metal shavings to a magnet. She really wasn't arrogant and he more than enjoyed her company.

"So, you ready for round two?" she asked while lightly punching his shoulder, bringing him out of his thoughts.

"What?"

"Another lap around the park." She jumped up.

"Mia, that was not a lap!"

"Well, what's a few more miles?"

"Go away, Mia Walsh. I have done enough in the rain for one day."

"Drizzle, not rain. Completely different precipitation. As a Seattellite, I would expect you to know that." She stood and extended her hand to him.

He took it and let her help him up. She was surprisingly strong. "How about we compromise, Mia? I will walk a little ways with you."

"Okay, deal." She squeezed his hand before letting go.

Jackson remembered a question he'd been meaning to ask. "Remember your dad's birthday?"

She looked at him sideways. "Uh yeah." She laughed and tapped his shoulder as they strolled. "I'd have to be pretty bad off not to recall that."

He crossed his arms, pretending to be offended. "Look who's got jokes."

Still chuckling, she said, "Sorry."

"Now, not that I was being nosy, but I heard that lady named Martha ask if you could help with the kids."

"And you want to know what it's all about?"

"Well, not everything, but you could say I was curious."

"I see," she teased. "Since you've been such a good sport, I suppose I can answer." She hopped around a mud puddle. "When I'm home, I volunteer at the Village Center. It's a childcare facility. I teach the kids art."

"Oh, yes, you mentioned you want to paint. What do you specialize in? Watercolors, acrylics?"

"I'm not sure I specialize in anything. I paint in oils mostly, and I work with pencils. I majored in Art History in college."

"Do you have a lot of works or pieces? I don't know what you guys call it."

She smiled at him. "Yes, I have a whole spare room full in New York."

"Have you had any shows?"

"Goodness no!"

"Why do you say it like that?"

She shrugged and then smoothly grasped his upper arm as if she'd been doing it all her life. He liked it. In fact, he liked it a whole lot. So much, he had to say, "Excuse me," because he missed what she was saying.

"I said, I love creating artwork, but I'd be a nervous wreck trying to sell it."

"Why? It's not like your livelihood depended on it. That should take a lot of the stress out of it."

"It's not only about money, silly. I created each and every one of them, so most would be hard to part with. They are sort of like my children. It would be excruciating to watch my babies being taken away or criticized." She threw off her hood again, releasing her wonderful hair.

"How about watching people compliment your children. No one can enjoy them if they are hidden in your house. Can't you have some kind of showing, where they're not for sale?"

Letting go of his arm, she ran her fingers through her hair. The outline of her body against her stretched clothing was enticing. "You sure are assuming a lot. You haven't seen my work you know. It's possible you might think it sucks."

"I doubt anything produced by you would suck." He shoved his hands in his pockets and moved behind her to avoid another jogger braving the weather. "I work with wood, and I'm not to humble to say I've built some absolutely beautiful coffee tables and rocking chairs. Guess what?"

She waited until he was beside her again before saying, "You've sold them all."

"Yep. I did take a picture first." Getting slightly ahead, he walked backwards so he could see her face. "Maybe one day, you'd like to see my album."

"I'd love too." She pointed while saying, "Watch out."

A lady with a high tech baby carriage was headed their way. It had three big wheels and plastic covering the baby. Jackson moved to let them pass. "Wow. Now that's dedication."

"It sure is." Mia agreed, turning to watch the woman.

Walking shoulder to shoulder again, he said, "I'd love to see your work."

Her shoulder briefly rubbed against his. He couldn't tell if the movement was accidently or not. "Maybe, just maybe, one day you will." Flinging her hands out to the side, she continued, "Who knows, could be sooner than you think."

They walked along in silence for awhile and then Jackson said, "Would you like to see something?"

"What?" Mia asked and before he could answer, she said, "It must be something special because you sound just like a little boy."

He shrugged. "It's not that spectacular, but I want to show you anyway."

"Then I'd love to see it." She grasped his arm and squeezed.

Chapter Six

Mia followed in her car, still a little surprised at herself for sharing so much. Something about the man was reassuring and calming. Her openness was weird, but she certainly didn't regret sharing. In fact, she felt relieved.

She wiggled in her dry jacket, getting more comfortable in the seat. She'd brought two coats, and the wet one was now in the trunk. She'd also put sweat pants over her shorts. She noticed that Jackson still wore his wet clothes and she hoped he didn't catch a cold because then she'd feel guilty.

They were about a mile away when she figured out they were going to her parents' second home. She wondered why he was taking her there. Did he want her to see the remodeled kitchen?

He parked and was out of the car before she'd turned off the engine. After holding the door open for her and helping her out, he led the way to the front door. She had to admit that she found his eager attitude cute.

"I just finished and delivered it to the house this morning," he said as they entered. "I tried to have it done before the birthday party, but it wasn't ready to be finished." He smiled boyishly. "Sometimes you can't rush these projects. They're done when they are ready to be done."

They weren't headed to the kitchen, so Mia was truly perplexed about what she was about to see.

"Also, I finished up the remodel this morning. Your parents are going to come and check everything on Wednesday and that's when I'll give it to your pops."

"Okay," Mia said slowly wishing he'd hurry up and get to the point. She'd never been extremely patient and all this build up had her anxious to see whatever it was he was talking about.

He led her to a small room at the back of the house. Ushering her past the doorway, he said, "Waaalaaa!"

"Oh, wow! This is absolutely gorgeous, Jackson." She exclaimed when she saw the piece. "My father is going to love this." Mia walked over and ran her hand over the wood. "How many games can you play on it?"

"Chess and checkers," he answered. "Your father and I have quite a match going. He's one chess game up on me right now. We've been playing once every other week for about a year."

Mia walked around the chess table, feeling every inch of the lacquered timber. "What is this?" she asked.

"Teak," he answered apparently knowing she was referring to the type of wood.

"This inlaid board is truly beautiful. Was it hard to do?"

"Doing stuff like this is the great part of what I do. I wouldn't characterize it as hard. It can be challenging, but it's a whole lot of fun."

"I love the grain pattern of these stools. You are a true artisan."

He bowed and said, "Thank-you, my lady. I hope Mathew is as pleased."

"My father is going to flip when he sees this. I'm sure he'll insist on playing right away."

"Good," Jackson said, nodding.

He held his hand out to her. "Come see the kitchen."

"Why don't you take off that wet jacket first, and I'll throw it in the dryer," she said.

"Sure." He stripped it off, and Mia almost bit her lip to keep from reacting. He wore a white tank top underneath, exposing glorious muscles that tapered into a trim waist.

She took the jacket and turned from him quickly. She felt the blood rushing underneath her cheeks, making them feel hot. "Get a grip," she whispered as she went into the garage where the dryer was located. He'd moved to wait for her in hall and as she drew nearer, he extended his hand again.

Grasping his slightly cold, big palm, she followed him down the hall, telling her traitorous body to behave. It was hard because she could smell him, the freshness of rain and the faint scent of cologne or deodorant. Damn, she thought, wet or not I might have to insist he put the jacket back on!

When then got to the kitchen, she found herself repeating what she'd said earlier, "Wow!"

Letting go of her hand, Jackson walked around, pointing and explaining what he had done. She tried to pay attention but the way his arm muscles twisted and rolled as he moved was very distracting, not to mention the way the way the tank gathered around the curve of his admirable bottom. She shut down the growl gathering in her throat.

"I converted it into a French style custom kitchen with an island and nook. I tried to downplay the appliances by surrounding them with wood. I was hoping it would make it warm and cozy because I personally love gathering in the kitchen."

Mia nodded, and then said, "Before you say anything else, let's celebrate this moment properly." She went to the refrigerator. "I risked my life walking in here when it was all torn up to put up a bottle of wine. I never got the chance to drink it, and I believe a glass now would be perfect." Also, she hoped it would mellow her libido. Mia turned, holding the bottle. "I hope we have a bottle opener."

"We do. I saw one earlier when I was putting everything back together." He opened a drawer and pulled out the opener. "May I do the honors?" He held his hand out.

"Of course." Mia handed him the bottle. "I hope you like Merlot."

"I love it." Jackson went to a counter and began uncorking the wine.

"I believe you accomplished your goal." Mia walked over and ran her hand over the dark green countertop. "This is definitely the perfect place for a family to gather. Is this granite?"

"Yes," he nodded. Retrieving two glass cups, Jackson said, "I hope these are all right. I didn't see any wine glass."

"They will do just fine." Mia accepted the cup. Their fingers brushed, giving her heart a little start.

"You've done a wonderful job, Jackson. I know my parents will be overjoyed. The old kitchen was so dingy and dismal. It's hard to believe I'm in the same house."

Jackson didn't reply, just looked around at his work as he sipped.

"To a job well done," Mia toasted.

The two cups clinked as they tapped them together.

Mia found herself looking at him and liking what she saw. However she knew it wasn't only the sight of him. "I enjoy your company very much." She felt her eyes widen when she realized she'd spoken the words out loud.

He turned and faced her fully. "Thank-you," was all he said as he moved closer. He leaned back on a counter near her and drank from the cup.

Suddenly nervous, she blurted, "Your jacket's probably dry. I'll get it."

"Mia, you just put it in. Unless you have a super dryer, I'm sure it's still wet."

Did the man not know what he was doing to her? The word wet made her acknowledge that her most secret self was definitely anointed in response to the vision before her. Her wicked mind took off on its own and she imagined what it would be like to kiss his chest? Would those glorious pectorals quiver beneath her tongue?

"Hey, are you all right, Mia?"

Good Lord, he was standing right in front of her. He was so tall she had to tilt her head back to look in his face. Be still my beating heart! The fact that the cliché jumped to mind made her chuckle. She looked down; thinking he probably thought she was quite odd.

"Is something funny?"

"No, no, there's nothing amusing going on here." Her eyes lifted to his chest and she did not look any further.

"Oh, yeah and exactly what is going on here?" his deep voice asked from above.

She shrugged. "Don't know." Standing this close, she could just make out the outline of his stomach muscles. She quivered.

"Are you cold?"

She wanted to say yes, but she knew she wasn't that good of a liar. She couldn't remember the last time she'd felt like a weak-kneed teenager.

"Mia?"

She realized she hadn't answered him. "No, I'm quite warm actually."

"Really."

His big chocolate hand lifted and with a thumb and forefinger, he caressed her chin before lifting gently until she met his eyes. "Hi, there," he whispered. She didn't think an answer was necessary. "You know what's about to happen. If you have some objection, let me know now."

Before she could take a proper breath, his warm lips closed over hers, mouth molding and shaping as his tongue flicked against the seam of her lips asking for permission to enter.

Damn, I love polite men! My hands will remain at my sides, she told herself, but it's okay to part my lips, just a little, for an itty bitty taste. To her embarrassment, she groaned just a little when his tongue dived inside, sucking and licking the roof of her mouth until she had absolutely no other choice but to lift her hands and fist them on the straps of his tank.

"God, I've been dying to do this again," he murmured against her lips. "I've been drawn to you since the first second I saw you. You are so cool and collected, but I knew a hot woman burned underneath."

As though her body wanted to prove him right, she found herself moving against the thigh that was now between her legs.

"Mmm, yes baby." One of his hands caressed her shoulder while the other strayed down to her bottom to help her hips move.

A small sane, rational corner of her brain shouted for her to stop before this went too far. Hell, who was she kidding? The silky strip covering her sex was drenched, a clear indication that this was already way out of bounds.

He was at her neck doing the most delicious things and of their own accord, her fingers caressed his nape encouraging him to drive her wild. All sensible thoughts evaporated when his mouth reached her chest. He lifted off her jacket, then nosed her tee shirt and bra aside as he devoured her skin.

Knowing where he was going, she looked down to see her own pebble hard nipple as it disappeared behind his lips. He sucked it deep into his mouth. Mia moaned and threw her head back. He responded by going to the other breast. Her hands moved to clench the fabric of his tank. She wanted to rip it from him, but didn't have the presence of mind to accomplish her task.

"Off," she whispered.

With a popping sound as he left her flesh, Jackson quickly complied.

The man was too sexy in nothing but sweats and his shoes, and oh, his glorious skin. She wanted to rub it, take it in her mouth, however, he had other plans. Lifting her up on the counter, he easily fit between her spread legs. Without actual thought, she lifted an arm and hooked it around his neck and found herself pressed up to the hard wall of his chest. Hot breath, then his teeth nibbling her earlobe caused her neck to arch again.

She jumped just a little when his large hand slipped inside her loose sweatpants. He grumbled in what she assumed was satisfaction when his fingers were greeted with slippery wetness. Mia was a little embarrassed at how aroused she was until a thick, blunt finger brushed her essence. Her hips rocked against his talented hand and she shuddered like an asthmatic when he slipped a finger inside or was it two? It really didn't matter when his thumb grazed her clitoris to give it some much desired consideration. Less than five strokes later, she was gone. The walls of her sex clamped down tightly as she climaxed and her shouts reached the high ceiling of the kitchen.

His kisses softened while he pressed gently against her mound as what seemed like endless tremors continued to rack her body. Slowly he calmed her as the sensations ebbed away.

"Are you okay?" she asked.

He chuckled. "Are you referring to these?" He softly moved the fingers that were still inside her, and Mia began to question herself when she felt a tingle. Is this man turning me into a nympo?

He removed himself from her body and lifted his fingers to his face where he slowly licked the ones that were wet. It was one of the most erotic things Mia had ever experienced.

"Nope, my hand is just fine," he said as Mia stared at his lips where they glistened. She moved forward and kissed him hard, catching his flavorful fingers between their lips.

He groaned and then she was being lifted, cradled against his wonderful muscles as he carried her somewhere. She'd meant to ask what he was doing, but her lips couldn't resist his flesh and he moaned as she placed kisses along his upper torso. She realized she was in one of the two bedrooms when he smoothly lowered her feet to the ground where he removed her clothing before helping her lay on the comforter covered mattress. Then to Mia's delight, he stripped, leaving her to gaze in wonder at his broad chest, narrow hips, strong legs, and wonderful glory that jutted quite a ways from his body in fierce pride.

Coherent thought was impossible as Jackson gazed at the beautiful woman below him. With her supple curves and long, gorgeous legs, eroticism radiated from her like perfume. She lifted a hand, motioning for him to join her and the gesture had bolts of electricity shooting straight to his groin. He was so aroused it was beginning to hurt.

He trailed a hand down her body, from her high cheek bones, across the full curve of her lips, down the taut smooth plane of her abdomen. He focused on what lay below. The part of her body he'd felt thoroughly but hadn't actually seen. Her pubic hair was a neat, square shaped patch of dark wiry hair over plump juicy lips.

Her breath caught when his palm touched, feather light, over the area letting him know she'd recovered from their adventures in the kitchen. He couldn't stop the smile spreading across his face at the thought that her rejuvenation was solely due to his touch. He remembered how she'd tasted on his fingers and that's what guided him as he knelt between her legs.

Without pretense, she drew her knees up to give him unimpeded access to what he wanted most at that moment. With his thumbs, he spread her plump outer lips, having a good look before filling his mouth with hot flesh. He forced himself to go slow, be gentle until her moans let him know how to move his mouth, where to place his tongue. Of course the hand at the back of his head was a big help as well.

He lapped at the hard knot of flesh at the top of her sex before circling it and sucking it. This rotation seemed to drive her wild as her pelvis rocked and bucked against him. His penis thudded with each whimper, moan, throaty purr she uttered and he feared he might disgrace himself in the sheets he grinded against.

"Oh, oh, oh, God Jack...," the rest of his name was lost in a loud moan as she began shaking against his mouth. He held her hips and quickened his motions against the hard knot. A fresh rush of liquid bathed his tongue and he found himself moaning as he lapped it up.

Mia gazed at the ceiling in wonder. She had to breathe deeply several times to fortify herself before looking down her body. Jackson was still between her legs, placing gentle kisses along her inner thigh. If she wasn't so besotted by the whole experience, she could have sworn his touches were loving.

Damn , I'm in trouble, she thought. She'd never responded to a man the way she was responding to Jackson. But then again, she'd never had someone treat her quite the way he did. It was hard to put into words, especially when she wasn't thinking very clearly.

Mia knew she was attractive and she'd had the pleasure of turning more than a few heads, but she'd never had someone look at her as if she were the most precious thing on earth. It was like he was seeing past the physical into her soul, making connections she wasn't sure she even understood, so she for damn sure knew she wasn't ready for the bond.

When he'd run his hand down her body earlier, it was as if he was trying to memorize and enjoy every single inch of her, or was he branding her? Somehow, the answer wasn't important when he'd buried his head between her legs, and kissed her like she was the most treasured, luscious, superb treat he'd ever tasted. She'd come so hard she'd lost vision for moment. Heck, no man had ever treated her anything like that! In her heart of hearts, she knew where this was leading, at least for her although she didn't want to admit it.

She watched, as if in a dream, as he lifted up over her, braced himself and kissed her so tenderly she wanted to cry or scream. Then he leaned away and ripped open a condom he got from God's knows where. He proceeded to roll it on with slow deliberation. She wondered if he was trying to whet her appetite for what was now inevitable because his mighty length sure look good as he handled it in preparation.

Well, damn, it's working, she almost whispered the words out loud and stopped herself from reaching for his penis. Then she thought, what the hell, and did caress his hip with her hand. He came towards her and she spread her legs wide to accommodate him. He slid in much easier than Mia expected because, after all, he wasn't a small man. He held himself still, trembling inside her, and Mia answered the unspoken question by flexing and squeezing around his length. He began to move, stroking out and in, in and out. He kissed her, the movement of his tongue in time with his lower body. She kissed him back, wrapping her arms and legs around his body.

As if unleashed, he moaned deeply before picking up the pace. Mia marveled at the sounds that seemed to tear from his chest each time she worked her muscles along his length. She reveled at her apparent ability to give him pleasure. Their bodies became slick, a mixture of oil and sweat. The sound of flesh meeting flesh was terribly erotic to Mia, almost as thrilling as the feel of his chest rubbing against her nipples. All of this was driving Mia to another peak. She didn't even question it as she tumbled again, coming for three times in one session for the first time. Something about Jackson was magical and she was in La La land when he tensed and groaned against her. Still feeling a tad bit faint, she managed to hold him tight as he released into her body before going limp.

"Wow," he uttered as he rolled off, pulling her on top of him.

She chuckled, her cheek pressed to his chest. "That's an understatement," she teased.

"Sorry, babe. That's the best I can do right now. Give me five minutes and I'll be more eloquent." He whispered the words against the top of her head. She liked the sensation of his breath ruffling her hair, tickling her scalp.

She breathed deeply and nibbled at his pectorals before saying, "Good Lord, what have we done?" She didn't expect an answer and kept talking, "Where do we go from here?"

"How about to the shower?" His arms tightened around her.

"Mumm," she murmured, "I like that." When she realized she'd spoken the words aloud, she was a little embarrassed. Then she berated herself for being silly. Why was she so off-balanced with this man? Suddenly, she began to shake slightly, which made her feel vulnerable. She needed to leave.

Yawning and stretching to create separation, she moved from his body and sat up. He lay there looking so good it should have been a crime.

Putting his hands behind his head, he said, "Time to go?"

"Afraid so," she answered.

He sat up and wrapped her in his arms. "I can see it in your eyes. Don't regret this. It was special and wonderful." He leaned back and looked at her. "When do I get to see you again?"

She giggled. "How about tomorrow, same park, same run."

"Nooooooo," he teased. "I have to go through that torture to see you again?"

"Thou protest too much. Running is good for you." She stood up and she had to admit that she liked how his eyes widened as he took in her body. Being appreciated by a man was a special thing.

Chapter Seven

Jackson did meet her at the park the next day and the next day after that. He obviously hated it and it warmed Mia's heart that he did so to please her. So she responded in kind and went to a Seahawk's football game although she hated the sport. Men running around in puffed up gear hitting each other held no appeal. And the crowds! It took them an hour to park and walk to their seats and two hours to leave! Mia complained good-naturedly, but she really didn't mind because she enjoyed Jackson's company. She assumed he had similar feelings because they saw each other daily for the next two weeks. They ate out, saw movies, and he coaxed her into the gym where he had her lifting weights until her limbs felt like melted jelly. But the best part for Mia was their conversations. They talked about everything from past relationships to how many different shades of green there were. Mia wondered if it was fate that they were both single at this point in time. Who cares, she decided. She was just going to keep taking pleasure in his mind just as much as in his body.

Speaking of such, she was returning to her parents' home late Friday after she and Jackson had enjoyed each others' company well into the night. Out of respect for her parents, she always came home before the sun came up. However, tonight it had been especially hard to leave the comfort of Jackson's strong arms. She smiled, imagining her face pressed against his chest as she shut the front door.

She turned and gasped loudly. "Mother! I didn't see you standing there." Marie was barely visible in the dim hallway light.

Her mother leaned away from the wall to stand up straight. "No, I suppose you didn't." Mia noticed a crooked grin on Marie face. "I'd suppose your thoughts were on whatever has you coming home late these last few nights."

"Mom, I'm in my twenties…"

"Shush," her mother interrupted while holding a hand up. "I was there when you were born. I'm well aware of your age." Her mother motioned to the couch and Mia obeyed and sat. Marie slowly lowered herself beside her. "You know when you and Mark were little, you were on my hands." Palms up, she held up her arms. "Now that you're adults, you're just on my heart. No matter your age, baby, you will always be on my chest." Her mother reached out with her right hand and held Mia's left. "You understand that, Mia?"

She nodded.

"Good, so next time you want to be out until the wee hours, we at least need a call so we know you're safe."

Geez, and Mia thought she was doing pretty good by coming home at all! Keeping her thoughts to herself, Mia kissed the back of her mother's hand, which was so much slimmer now. She kept her grip light because she didn't want to accidently hurt her. "Sorry, Mom, you're right. I'll call."

Her mother sandwiched Mia's hand between hers and rubbed. "I'm not getting all up in your business, but I know you've been spending lots of time with Jackson. That and the late hours you keep lead me to some conclusions."

Mia felt her face getting hot. She hadn't discussed the opposite sex with her mother since her sophomore year in high school. She certainly didn't want to discuss what was happening with Jackson. In fact, she refused to. She squirmed in her seat. "Mother, I'm fighting exhaustion here."

"Shush, and relax, dear." Marie released her hand and patted her knee. "You're father and I really like Jackson. He's an exceptional craftsman and a genuinely nice person. He's our friend as well as yours. Take that into to consideration as you two do whatever you do. Strife between you would affect us all."

Mia felt like they were reaching the Outer Limits, a strange place she didn't want to go with her mother. "Mom, you're assuming a lot."

Her mother nodded. "I know, but I felt something between you two at your father's birthday. Tread carefully because all may not be as it seems."

What? Mia had wanted to ask but her mother kept talking. "I will not lose my daughter, yet I would hate to lose a friend."

That sentence brought all the previous hurt to the surface. In the faint light from the hallway, she met her mother's eyes. "I would hate to lose my mother." She didn't have to say anything else. Marie knew exactly what she was talking about.

Her mother sighed deeply before saying, "You weren't here, dear. I didn't want to disrupt your life unless it was absolutely necessary."

"You're my mother and I found out about this by accident!"

"Shush, Mia, you'll wake your father. I'm sorry you found out that way. If I had realized what fate had in store, I would have told you first."

Mia struggled not to cry. "How could everyone but me know, mother? Do you think I'm an imbecile who can't handle hardship unlike my brother who you told right away?"

"It was in my plans to eventually let you know."

"When, mother? When? Heaven forbid, after the fact?"

"Stop it, Mia." Her mother smothered her in a hug and that's when she realized tears were streaming down her face. "I was wrong, babe. Parents make mistakes, too. I should have told you right away. I didn't because I wanted you to be free to enjoy the big city and live your life. I didn't want you to have any regrets and all I did was create regrets for myself." Her mother spoke in a fast, low murmur that connected with Mia's soul. "I didn't want anything happening with me to interfere with your … joy of life."

"Oh, mother." Mia held her back, face in her neck. "What good is my life if I can't be here for the ones who loved me and raised me?"

She felt her mother's nod against her head. "I'm sorry. I promise you'll know all in the future. Do you want me to tell you about it?"

Mia nodded while letting her mother wipe away her tears.

Sitting on the living room couch, during the wee hours of the morning, Marie told her daughter how she discovered she had cancer, who she told, and the details of how it was treated. Mia pressed a hand to her mouth in what she hoped was a casual gesture but she was really trying to quell the sudden nausea as her mother talked straight-forwardly about the operation, telling her that the doctor scraped the poison right.

Suddenly her mother switched subjects. "So now you know and I'm tired of talking about that. I want to tell you how proud I am of you. Going to law school in the Big Apple, I can't wait to come and see you do something lawyerly."

That brought fresh tears to Mia's eyes which quickly began to flow.

"Good heavens! What is it, Mia?" Her mother wrapped her in another tight embrace. "Let it out, child." Marie rocked her. "Let it out, then tell mamma what's wrong."

Eventually, the tears subsided. She leaned away from her mother's wet shoulder to rub her face vigorously while uttering a few choice words. "Sorry," she whispered when she gazed into her mother's kind eyes.

"It's all right, baby." Marie's hand ran over her head.

One more look in her mother's eyes, and Mia let the words flow. "I feel like such a failure. I spent all that time in law school and it's not what I want, mamma. I don't want to be a lawyer." Now that the words were out there, she rushed on, wanting to explain before her mother could berate her.

"I've known for a year. I forced myself to finish school, but the bar was another matter. I just couldn't do it, mom. I had these…attacks. The doctor said they were caused by anxiety. I couldn't…didn't pass the test."

"Baby…" Her mother stopped for a moment as if afraid her voice would break. "My poor baby."

Marie's voice full of pain and sympathy was unexpected, but then Mia told herself she was being absolutely silly. Her mother had always been supportive. Why would she fail to do so now? Feeling a rush of gratitude, Mia fell into her mother's arms again. "Thanks, mother."

After a time, her mother asked as she rubbed her head. "Do you know what you want to do?"

Mia whispered, "I'm not sure." She was quiet, then decided since this was revelation time, she'd be completely honest. "Well, actually I do have an idea."

"What, baby?"

"An artist. I'd like to try and sell my paintings."

"Mia, that's a great idea! You've always loved it. Why not make money doing something you enjoy."

Mia rubbed her face and sat up. "Really, mom? You know people are going to say I wasted all that time in school, especially your son."

"Baby, how can knowledge ever be a waste? Law school was just part of your journey. Maybe it was something you had to experience to find your true passion." Her mother grabbed her shoulders and shook her slightly. "Go for it, girl."

Mia felt as if the elephants sitting on each shoulder had gotten up and lumbered off. She basked in the glow of her mother's acceptance. They sat for awhile and Mia must have dozed off.

"Come on, baby, let's go to bed." Marie was shaking her gently. Mia yawned and stood up, then let her mother put her to bed.

The next day, Jackson drove down Broadway in the center of Capitol Hill, speeding just a tad. It was hard to go fast on Broadway because the street was always crowded. Every time he came to this neighborhood just north of downtown Seattle he was amazed at the diversity. The place had some of the biggest, grandest mansions in all of Seattle and Jackson knew because he'd worked on a few. It was also the center of gay life and home to most of the counterculture in Seattle, Jackson mused as he watched an Asian kid walk by with his hair styled into a ten inch, rainbow Mohawk. Jackson shook his head and slammed on his brakes to avoid hitting a jaywalker. He did a double take because the black woman reminded him of Mia. Hell, everything reminded him of the woman. He couldn't get her out of his mind.

He stopped at a stop sign and had to wait extra long as hordes of people walked in front of his car. Yes, the area was crowded. A fact that Jackson appreciated since he'd been hired to do multiple remodels in the area. Of course, his friend, Shannon Drake, had a lot to do with that. Shannon, an architect, was the one he was rushing to meet. His friend lived and worked on Capital Hill, and he was always sending people Jackson's way.

Resisting the urge to beep his horn, Jackson remembered meeting Shannon in his high school chemistry class. Shannon had been and still was tall, skinny, with large features in all the wrong places. He'd kind of grown into his big nose, enormous ears, and long feet. At least now he didn't trip on them anymore, but in tenth grade if you'd looked up the word awkward in the dictionary, his picture would have been front and center, a fact that made him very popular with the bullies at Garfield high.

All that changed when Jackson sat in Chemistry feeling like his head was going to explode trying to follow the rambling teacher who made no sense to him. It was the last class of the day and he sat there at the end forcing himself not to panic because he hadn't understood a word the man had said since the first day of the class.

Shannon, who sat next to him, reached over and grabbed his book. "Look, it's not as hard as he making it. Here's what he said…" Shannon put it in a way that was easy for Jackson to follow and the two developed a lasting friendship. After that day, no one messed with Shannon and by the next year, he was known as the cool geek.

With a tire screech, Jackson pulled up to the B & O Espresso. The place was historic, according to its website, which claimed it was the first of its kind in Seattle since they opened their door in 1976. It continued to thrive, Starbucks be damned.

Looking through the large windows, Jackson saw Shannon's blond head and realized he and his son, Sam, were already seated. Jackson rushed inside and the brown- headed, four year old ran to greet him. He picked him up wanting to swing him around but there wasn't enough room in the crowded, tight restaurant, so he settled for tossing him up high and carrying him back to the table like a football under his arm.

"Hey, Shan." He hugged his friend and sat down with the squealing and laughing Sam on his knee.

"Hi, buddy." His friend sat as well. "It's good to see you. As you can see, Samuel's excited." Shannon's hands floated in the air as he talked.

"So am I." Jackson admitted. "I just don't show it like Sammy, here."

Shannon leaned his elbows on the table and Jackson noticed his fruity perfume. It made his nose itch. He ignored it like he usually did and tickled Sam. "How is your world?"

"Pretty good. Lots of work, "Jackson answered. "How about you? How's Tom?"

"My better half is excellent." Shannon crossed his Levi clad legs, making his bright red, old school Converse's stand out. "And I have great news." Shannon bobbed in his seat, bouncing his hands off his knees. "Samuel's adoption is now complete. He is officially our son!" He screamed the last part.

"That's great news!" Jackson knew this was the end of a two year ordeal for his friend. Shifting Sam so he didn't squish him, he reached across the small table and clapped his friend on the shoulder.

Shannon grabbed his hand and kissed the back. "Thank-you for being so supportive, Jack." Jackson squeezed his hand and let go. Then he was surprised when others began clapping and congratulating them. It wasn't worth the effort to explain he wasn't the third in this happy little story, but he sure wished he had when he turned and was startled by a pair of very wide eyes.

"Mia," he whispered.

She sat about five tables away with two other women, looking absolutely gorgeous in a brown skirt and green blouse with a modest scooped neckline. Jackson inwardly stilled at the sweet memory of what those clothes concealed. A waiter moved quickly around her table, setting down menus. The man said something that made her friends laugh, but Mia paid them no mind. Her eyes bore into his and he could feel the heat of her anger all the way across the restaurant.

Jackson's stomach plummeted as he speculated about what she must be thinking. He knew she had the absolute wrong impression and he wanted to jump up and explain. But then some part of him asked, why should I have too? If she's the type of woman who jumps to conclusions, this thing is doomed from the start! Hell, can't I meet with a friend in a coffee shop without drama?

Apparently not, Mia blinked several times and then looked away. This shit is ridiculous! Jackson sat back in his chair and Sam thumped his chest with a little fist. "Uncle Jack, what's wrong?"

"Nothing, buddy." He ruffled the kid's hair and tickled him. "I'm gonna eat up all your cake if you don't get to it." He grabbed a fork and reached for the apple pie he knew was Sam's.

"No!" the kid screeched and leaped off Jackson to run to his seat and reclaim his property.

Jackson glanced over to Mia's table and saw that it was empty. Several choice words went through his mind as he cursed how unfair life could be.

Chapter Eight

So, that's what mother meant! The thought seared through Mia's mind. Dammit, why do I have to get the fine brother on the down low? But heck, he's on the up low, meeting his partner and boy in coffee shop.

Mia slapped the steering wheel of the Lexus she'd recently bought. "How could I be so stupid?" she yelled. Her cell rang. She removed her phone from her hip. Seeing Jackson's name, she threw the phone in the passenger's seat. She fumed more thinking about her friends. They certainly thought she was crazy because first, she insisted they leave the B&O and then, she told them she had to leave!

She was too upset to go to her parent's house. They'd notice something was wrong right away and she couldn't answer questions right now. Besides, she was too old to be bothering them with this type of crap although her mother apparently had a clue. Why didn't she just tell her Jackson was gay or bi or whatever? No, she didn't want to look at her mother right now. She drove aimlessly for about an hour then she found herself at her parent's second home. Where it all started, she taunted herself.

She sat in the car for moment as memories of her time with Jackson in this house flooded her mind. "Fuck him," she whispered. She was going to sit in this house and get herself together so she could go back into the world without growling at everyone.

"Damn," she muttered as she entered the front door. "At least I don't have to worry about disease." Soon after the first encounter, she and Jackson had exchanged papers showing they were both clean. She plopped down on the couch and fought the water that wanted to burst from her eyes. "I refuse to cry over that man," she said loudly as if the volume of her voice would make it true. "This is so stupid, Mia," she whispered. "You act like you're in love and that would be absolutely ridiculous!" She rubbed her head vigorously, messing up her hair.

The knock on the door startled her and she jumped from the couch where she sat. Seconds later, the doorbell began ringing insistently.

"Dammit, go away," she whispered after looking in the peephole and seeing the person she least wanted to see.

As if reading her mind, the irritating man yelled, "Open the door, Mia. I'm not leaving until we talk!"

She leaned her back against the door and crossed her arms.

"Mia! I'm trying to be polite, but I do have a key!" Jackson pounded as he yelled, shaking her whole body literally and figuratively. Suddenly, she turned and hit the door back as hard as she could. Then, she flipped the locks and flung it open so hard the door stop bent and the wood banged against the wall.

Jackson stepped through the entrance way and looked at the hole in the dry wall she'd just caused. "I'll fix that for free." He smiled faintly and Mia wanted to hit him. He probably wouldn't dent as easily as the plaster.

She clenched her fists to avoid doing what she wanted to do. "You really don't realize how much I want to hurt you right now. If you did, you wouldn't be standing there smiling."

"I can't help it. You're gorgeous when you're mad."

She hissed.

He held his hands up in a conciliatory way. "Listen, you really don't understand.,,"

"Is the boy your son?" she rudely interrupted. "Are you bisexual or just plain gay?"

Jackson laughed.

Without a clear thought, her hand raised and she advanced to be quickly spun, ending up with her back to his chest. His arms wrapped around her, he held her close and voice just above a murmur, he said, "Damn trying to explain. I'm not gay and I'm tempted to show you right now how much I do like women, particularly the one pressed against me now."

A part of her believed him, while the other part shouted, You're a fool! She managed to elbow him. "Let me go!"

"No," he said in a playful voice.

She stamped the top of his foot with her hard flats.

"Ouch! That hurt, Mia. Stop it." He bent and nuzzled the side of her face with his cheek.

She was paralyzed. It felt so good that she wanted to scream in frustration. Instead, she just stood still as his lips moved from her temple to her chin. She didn't even realized he'd let her go until she suffered momentary weakness and Jackson quickly put his hands to her hips to brace her.

Slowly he turned her to face him. "I'm not gay." Then he kissed her expertly, making her tongue curve this way and that way so well that she wouldn't have been surprised if it ended up in a bow! She relaxed and next thing she knew she was moving like the island girls she admired at the dance clubs in New York-lots of pelvis swivel while her upper body barely moved. Jackson groaned and moved his hips in kind.

Jackson's hands squeezed and weighed her breasts and Mia tore her mouth from his breathing heavily. Mentally, she threw caution to the wind and pulled his head down. Like a homing pigeon, he ripped open her blouse, pulled down her bra so his tongue could devour turgid tips, while his mouth sucked her in deep.

Her body trembled, pinned between him and the hallway wall. Her back arched as the hidden thread connecting her breasts to her clitoris was drawn tight. Both hands were at the back of Jackson head, but one strayed down to touch between her legs. Jackson shifted and soon her pants were around her ankles and his hand had seized her stuff. She couldn't have stopped her body's reaction if she'd wanted to. She was a willing prisoner of the pleasure this man produced and her legs spread as wide as they could to give him as much access as he wanted to the fire below.

Mia gasped loudly when Jackson hands massaged her slowly and thoroughly. His forefinger slid open her folds and dipped into the honey then spread the slippery stuff all around the opening. She clutched the back of Jackson head and he nibbled her nipple just the way she liked it. She writhed in ecstasy realizing his fingers weren't enough. She wanted the real thing.

"Now," she whispered harshly.

She almost fell when he moved back slightly and ripped off his clothes with animal intensity. As he yanked protection from his wallet, she tried to focus on removing her bra. Arousal made her fingers feel thick and clumsy. "Wait," she told Jackson before he ripped the package open. He must have assumed she wanted assistance because soon he was helping her remove her clothes. But that's not what she wanted. The instant she was naked, she sank to her knees, fisted his wide girth and drew him to her face. Mia held him as she enjoyed the head before licking down one side and up the other. Then she took the majority of him into her throat as she gently grasped his sac and rolled his jewels with her palm.

"My God!" Jackson yelled as her fist and mouth moved on him. "Too much," he groaned and his hands went to the side of her head. She released him with a loud pop. "You drive me crazy in more ways than one," he murmured against her mouth while putting on protection and kissing her senseless. The man sure could multi-task. Jackson lifted her with his arms beneath her thighs, so she could accommodate him, and soon she was filled to the glorious hilt.

It was excruciatingly delicious as he ground against her before beginning the delicious out and in. Mia relaxed her muscles on the inward stroke and squeezed on the outward one. The hallway filled with the sounds of flesh meeting flesh, harsh breathing, and moans bumping up against groans.

Mia bit his shoulder as he pistoned inside, her arms locked around his neck. Jackson pounded without mercy and too soon she was screaming against his neck as she spasmed and jerked into oblivion. Jackson was right behind her yelling loudly, shuddering and supporting her on trembling legs.

"Unbelievable," he whispered as he gently lowered them both to the floor. They lay in a silent heap for a long time as they recovered.

How did I let this happen? Mia chastised herself as the glow slowly ebbed.

With a finger under her chin, Jackson lifted until her eyes met his. "I've known Shannon since high school. To make a long story short, he helped me with academics and I made sure he wasn't bullied." He stopped to kiss her lids before continuing, "I hope you're not so homophobic that you can't believe we're just friends."

"Homophobic?" Mia almost laughed. "I'm anything but. I saw him kiss you, Jackson!"

"On the hand, Mia." He kissed her palm. "Shannon was overjoyed because the papers just came through on his son's adoption. Sam is also my godchild. Do you have a problem with that?"

"No, but that doesn't explain my mother."

"Your mom? What's she got to do with this?"

"She warned me about you, told me that all wasn't as it seemed."

Jackson laughed again.

She thumped his chest. "It's not funny, Jackson. This isn't humorous."

"All right, all right, love." The word just rolled off his tongue and struck Mia in the heart. Love!

"You're mother is always chastising me about being a womanizer. I'm sure that's what she's referring to me, not my sexuality. I'm all man, baby. Should I prove it to you again?"

Baby. She liked love better. "Watch out, Jackson. You're drifting dangerously close to male chauvinist pig area."

"I am piggish when it comes to you, Mia." He kissed her nose, then looked suddenly shy. It melted Mia's heart. "I may have thought I was in love in the past, Mia, but it was nothing compared to what thunders in my heart for you." He looked so sincere. "I don't want to be hasty with you. I want whatever is going on between to have a chance to grow and confirm what I think is happening. Time will tell, but I believe I'm falling in love with you."

There is a God! She thought as he enfolded her into a bear hug and she held on furiously. A trembling started deep inside, vibrating places she didn't know were in here. The truth rumbled inside of her and she committed it to air. "I falling for you, too, Jackson," she whispered, a part of her waiting for the sky to fall or worse, for Jackson to say he was teasing. "I've decided to move to Seattle, try the art thing, and let this thing between us grow to a happy ending."

Instead, he growled before saying, "I like the sound of that!" He smiled and planted small kisses all over her face. He ended up staring into her eyes before uttering, "Oh, baby." Then, he buried his nose in her neck and neither spoke. They both understood the moment and more words weren't necessary. They could and would come later.

A Handy Man
By
J.M. Jeffries

Other Titles by J.M. Jeffries

Chapter One

The instant he saw the beautiful and graceful 'Lady' Taye Davis fell in love. He couldn't wait to get his hands on her to give her his special touch.

She was old and worn, tattered around her façade, but once upon a time the Victorian had been a grand house.

His heart began to race. He hadn't worked on a one of these babies in a long time. Normally his construction jobs ran to refitting newer houses with custom remodels. But with the sad state of the economy people weren't buying houses unless they could get a repo or foreclosures and doing the work themselves. Many of the jobs he took now were to correct the homeowners' mistakes. He was doing okay, but he wasn't swimming in work.

He stood on the sidewalk and studied the grand old lady. One side of the wraparound porch sagged. Paint peeled in long curling strips. Missing risers on the stairs, an ill-fitting front door and two cracked windows suggested the house had been vacant a long time. The turret had pieces of wood missing from the siding. At one time someone had painted the house a boring gray and gray it still was except for some rose colored trim along the eaves that had faded to a washed out pink.

This Painted Lady was going to take time and money to restore and hopefully Ms. Erica Walsh had plenty of both. The front lawn was a patch of overgrown weeds. Two trees flanking the cobbled stone walkway to the porch were badly in need of trimming and shingles were missing from the roof. Taye opened the squeaky wrought iron gate and one of hinges, rusted through, fell off.

Though house was in one of nicer neighborhoods in Riverside not too far from the university, it was definitely an eyesore.

An arctic breeze blew by him and he shrugged deeper into his jacket to ward off the chill of this unusually cold day. Riverside was rarely so cold in September with temperature still in the 90s, and he wondered if the chill signaled a cold winter.

He checked his watch: fifteen minutes to three. He was a little late for his appointment with Ms. Walsh. A silver Lexus parked next to a covered patio told him she was already here. The patio cover had a wicked lean to it. That would have to be fixed. A stiff Santa Ana breeze would knock it down. Maybe if he was lucky Ms Davis would like a garage since the original one was a pile of rubble at the back of the patio. He started running figures in his head. Depending on how the inside looked, he could repair this at a decent price with enough work to keep him busy through the winter.

He walked up the stairs and hearing the squeak beneath his feet. He cringed, whoever had this baby let it go to hell in a hand basket should be shot. What a shame to see a house meant to loved, respected, and cared for abandoned like this. These 19th century houses were built to last and with the right touch and a lot of love the house would last another for another hundred or more years.

He grasped tarnished cherub door knocker. The knocker came off in his hand with a little plop. The little brass angel smiled up at his and he felt as though he'd broken off some little kid's finger. This he'd fix for free.

"Careful or the door will fall down on your head," came a cheerful woman's voice. A small slender woman, dressed in workout clothing, walked up the cobbled stones, smiling.

He stuck the angel in his pocket. "Ms. Walsh?"

She stopped just before she reached the first step, but kept walking in place. She held one hand pressed to her throat while she checked her watch. "Another minute, please." She kept stepping but not moving.

Her skin was coffee brown. Her face was a perfect oval with full, generous lips. Legs encased in black spandex were long and slim for such a short sister, but they were nicely muscled. He couldn't tell much about her upper body because she was sporting a bulky red jacket. Other than the very kissable mouth he couldn't see much of her face, because a blue and gold UCLA baseball cap was pulled down to shade her eyes.

"Twenty extra minutes and there is ice cream in my future." She stopped walking and looked up at him, her luscious lips curved in a pleasant smile. Her eyes were a beautiful golden brown that reminded him of fine Baltic amber.

Taye couldn't help but smile. At nearly forty he got excited when he could eat ice cream too.

She wiped her hands on her legging and climbed the stair one hand out-stretched. "You must be Mr. Davis."

He shook her hand and her grip was firm. "Call me Taye, Mr. Davis is my father."

She smiled. "Jen Bradford said you had the best hands in the business."

Since he'd remodeled Jen's kitchen and dated her at one time, he wasn't going to touch that one—not by a long shot. "I don't know about that."

"Let me get you inside so you can see what you have ahead of you." She took a key out of her pocket. "I see Charlie finally gave up the ghost."

"Pardon me?"

She pointed to the space where the door knocker was supposed to be instead of hidden in his pocket.

"I called my angel Charlie you know from the Jimmy Stewart movie."

Taye felt foolish. "He's in my pocket."

"Don't look so guilty, him falling off was the least of my worries." She opened the door. "See what I mean."

Taye walked into the house and tried not to wince. The house was gutted. Hell it was a hot mess. Plaster lay everywhere on the elegant walnut wood floor that were badly in need of refinishing. The living room on his right had huge holes in the walls exposing the electrical wiring that looked as though it was original to the house. Patched of ceiling plaster lay on the floor.

As Taye walked through the house, he felt his stomach sink. This was more damage than he could imagine. Yet the bones were good.

Even if he bottom lined the estimate he could make money off this job and make the work last until next summer. "Who tried to kill your house?"

"Ever hear of Sam Hayder?" Erica Walsh lost her smile. Her lips thinned into a straight line.

Taye had heard about Sam Hayder and in his opinion the man was a walking talking con job. Sam's lack of ethics and skills put a lot of money in his bank account, but left a lot of unsatisfied customers some of whom had turned to Taye to fix everything right.

"Unfortunately, I have," Taye said.

She sighed and glanced around. "Can you fix this mess?"

Taye could repair just about any type of house. "Shouldn't we talk money first?"

She rubbed her head. "Why don't you take a look around first. You might not want to make this kind of commitment until you see all damage that is now my house." The cheer was gone from her voice replaced by sadness.

Some work had been done. Normally this type of house had a lot of small rooms, but he could see she'd decided to go with a more open floor plan. Some walls had been removed already, but others had been left as is because they were bearing walls, though Taye was surprised Sam recognized a bearing wall from a stud. The work was shoddy, but fixable. "Was this a repo?"

"No, the lady who owned the house before me was quite ill the last few years of her life and the house went to hell. Her kids didn't have the time or money to keep it up, so I pretty much got it for a song, but the repairs are going to make up for the cheap price."

He could see that. The walnut floors were solid under his feet, but the rooms were dark. The right paint and wallpaper would give it a more open feel. "Give me about an hour to look around and then we can sit down to talk money."

"While you're doing that, I'm going to run over to my apartment grab a shower and hurry back. It's getting late, do you like Chinese?"

Her offer of food was unexpected. She was going to feed him and talk—was that a good sign or not. "I'm all about the Mongolian beef."

"I'll call and Chan's delivers here." She turned and headed out of the house. "See you in about an hour."

She turned and he found himself enraptured by her cute little bubble butt as she headed out the door. He'd been a lonely man for awhile now. Between chasing down every job he could get and finishing up his master's in business management, he didn't have a lot for time for dating.

A part of him that wanted to turn down the job so he could ask her for a date instead, but he needed the money more then he needed a date. Sam his oldest son had just been accepted to Penn State on a football scholarship, and he would still going to be money to keep that boy in sneakers and protein shakes. He sighed. Damn shame that she was a fine looking woman. Maybe he couldn't ask, but he could certainly look. He grinned as he started his inspection of the house.

Cool water washed over Erica's skin. She didn't like cold showers especially on cold days like this one, but after getting a view of the handy man, she was hot all over. He was one fine brother and knowing her girl parts were still in working condition was enough to make her sigh. After the bit of nasty her life had taken over the last couple of years, frankly she was done with men.

Just because Taye Davis looked like a tall molten chocolate dessert didn't mean she was going to act on her desire. Okay she was going to enjoy him visually, anything else she didn't have the stomach for. All she wanted to do was get her life back on track and that didn't include men—at least not for a while. And not with someone who worked for her. Hadn't she learned her lesson with her ex husband?

She stepped out of the shower and dried herself off. Checking her waterproof wrist watch she had twenty-five minutes to spare. Luckily her apartment was close to her new home and her work.

With the towel wrapped tightly around her, she opened a drawer and pulled gray sweats. No, they wouldn't do, which was ridiculous since she was going to be working in her new house.

She reached for a pair of jeans. Her skinny jeans, the ones her sister Carmen told her made her ass look like an apple. She pulled them on and took a gander at her behind. The dark denim made her butt look fabulous. This baby did have some back. After her get-revenge-skinny-diet she was glad she hadn't lost one of her best assets. See what a nasty divorce will do for a girl. She got to have skinny jeans. At least she had her money and her career together.

Lose a cheating ex and get a new wardrobe. She smiled. This is where she came out ahead. And she now had a dream house and a great job. She needed to get back on the publishing track again. Her book wasn't going to write itself. Focus girl focus, that's how you will get done what you need done. Don't let a man get between you and your career. That had already happened and hadn't turned out so well.

She slid a soft red cashmere sweater on, then she stopped herself. Why she putting the semi-glam on? Taye Davis was hot, but she didn't have any plans to take it any further then staring at his oh-so-fine behind. After taking the sweater off, she threw it on the bed and yanked the jeans off replacing them with the sweat pants. Damn it. After ten years of marriage she'd forgotten how to act around a man. She intended to hire him to fix her house, not her.

For all she knew he was another one of those fly by night contractors planning to suck her dry and leave her holding the termite infested bag.

She checked herself in the mirror. "Girl what has your life come to?" She ran a hand through her black razor bob. "Thirty-five years old and starting all over."

It could be worse. She could still have her low-down, dirty-bastard husband Marshall along with her cushy job at Georgetown University and her house overlooking the Potomac. A long sigh left her lips. But then she'd have to keep the husband and his mistress.

Now she was head of her Department at University of Riverside. Not too shabby. One of the best schools on the west coast. She was in a financial think tank more interested in being cutting edge then old fashioned. She shook her finger at herself in the mirror.

"You know what, girl, you landed on your feet." She was back home in SoCal fifteen minutes from her sister in Mira Loma and twenty minutes away from her mother in Norco.

And she had her dream home, sort of. Be positive, she ordered herself. She had a good feeling about Taye Davis that had nothing to do with his handsome chiseled face and sultry brown eyes. This man was committed to the job and doing it right. He was going to make her house beautiful again. He was going to make it into a home again. A place that was hers. And she was going to help him. Whether he wanted it or not.

Chapter Two

"I want to help you with the remodel," Erica Walsh said.

The red chopsticks halted about half way to his mouth, a piece of Mongolian beef dangling between the pinched ends. "You want to what?"

They sat at a card table set up in front of a fireplace that had been bricked up and left as an ugly eyesore in the dining room.

"I want to be very hands on during the project."

The meat dropped in his lap. Right on top of his boy. Good manners forced him not to reach down and snatch it right away. "I have never had a customer who wanted to help me before." He discreetly reached down and flicked the meat off his pants and then picked it up from the floor. He'd never even had a customer who understood what he did, much less want to participate in the remodel. "Why?"

"Because," she said presenting him with a defiant look, "I should know how to take care of my house. I have no idea which end of a hammer to use."

Nobody was that helpless. A hammer was a hammer. "That's not a ringing endorsement."

"I'm a fast learner," she continued, "and I'm not going to mess up a job because my ego got in the way. And think about this way. If I mess it up you get paid to fix it."

Was that the sound of cash register ringing in his head? "That's very logical."

She stared at him with big, sincere brown eyes. "I am, for the most part, a very logical person."

He didn't doubt that. "Don't you have a husband to do these things around the house?"

Her pretty eyes narrowed and the full lips thinned. "Not anymore and the only thing he knew how to use was use the telephone to call someone. I don't want to be that kind of person anymore."

Her statement said a lot about her and he suspected she was a bit of a pampered princess. Not that being pampered was a bad thing, but the interesting thing was that she didn't want to be that person anymore. He felt his admiration quotient kick in.

Intrigued, he said, "What do you mean you don't want to be that kind of person anymore?"

She glanced away looking ashamed. "That sort of slipped out. Ignore it."

He shook his head. "I one of those guys who don't believe there are any accidents." This was turning into an interesting conversation. He liked that. He liked her. Or at least what he already knew about her. "So explain it to me."

She rested her chopsticks on the edge of the Styrofoam carton. "We've only just met."

"I'm easy to talk to. And the more I know about you the better I can get this house to where you like it and can be comfortable."

Erica leaned back in her chair and crossed her arms over her small breasts. "Are you analyzing me?"

Yeah he was. That's how he worked. "Not in an I'm-your-shrink kind of way, but in an I-want-this-job way."

Her head tilted to the side as she studied him for a second. "For a contractor you're very honest," she said a slight tone of disbelief in her melodious voice and surprise in her eyes.

"Most people in construction are honest, hard working people; we just get underbid by the shady ones. And then we suffer the backlash." He hoped he didn't sound angry, but the thought of all the Sam Hayders in the world irritated him. They gave a good profession a bad name.

"Isn't that the way in every profession? I'd love to smack every bad professor I've run into for making my job just that much harder."

She was a cagey one.

"You are good," he said.

"What's that?" Erica uncrossed her arms and picked up her chopsticks.

"Avoiding questions you don't want to answer."

She pointed her chopsticks at him. "And you have a good memory."

"It's an asset in my job. So reward me with the answer."

She speared a piece of sweet and sour chicken. "What was the question?"

"You said you don't want to be the kind of person who has to call someone to change a light bulb anymore, you want to know how to change one for yourself. Why?"

"I don't recall saying anything about the light bulb part."

Taye couldn't help a smile. "I'm embellishing. Stop stalling."

She gave him a mischievous smile. "You are demanding."

He felt a tightening in his gut at the look in her eyes. Don't get involved, he told himself. But he already was. "Yeah I am."

"This might take a while." She tapped a finger against her chin as though pretending to be thinking.

"I have time." Grabbing a piece of beef, he lifted it to his mouth. "I'm all ears." He sucked the spicy meat into his mouth and chewed.

"You're relentless."

He chuckled. "So I've been told."

She gave him a dazzling smile and his heart raced. She was such a beautiful woman and all he could think of was how cute she looked in her sweats.

"I had a pretty cushy childhood," she said. "Both my parents were professors at UCLA. My father taught at the law school and my mother was the writing professor."

"And you're a professor of?" he asked.

She nodded, pride in her tone. "Economics."

"Good with money?" He was impressed.

"Very good."

Smart woman. God, he loved smart women.

"I married well. So, yeah, I was pampered, along with my sister. As a consequence, we never got a basic education in the real life, like learning how to change a light bulb."

Taye leaned back in his chair and studied her beautiful delicate face, the teasing look in her eyes and he tried to keep a grip on his own version of real life, the kind that made him ache to touch her. "So now you want real life?" Or what passes for real life.

She took a deep breath and speared a bit of rice. She popped the rice in her mouth and chewed thoughtfully for a moment. "There are very few things in life a person can depend upon. Like until death do us part…" Pain filled her voice, but it hardened as she continued, "but a woman can learn to rely on herself."

'Til death do us part, he thought. Yeah, he remembered those words. And he remembered the bitterness of his own divorce. He'd walked away feeling like a failure. No matter that he and his wife had just grown apart, moving in different direction once the kids were almost grown, but the bitterness at his loss never quite went away. "I'm divorced, too."

She looked at him oddly. "Do you know where to take your car when it needs maintenance? I don't. I didn't even know where my husband took my car to be serviced. And when I finally did need to take it in, the service manager talked me into a whole slew of maintenance my car didn't need. I agreed because I didn't want to be stranded somewhere on a dark night and…well, you can guess what the service manager implied. You would never have fallen for such an obvious ploy."

"You make yourself sound like an idiot," he returned, hot at the idea of her being conned into work the car probably didn't need. On top of the contractor who'd ripped her off, he could see why she was sour on life. He didn't want to tell her, but everything that had happened to her was real life, too, just a slightly different reality.

She shrugged and looked ashamed of herself. "I'm not. I'm book smart. I have common sense, but I have no idea how to change a light bulb." She started to say more, but clamped her mouth shut over the words and looked down at her food.

He would have loved for someone to take care of the day to day details of life for him, leaving him free to do what he wanted. That real life shit was overrated and just plain annoying. "I suppose you want to learn to use power tools, too?" He hoped he didn't look as afraid as he knew he sounded.

She grinned and half laughed. "Don't look so frightened. I know you'll teach me how to handle them properly and you won't have to worry about me skewering my hand to a two by four."

"What about your teaching job? Don't you have to shape young minds for the future of the world?"

"I only have one class this semester, not including office hours. I'll be home by one, two at the latest even walking to and from campus."

Taye hitched his thumb over his shoulder remembering the sporty Lexus in the driveway. "You have that sweet ride out there and you want to walk to work?"

"Have you seen the price of gas?"

"I drive a Ford truck. I feel the pain every time I stop at the pump." Hell, if he could carry his tools on his back, he'd leave the gas guzzler at home, too.

"Besides, walking is my exercise, which means I don't have to pluck down a hefty gym fee. I love to eat so I have to exercise."

"You seemed to have everything figured out."

She glanced around the room, at the mess, the peeling wallpaper, the plaster dust everywhere. "I hope so. I really want to put my money in my house."

She would be sinking a small fortune into getting this beauty back into her groove, not that he was complaining since she was paying him to do it, but in this economy he had to wonder. "Why this house? You knew it was going to take a lot of work?" There had to be a dozen others that weren't in such bad shape.

"I crushed the numbers, even with the remodel I'm still saving money. I'm close to work, close to my sister, close to my mother. All in all it's pretty perfect for me. This is an established neighborhood. The market value is holding so it was a good investment."

That was impressive. Everything about this woman was impressive. "Very logical, but I'm sensing more than just all the reasons you laid down."

"Okay I'm really a sucker for classics."

"Me too. This old girl was built to last."

She leaned forward. "So how much is this going to set me back?"

"While you ran to your apartment I did a run through of the house." He slid a piece of paper over to her which listed all the problem areas and how much he would need to get this house in shape." It was an straightforward figure. He wasn't cheap, but he was honest and he was the best.

She let out a long breath. "Well your estimate is a bit higher than two of the people I had out here."

There was a spark of pride in his tone. He backed his shit up and didn't quit until it was right. "My work speaks for its self."

"Frankly I didn't like them and you are having dinner with me. One of them just about had a cow when I told him I wanted to work with him. You at least ask me why?"

"I thought it was a trust issue."

"After the first bozo, can you blame me?"

"No. Not really."

"So will you teach me?"

Like he was going to turn down a chance to spend time with her. "Yeah I will."

She smiled. "Okay you're hired."

Relief spread through him. He needed this job. And If teaching her to be a handy woman part of the gig. He could do it. And a part of him thought he would enjoy spending time with the lovely professor. That was an added bonus. And he always liked life's little bonuses.

Chapter Three

Erica stood back and admired her handy work. Her new white claw foot bathtub looked perfect in her newly remodeled bathroom. The walnut floors gleamed. How anyone could cover that with lime green shag carpet was nuts. Stretching her tired muscles, she watched she took a deep breath. The sharp aroma of drying paint invaded her nose. She walked over and opened one of her brand new double paned windows, to let in some air. Although September in D.C. was already chilly with snow just around the corner, but in Riverside she could still wear shorts. Not that she was. This last two weeks she had banged herself up pretty good. Sacrificed her manicure, big toe and nearly and killed Taye with the nail gun. But her new bathroom was beautiful.

She was glad that she let Taye talk her into knocking down a wall and combining two of five bedrooms up top to enlarge the bathroom and the closet. Yes it cost her extra, but what did she need five small bedrooms upstairs and only one bathroom. But her sister and mother had wept with envy when they saw the size of her closet.

"I like how you're decorating in here."

Erica turned around and saw Taye standing in the door way holding one big red ceramic pots. She smiled. That man could take her breath away any day. "It's not too girly for you?"

He dug small digital camera out of his tight jeans pocket. "Red walls, claw foot tub and a pedestal sink. Look kind of sexy to me."

She felt a heat flush creep up her cheeks. "Bathrooms aren't supposed to be sexy, they are functional. She looked at the white pedestal sink that was shaped like a flower. The beveled mirror medicine cabinet that would hide all of her toiletries. The bathroom did have an old fashion feel to it, but her house with her husband was a modern monstrosity that cost the earth but had no soul. The only she liked was the location. "Actually I was going for an anti-Marshall look?"

"Marshall is the ex?" He stepped into the bathroom and put the ceramic vase into the window sill. It was the perfect location that would hide her sitting in the tub from prying eyes.

That was exactly where she was going to put it. The right silk flowers and it would be done. "He would hate this house, it's location, and it's style."

"Didn't go for classics?"

"He liked brand spanking new every five minutes. That's why he traded me on a younger, fresher model." Okay she said that and it didn't even hurt this time. She was going to put that feeling in the win column. Yippy for her.

His eyebrows rose as if he couldn't believe her. "How old are you?"

"I'm going to be thirty-eight in December." A youngster just really starting out on her own at thirty-eight.

"How old is the new wife?"

"Fifteen."

He scored major points for looking mortified. Up until about three weeks ago, she was still horrified. "Jesus."

"Not really. She's twenty-four I think. He caught me when I was young. I'm number two. Miranda, my sister likes to say that wife number six is just getting out of the third grade."

He chuckled. "Ouch."

"Hind sight is a beautiful thing. I thought he thought I was mature for my age. He just likes to plow new pastures every few years."

"How long have you been divorced?"

"Two years, nine months, three weeks and four days."

"Do you know the time?"

"Ten fifty-eight A.M. eastern standard time. Marshall's a judge. He got the first courtroom in the morning, so he wouldn't miss his tee off time." Okay that wasn't the real time but it sounded good.

"You're funny."

"That's good I was hoping I didn't still sound bitter." If he'd met her a few months ago she wouldn't have been able to find the humor in this situation, but now she was better.

"Are you?"

She bit her lip. "Not so much anymore. I'm relieved. I feel like I've grown up a lot these last two years." God, did she just reveal way too much about herself. He was so easy to talk to and didn't seem to judge her. She knew he worked for her, but he seemed genuine in a way she hadn't seen in a long time. It was really nice that he made her feel comfortable.

"By the way, pizza's here?"

Good now she could stop opening a vein in front of him. "I'm starving."

She followed him downstairs noticing and, not for the first time, how much his jeans just loved his butt. They clung to his beautifully sculpted ass. A hot flash of lust sizzled on her skin. She didn't know whether to be shocked or relieved that she had rediscovered her libido. It's not like she was going to do anything about it. But it was just nice to know she was on the road to getting over her ex-husband and not just angry anymore. Starting her life near the people who loved her had begun to heal her broken heart and battered pride.

Taye pulled a chair from the card table that severed as ground zero of her house.

Erica sat down. "So what do we have tonight?"

Taye sat down across from her. "Canadian Bacon and pineapple."

Erica's face scrunched up. "Eeek"

He flipped the top of the lid. "Half sausage, onion and bell pepper."

She smiled. Her ex never got it right and just figured everyone liked anchovies on their pizza like he did. "You remembered."

"Always do what the lady wants." Taye pulled a paper plate out of a plastic bag and put it in front of her, then did the same for himself.

She realized that they never talked about him. It was time to change that fact. "How did you end up divorced?"

"I don't know."

For a man with a lot of insight he wasn't very good about sharing about himself. "Really?"

"I was busy chasing the dime and my wife got lonely."

"How long have you been divorced?"

He blew out a long breath. "I can remember four years. Actually I was going to school working and running the kids around. There was never any time for us."

"You have kids?"

He held up two fingers and his face glowed with pride. "Two boys."

"I didn't know."

"You okay?"

She should have children. She wanted them, but her husband thought they would interfere with his fun. Now she was glad she didn't have any. That would have made a contentious divorce even nastier. "Yeah, I am." Or at least she would be.

Chapter Four

Taye couldn't help but stare at Erica tight little ass on the ladder as she secured the frosted glass door of the last kitchen cabinet. Not only did the woman have the finest booty in the free world, she really got the hang of home remodeling. The whirl of the electric screwdriver stopped.

"Ta da." She waved the power screwdriver in the air. "I am the kitchen goddess."

Looking up at her happy excited face, a shot of hot burning desire ran through him. "Yes, you are."

She took a step down and her foot slipped and she dropped the power screwdriver.

Taye caught her around the waist with one hand and the power tool in the other. His heart was racing as he pulled her close to him. "Are you okay?"

Her entire body was shaking. "The kitchen goddess has been overthrown."

Taye let her small body slide down his until her feet touched the floor. He couldn't speak as the tiny body pressed against him. "You're shaking."

Her eyes were wide with fear. "I thought I was toast."

As if he would let that happen. "I can't let anything happen to my best student."

A slow seductive smile spread on her full berry colored lips. "Maybe you should let me go."

He did so, reluctantly. He liked the way she felt in his arms as if she was supposed to be there. "I'm sorry."

"No it was my fault. I shouldn't have bragged until I was on solid ground."

She had every right to be impressed with herself and he had to say getting her in his arms was a bonus. He was not made at all. "Hey, you did a great job. I'm impressed. I'd even take you on as an apprentice."

She rolled her big brown eyes. "Stop. Please it's all going to my head."

He loved her sense of humor. He loved that she could laugh at herself. This was a rare trait in most people. "You have no idea how much I make a year going in and fixing owner's mistakes."

She laughed. "You aren't mad at all those home improvement shows on TV?"

He hoped they never ended. "Hell no. I've been surviving on fix-it jobs for the last few months."

The door bell rang.

"I'm hoping that's the dining room table and chairs." She clapped her hands together like a happy little kid.

"I'll get the door. You get all your materials ready to do the backsplash and the kitchen sink."

Her little body just vibrated with pleasure. "I'm going have a great kitchen. I'm going to have to learn to cook."

He laughed as he left the kitchen. What he would give to get her into bed. He needed some time away from her so he could cool his jets. He'd been working at her house for nearly three weeks. Things were coming along at a nice pace. She was a great help and a fast learner and seemed to enjoy what she was doing.

His ex Chandra would hate doing all this stuff. Not that he held that against her. She was one of those women who believed there was man's work and there was woman's work. She never expected him to wash a load of laundry and always seemed surprised when he did. Davis men were self-sufficient. He was. His father was and he made damn sure that his sons were. Much to his ex-wife's horror.

Taye opened the front door which no longer creaked on squeaky hinges to find a tall well-dressed brother standing there with a scowl on his handsome face. This was not the furniture delivery man. "May I help you?" Maybe he was lost because he didn't look like he fit into this homey neighborhood.

"Is this Erica Kent's residence?"

The voice held a bit of the upper crusty South in it. So that was her married name. Was this the ex-husband Taye wondered? "No." It wasn't really a lie.

The man looked annoyed. "This is the address that I was given."

Taye shrugged his shoulders. "Sorry I can't help you, man." And he began to close the door.

"Marshall?" Erica came to stand next to him. "What are you doing here?"

"Apparently getting lied to." Marshall shot him a narrowed gaze.

Taye shrugged again. It was no sweat off his nose. "Her last name is Walsh. Single woman can't be too careful."

Erica slid her arm around his waist. "Taye likes to joke a lot. It's one of things I love about him."

What? Is she telling this guy she's my woman. Now that was interesting. "What can I say? Ladies love to laugh." He slid an arm around her tiny waist. He could play along. Hell it was going to be fun. "I'm a joke a minute kind of guy, isn't that right?"

Marshall simply stared at them. "May I come in?"

Taye turned to Erica. "Baby?" Please say no, he thought trying to shoot her a mental message.

She flashed him a big grin. "Of course."

Telepathy didn't work.

Taye stepped aside and Marshall walked inside the house and stopped dead.

"How quaint," he said a hint of scorn in his tone.

Taye still had his arm around Erica's waist and he felt her go stiff. He looked at her face and her black eyebrows were drawn together and her dark eyes were narrowed. Okay this was about to get ugly up in here. And he had a front row seat to the action. Sweet.

"The word is historical," she said.

Marshall bent over to try and kiss her and she stepped back and broke contact with him.

For a second the poor man looked shocked but he recovered well. Point to him.

"What are you doing in California?"

Marshall smirked. "I've been offered a federal judgeship here."

There was a couple seconds of dead silence. "Are you going to take it?"

"I haven't decided." He studied the room with a little sniff.

Erica put her hand on her hip. "How did you get my address?"

Taye could feel the tension radiating in her tiny frame. Obviously she wasn't a happy camper.

The man had the nerve to look offended. "I still have my connections at Georgetown."

Taye wondered if he was trying to hook back with Erica. Oh hell no. Not as far as he was concerned that wasn't going to happen.

"Looking for a new wife?" she said.

Taye cringed. This woman wasn't cutting ole Marshall a single break. Good for her.

"That's beneath you."

Taye didn't think so.

She tilted her head and studied him like he was a bug on a glass slide. "No, it's not. Why are you here?"

"Can't I just want to see you?"

She shook her head. "No."

All righty then, Taye thought. Erica had some issues and this guy wanted something from her. He figured she was okay by herself and he was a little embarrassed for her ex. It went against the man code to watch a sister slice up a man's ego. "I'm going to go work on the backsplash."

"No, I want to do it?" She grabbed his arm stopping him from turning around.

"Are you working on the house yourself?" Marshall asked.

Oh here it comes, Taye thought.

She squared her shoulders. "Yes, I am."

Marshall barked out a laugh.

Taye cringed. Erica looked as if she was going to bring on the pain, and he was thankful it wasn't going to be directed at him. He was laying money on her, cause she'd been working hard and had some serious muscle tone now and the man—well he looked kind of soft. Plus Erica had that rage thing going on.

"I'm surprised you know one end of a hammer from another," Marshal said with another sniff.

She did the sister neck roll. "I'm not as stupid as I used to be."

"Really?" Marshall's eyebrows shot up.

Now. It was going to happen right now, Taye thought.

"If I can figure out free market economy, I can learn how to operate a power drill." She smiled and lifted one of those perfectly shaped black eyebrows. "Well most people can."

So this is how high-brow people fight. It was kinda fun in a bloodless sort of way. Taye settled back to watch the battle.

Score one for the little lady. "Do you want me to leave?" Taye asked.

"Anything he has to say, he can say in front of you, sweetheart." Erica stood on her tiptoes and kissed his cheek. "Right?"

His cheek sizzled from her kiss and his palms started to sweat. "Ah yeah sure."

Marshall pointed at him. "You two are together?"

Taye swung his gaze to Erica's smiling face. He was going to let her answer this one.

"Did you hope I was still pining away for you?"

"Erica. we're grownups. Of courses you're allowed to go on with your life. After all I'm the one who left you. I'm glad you have someone. He is just so…unexpected."

Like the left jab I'm about to give you,Taye wanted to say but he didn't.

Erica let out a long sigh. "I'm hope you're not being a pretentious snob, Marshall, I always hoped you would have moved on from that by now."

Taye clamped his lips together so he wouldn't laugh. He really wanted to know what this guy had to say.

Marshall cleared his throat. "I've had an offer on the Berkshire property. I wanted to see if you wanted to counter it?"

Both of her eyes brows rose. "That's it? You came to ask me about our summer house?"

Taye was asking himself the same question even if he didn't have any idea what they were talking about, so he just looked like he was interested.

"You always loved it there."

"If I had wanted it I would have asked for it in the settlement. I could care less."

Marshall's face went blank. "But you loved it there."

"You and your tootsie kind of ruined it for me. Sell it."

That was a story Taye really wanted to hear. Hopefully she'd volunteer because he didn't have the stones to ask.

"But--"

"My life's here. I moved on. So should you." She smiled and moved to the door and opened it. "Have a good day."

Marshall looked as if he'd been dismissed so quickly. "Erica?"

"Would love to talk, but I have a backsplash to put in. I've been waiting all week to learn how to use a hammer," she said in a caustic tone. Marshall cringed. He gave Erica one last searching look and then walked out the door.

Taye watched him get into his car, but had the feeling that this wasn't the end of Marshall. Erica closed the door with a firm snap.

"Asshole," she muttered.

"Are you okay?"

She looked ready to blow a gasket.

She crossed her arms over her chest. "You know when your life is going fine and you think you're on top of the world and then something happens to let you know you're really not in charge?"

"Yes."

She shook her fists in the air. "Well, how do you feel after that?"

He took a deep breath. "If I hold on it will pass."

She touched his arm. "Thanks for playing the part of my new love interest."

Happy to help a lady out anytime he could. Especially if it made her ex feel like the ass he was. "You're welcome, but why did I have to?"

Erica look a little chagrined. "It just seemed like a good idea at the time."

Marshall wasn't just here to sell her some land. He wanted her back. "I think he's fishing for something."

"This trout is not interested."

There was a part of him that was a bit skeptical. "Are you sure?"

She rolled her eyes. As if she couldn't believe that he didn't believe her. "Yes."

"Just wanted to be before I do this." Taye wrapped an arm around her waist leaned over and kissed her.

Chapter Five

Erica knew the kiss was coming and a part of her wanted it, but she tried to step back the second his arms went around her.

When his lips touched hers, her mouth opened and his tongue slipped inside her and heat consumed her body. She stood on her tip-toes and put her arms around his neck and let herself fall into the sensation.

Her heart raced and she knew she'd never been kissed this thoroughly before. His lips were firm and masterful. His arms were strong and she felt safe inside his embrace as if this was where she was supposed to be. She arched her body into his. His body was muscular and all man. Marshall never felt like this and she'd had very little to compare other men to. Taye was what a man was supposed to feel. Strong supple powerful. And he smelled so wonderful. Like musk, sandalwood and man. The very scent of him seduced her. His callused hands moved over her body and cupped her butt pulling her closer to him.

The thoughts inside her head were swirling. She wanted more, she knew this was wrong that they were both in the wrong place to have a relationship, but then again she didn't care. All she could focus on was her need.

The doorbell rang. "Riverside Antiques," came from the other side of the door.

Suddenly Taye pulled away. Erica looked up and saw the desire plainly written in his eyes, but she also saw guilt. Frankly he confused her.

"Erica, I'm sorry."

She resisted the urge to touch her mouth. Her lips tingled. Marshall never made her lips tingle. "Don't be. I'm not."

Taye ran a large hand over his short cropped hair. "You aren't?"

She almost laughed at the surprise in his eyes. "No. It's my fault."

"No it's not."

The doorbell rang again. "Ms. Walsh, Riverside Antiques."

Well she didn't think that was going to happen again. Strangely enough the though made her sad. She liked the way he touched her. "Let me get that."

Shaking his head he turned around. "Yeah, I'll be in the kitchen."

Erica opened the door and three men in federal blue uniforms were standing there. She saw a big truck parked on the curb in front of her house.

"Erica Walsh?" The short one asked.

"Yes."

"We're here to deliver your dining room table."

"Great."

She watched the men walk back to the truck.

Taye walked up to her carrying his toolbox. "Listen, I'm going to call it a day."

She had the wild urge to grab him and stop him, but she could see by the set of his broad shoulders he was determined to get the hell out of Dodge. "But--"

"We need some down time. We'll talk about it later."

Eric watched him walk down the stairs and get into his truck and she knew somehow everything had changed between them, and she wasn't sure if it was for the best.

Chapter Six

Erica was sitting on her steps as Taye pulled up to her house. He thought she was working late today. He intended to sand the spare bedroom and office floors today and varnish them and hopefully get out of here before she made it back. No such luck.

He slammed the truck's door shut and started walking up the cobbled walkway. Her bland expression didn't surprise him. He'd already figured still waters ran deep with her.

Taye knew he had to apologize for kissing her. Well she really kissed him, but he wasn't fighting in anyway. As a matter of fact he couldn't seem to get that brief kiss out of his head. All weekend he had a hard time concentrating. Even a trip to the USC football game hadn't gotten her out of his mind. Which meant he had it real bad. "Hi."

"Hello."

"I thought you had a couple of meetings today."

"Cancelled."

Normally her every thought was easy to read, but now she had her teacher face on and he couldn't read a thing. "Great."

"Don't sound so excited."

He didn't say anything but raised on eyebrow.

"That was sarcasm just in case you missed it."

"Oh I caught it." And ran it in for the touchdown, but he didn't say that. Football metaphors irritated women.

She stood up. With her standing on the second step they were almost eye to eye. "We need to talk."

Even when he wasn't dating a woman he hated to hear those words. As a matter of fact he'd prepared himself to lose this job because of what happened. He sat down next to her. "What do we need to talk about?" Be cool Taye, he told himself.

"I'm sorry about the other day." She looked down at the ground.

"You really don't need to be sorry. I was feeling the vibe myself."

Her eyes widened. "You were?"

Damn was he losing his touch? "You couldn't tell?"

"I'm out of practice."

Please don't let me look relieved. God, that would just be wrong. "That's a damn shame."

Erica blew out a long breath. "I've dated two guys in my entire life and one of them I married. I'm thirty something years old and I'm still trying to figure out the man-woman thing."

"I've dated plenty of woman so when you figure out the man-woman thing, break it down for a brother would you."

She smiled. "You're kidding me, right?"

Sometimes honesty really worked. Hope he told that to his boys. "Nope."

"So what are we going to do?"

He reminded himself to let her lead this. "I don't know. What do you think we should do?"

A shy smile curved her mouth. "Well to be honest, I am attracted to you."

"That's start." He wiped his sweaty palms on the back of his jeans. He was about ready to do the happy dance.

"But I have to admit, I'm leery about getting involved with any one at this point in my life."

"Why?"

She sat on the porch step and put her hands around her knees. "I'm starting over."

He suspected she was hoping he'd talk her out of dating, but he wasn't that stupid. He joined her on the porch step, happy that was the first thing he fixed for her. "Dating someone is a part of that starting over."

Erica let out a long breath. "No I've started my entire life over. I moved, got a new job, bought a house and have to make friends here."

"No time for some romance?"

"Does it sound like I have time for romance?"

"You have to make time for fun." He learned that the hard way. If he had figured that out he wouldn't be divorced. But then again, he also wouldn't be sitting here next to this gorgeous woman feeling the heat of her body and knowing he was too attracted to her to stay away.

She rolled her big brown eyes. "This comes from the man who works here twelve hours a day, goes to class and tries to study while raising two sons."

He held up his hands. "I do make time for fun."

Her shoulders sank. "I'm jealous."

"So I'm not fired."

"Hell no."

Relief flooded him. "Thanks."

She ran her hand on the wooden handrail slowly. "I think you love this house almost as much as I do."

Okay he had a flash of her doing that to him. A hot shiver ran up his spine. "If I were in the market. Yeah this one would have been at the top of my list."

She smiled. "I'm glad someone loves it besides me."

"Your mom still talking madness." He had to get back to some neutral territory before he just jumped her.

"That modern monstrosity she bought has no soul." Her huff was barely audible. "But it came with granite counter tops. And a yard the size of a postage stamp." Squeezing two fingers together, she shook her head.

Wait until you decided to landscape this baby, he thought, then see who the smart one is. But wisely he kept that to himself, because he was doing really well with her. "She can cut her grass with nail scissors in five minutes."

She pointed to a huge orange tree in the front yard. "I have fruit trees. I might even learn to can."

Taye laughed. "Stop you're making me laugh."

"I signed up for a cooking class."

"What?"

She slapped his knee. "You heard me. I'm going to learn to cook."

"This from the woman who bought a stove because it looked good in her kitchen not because it was functional. And let me quote. 'I'm not going to learn to cook with it; I just want it to fit the design integrity of the kitchen.'" Though the old fashioned stove was more functional than it looked, but he couldn't help teasing her about it.

Erica raised her hand. "That would be me."

Taye laughed at the fact that she looked so unashamed. "What the hell brought this on?"

"I figured out why my husband married and divorced me."

After meeting the man he she should have divorced him. "Lay it down for me sister."

"I was decoration."

Taye wondered why that was a bad thing. "You are a beautiful woman, but you are also smart and had a job. Right?"

"Not a trophy wife in the traditional sense, but still not a partner wife."

"Okay I have to catch up on my Oprah watching cause I'm lost here."

"I'm not bragging, even though I'm pretty accomplished, I wasn't a threat to my husband in any way."

He liked that she was all of those things. "Okay that I get."

"Our fields were different. I was in academia and I was for the most part happy just being teacher Erica, but I did an article on women and finance and I started getting a lot of attention from all different directions. Political, educational, and financial. I even testified for the Senate Finance committee. I noticed my husband started getting kinda funky."

"Funky?" Then it hit him she'd started raining on his glory parade. Stupid man.

"When we went to a party, people talked to me about my business, not just my golf handicap or what caterer I used."

"You golf?"

"Yes. Then I was asked to consider heading the finance department."

"Impressive."

"I would have been the first woman and African American to head that department. And I was young."

"Hey now a triple threat."

She shook her head. "Only to my marriage."

And if he were honest she was to him. "I'm beginning to see the picture."

"Marshall is one of the most respected judges in this country and he got all bent out of shape because now I was getting attention and he wasn't."

"Did you want the attention?"

She ran her hand through her short cropped hair. "I wanted to be a great teacher. I wanted people to understand that economics is an interesting exciting field of study."

Okay maybe in some alternate universe. "It is?"

"The history of the world, my friend." Erica shook a finger at him.

Holding his hand out he was now informed. "I had no idea."

"Economy is the bedrock of any society."

"I thought that was church."

"Don't make me tell how churches are influenced by money. Matter of fact I'm thinking about doing an article on that very subject."

"That will piss your ex off."

A sly smile now curved her mouth. "Yes it will, but that's just an extra perk."

He liked that she wanted to get even. It was kinda healthy in a way and it meant she didn't want Marshall anymore. "You are bad. So he went off the deep end."

"Then he found himself a replacement for me and filed for divorce."

"And you ended up back in Riverside."

She stood up and put her hands on her hips. "You make that sound like I'm a sad pathetic divorcé."

"Are you?"

"Do you want to sleep with me?"

For a second he wasn't sure he'd heard what he'd heard. "What did you just say?"

Chapter Seven

Erica headed to the stairs. "You heard me." She put her foot on the first step.

Hell yeah he did but he thought it was just his own head talking.

"Why are you waiting?"

He shrugged. "I'm a dumb ass."

Her lips quirked and she moved up the staircase. "Live a little." She stopped at the top and lifted her foot and took off one on the shoes.

A low wolf growl came out of his throat as he caught up with her. "This is really happening, isn't it?"

"I hope so."

He had to remember to thank her ex-husband for cutting her loose like he did. Today he felt like the luckiest man alive. "You have no idea how long I've waited for this." He trailed behind her to the bedroom.

She smiled and sat on the bed. "Me too."

Before he could reach for his belt buckle she was already unbuckling it and unzipping his jeans. She had his already erect cock out before he got his next breath. "We have time."

"I don't." She leaned forward and kissed him.

Her lips tasted sweet and hungry. Just like he liked his women. He pushed her back on the bed. Her breasts rubbed against his shirt and he could feel her hard nipples through the thin silk of her blouse. They wrestled around and got their clothes off.

Erica grabbed his wrist and guided his hand between her legs. She was hot and wet and so ready for him. She smelled like sex. Burying a finger inside her drenched heat, he felt her tighten around him. He stroked inside of her hitting her clit. Her body shook as his finger moved deeper.

Her back arched and her legs clinched around his waist. "You like that don't you."

"More."

"Far be it from me to disappoint a lady," he said. Taye reached for his jeans and pulled a condom out of the pocket. He ripped it open and put it on. He rolled onto his back and pulled her on top of him.

Without even thinking he shoved himself into her balls deep. Damn she was a hot woman. Tight and wet. Her ex should have chained her to the bed. Gritting his teeth he prayed to God not come too soon. This was four alarm ride and he wanted to savory every second.

She wriggled taking him in deeper. When he caught his breath, he started stroking in her nice and slow.

"That's it baby. Harder. Harder," she groaned, arching her back her

breasts full and heavy in his hands

He could feel her tightening up on him as he continued to stroke her hitting her hard clit every time.

The heel of her foot dug into his thigh adding to the sensation. Sweat covered her body as her pert breasts bounced in rhythm to his thrusts. She was so primed. She started stroking her own clit, but he didn't want her to help herself. He wanted to make her come alone. He grabbed her wrist.

His balls tightened and he knew it wouldn't be long until he exploded; he just wanted to take her with him. Working himself inside her harder, he felt her body convulse. He started moving faster, harder, deeper. Gritting his teeth, he just had to hold on another couple of seconds.

A low keening wail escaped her. Her tight internal muscles started milking him and it was all over except for the clapping. Taye let go and came with such intensity he cried out. Erica went rigid as her orgasms rolled on until she collapsed on top of him.

He lay beneath her running his fingers down her back. He didn't think he'd move until August. Course the damn heat would melt their bodies together.

He lay there, unable to speak. Her skin pressed hard to his. How was a man supposed to recover from this and move on with his life.

Erica smiled and stretched her arms over her head. "Well I can check that off my list."

She looked so sexy, Taye wanted to rip her clothes off again and go at it here on her brand new antique dining room table. "What list and do I want to be on it."

"I wanted to have anonymous sex with a stranger." She giggled. "That was redundant, wasn't it?"

"I'm still on the list thing." His eyes narrowed. "I'm not ready for grammar." He took a sip of wine from the elegant stemmed crystal glass as he watched her. Containers of Thai food were spread in front of them.

"After I met you I didn't want to have random sex anymore, I wanted to have it with you." She glanced at him shyly.

Okay he thought that was so bad. 'Anything else on the list."

"I'm going to the animal shelter to get a pet."

She didn't seem like an animal lover to him. Her house was going to be to perfect for an animal. Not that he was judging. "Dog or cat?"

She lifted her glass of wine and toasted the air. " Not sure yet. The ex hated animals. Which I find really strange because he grew up on a farm in Arkansas."

"Some people like to leave their past behind them." That sounded wise and profound. Damn he had no idea he was this deep.

"He wanted to bury his." She stared into the garnet depths of her wine lost in thought.

He could get used to sex, wine and Thai food after sex. "His loss."

"That's how I'm looking at it.

"What kind of pet?"

"I'm not sure. I thought I'd start small."

"A goldfish?"

"You can't interact with a fish." She shrugged her shoulders. "Why bother?"

"Dog? Cat? Ferret?"

Her face scrunched up. "I'm not a ferret kind of girl. Do you like ferrets?"

Taye laughed. "My son Roy wanted one. I was gratefully to find out it's illegal to own one in the state of California."

"Are we cool with this?" She changed the subject abruptly.

So the pet talk stopped. Good because it was out of his league. "What do you want to do?"

"Honestly?"

"No lie to me."

She jiggled her eyebrows. "Wouldn't mind doing 'it' again."

"You know this could get serious."

She nodded with the most earnest look on her face. "I understand that."

He hadn't been serious with a woman in a long time. Longer than he cared to admit. It was easier not to get involved. "But are you ready for that?"

"We're not getting married, are we?"

"No."

"You're not seeing anyone are you?"

He didn't want to see anyone, but her. "With my schedule?"

"And here I am trying to fill up my time."

That struck him as a bit sad. "Why?"

She blew out a long breath. "I think I have a lot of living to catch up on."

And he was avoiding living because it was messy. Oh hell yeah they made a hell of pair. "You make it sound like you are dying next year."

"I've been stuck in a cage for a long time."

"So you want to live?"

"Yes."

Taye leaned over and kissed her. He wanted to live again. And he wanted to do it with her.

Chapter Eight

According to decorating divas red was not a good color for the bedroom, but Erica didn't care. She'd wanted a red bedroom since she'd been a little girl. Being single and grown up she got herself one. She fluffed the red and gold throw pillow and combed out the red tassels until they lay spread prettily on the cha cha red duvet that covered the brand new mattress that had been delivered only a hour after the new bedroom set. She'd chosen an Arts and Crafts style bed and matching dresser. She painted the walls cream and found an antique Victorian sofa and matching chair in a lighter red and gold striped brocade that had been delivered a couple days earlier.

"Wow!" Taye said when he walked into the room. "This is a lot different than the last time I saw it."

Which had only been last night. "I know it looks like a brothel, but I don't care." She rubbed her hands together.

"I like it."

"You do?" She shouldn't be surprised they had a lot of the same tastes which was nice. He gave her a lot of input into the house's decoration.

His beautiful mouth curved into a seductive smile. "It looks like a bed a man can have a lot of fun."

Even though they'd been together a few times this really made her blush. "Really?"

"Oh yeah."

Erica patted the bed and jiggled her eyebrows. "Wanna give it a shot?"

Before he could answer there was a loud clanging sound. "I have to paint."

Erica put her hand on her hip. "You are turning me down to paint? What are you painting?"

"The exterior of the house."

"I thought you were you going to save that until ..."

He shook his head. "We having the hottest October on record, my sons are available and they are cheap labor."

She just loved that he was saving her money as well as doing a great job. "Oh."

"If you feed them we might even get it done today."

"You are fast."

"We use sprayers."

Raising her hands to the heavens she was grateful. She had the ugliest house on the block and it was getting kind of embarrassing. "Thank God for modern technology."

"We should be done with the primer in about six hours."

She looked at her watch. "I'll have something ready by five."

"Don't do anything fancy. It would be wasted on them."

She was thrilled at the chance of trying out her new cooking skills. "I'll do lasagna. Kids like lasagna. My cooking classes are so much fun."

"That works." He walked over and pushed his hand down on the mattress. "I like the new mattress. Pillow top? Soft and great for ..." He simply grinned at her, the look on his face telling her he was remembering last night and the night before and the two weeks before that.

"Of course you know I'm delicate." She splayed her hand on her chest.

"And you do like your comfort."

Most men would be judging her but he wasn't. She liked that about him. "Yes, I do."

"Me too."

"And it is brand new, so it hasn't been broken in."

"What are you going to do with your old furniture?"

"The furniture is rented. The rental company is coming tomorrow to pick it up. I didn't want anything from my marriage except the things I brought to it."

"You didn't get a divorce settlement."

She gave him this big duh look. "I took the cash."

"You make it sound like your divorce was painless."

"No, but part of the healing process was starting out fresh."

"And now you ex shows up with no wife."

As if that mattered, but she sensed he needed to hear it. "I've forgiven the man because I have to, but I'm never going to trust him again."

He studied her for a moment. "Then why are you letting him back into your life?"

"Because behind this reasonable practical economist is a vicious sadistic streak." She should be ashamed of herself but she wasn't.

He cringed. "Ouch, I'll remember that."

She pointed to the door. "Good now go paint my house."

"Yes Ma'am."

Erica watched him walk out of her new decorated bedroom. Wow indeed. Things between them were taking an interesting turn. They should have never been together. The Professor and the blue collar stud. But she liked him. With her and Marshall it was a meeting of the minds and not much else. But Taye was smart. He had a mind like a steel trap and she liked that. But he also knew how to have fun. And he made her feel special as if she were more than an appendage he could take to a cocktail party and show off. He was threatened by her success or her job.

That was just so weird. She always had the misconception that blue collar men didn't like smart white collar women. She should slap herself for having such a petty prejudice. It's the man not the job.

Her cell phone rang and she dug it out of her pocket. Although she had deleted his number from her data base she recognized Marshall's cell phone number. What did he want now? She'd been avoiding him for two weeks. She sent the call to voice mail. She had left her past behind. All she wanted to do now was concentrate on her future. One that included a handsome handy man.

Taye looked at Marshall standing in the door way. Damn this brother just always looked so smooth. He wondered if the man ever sweat. "What can I do for you?"

Marshall tried to look over his shoulder. "Is Erica here?"

"Nope." He started to close the door in the man's face.

"May I come in?" He planted his palm against the door.

Taye had about three inches and twenty pounds on the guy, if he wanted to force the door closed he could, but he could be generous up to a point. "You are polite. You got good home training."

Marshall didn't remove his hand. "Does that mean I can come in?"

"Not really."

"Isn't this Erica's house?"

"And she's not here, so good manners would dictate that I don't let you in unless she's specifically told me you can be here." Wow! He was tired after that long speech."

His nostrils flared. "I see."

Taye was almost impressed. "Maybe I can help you?"

"You could." His beady eyes narrowed. "I want my wife back."

Taye gave the man some points for finding his brains. Too late but hey at least he tried. "No can do."

"What makes you think you have any say in the matter? Do you think you can hold on Mr. Handy Man?" Marshall said in a very condescending tone.

Now it was time to lay down some truth. "I don't have to hold her, she staying because she wants to."

Marshall snapped his fingers. "I can get her back anytime I want."

It took every ounce of willpower not to laugh in his face. "You can try."

"I will."

Taye shrugged. "Okay."

"What kind of man are you to be so casual about a woman?"

"I didn't let her go in the first place."

"I made a mistake."

"Yeah you did." Call him a sadistic bastard, but he was really enjoying this conversation. "Only thing I can't figure out is why."

"I was ... mistaken."

That must have taken him a lot to admit. "Dumb is the word I would have gone with, but that's just me." So he rubbed a little salt on it. Sue him.

"There is no need to insult me." He squared his shoulders as if he was going to do something.

"True, but it is kinda fun."

Marshall's looked him up and down. "I can see what your appeal is, but Erica is the kind of woman who needs mental stimulation."

Ah ha! So that was the issue. The new bride hadn't been mentally stimulating enough. Also, with all the attention Erica had gotten, having a dumb wife said something about Marshall. "You're assuming that because I work with my hands I don't have anything intellectual to offer her." Did the man think he was too stupid to get the insult or was it just him?

"Do you?"

He was never going to win a Noble Prize but ... "A few things."

"Such as?"

Pretty much everything that was important to her. "I listen to her. I understand that was a problem you had."

Marshall looked...almost embarrassed. "I listened."

That was a direct hit, Taye thought. "No, you talk and she listens."

"We have many of the same things in common. Frankly I can't picture you at the ballet."

They did go and see The Color Purple last week did that count. There was some dancing in there. "I'm interested in her work."

"And I wasn't?"

Taye leaned against the door jamb. "What is the title of the article she got published in Newsweek?"

"That was almost three years ago."

Wrong answer. "No that was the article she published in the Economist. Three weeks ago she published an article in Newsweek."

"How do you know?"

"I can read."

"Did you understand it?"

"The Erica Walsh version of the trickledown theory?" He smiled. "I got the gist of it."

"The what?"

"Basically it's about your own self-interest. If you use stores and businesses near your work or your home, the money you spend will come back to you faster. It was a long article. You should read it. You ex-wife has a very clean writing style." And the article had changed the way Taye spent his money.

"You don't need to tell me about Erica's virtues."

"I didn't divorce her." With that he closed the door. He'd wasted enough time with this man and he had smoke detectors to put in.

Chapter Nine

Erica's lips were soft and yielding under his. She tasted of chocolate and coffee. Her mouth under his and she slipped her tongue inside his mouth. Yeah, she was really making up for lost time with this kiss.

"Am I interrupting something?"

Taye felt Erica's body stiffen, and then pull away from him.

The ex stood at the bottom of the porch steps with an annoyed expression on his face.

"What do you want, Marshall?" Erica's tone was less than kind.

He held out a bottle of wine. "I wanted to give you a house warming present."

Erica reached out and took the bottle. She set on the porch railing without even looking at it. "Thank you that was very kind of you?"

Taye had to resist the urge to toss the bottle back at Marshall. "Thanks dude, I'm sure we'll enjoy it."

Marshall's lips thinned. "It an Alain Graillot Crozes Hermit Age Rhone. One of your favorites."

Erica widened. "You remembered?"

Taye suspected that the guy was waiting for an invitation to have a glass of wine and he was enjoying watching him squirm. Oh what the hell. "Would you like to join us for a glass of wine? All we have is paper cups but I'm sure that would be okay."

"I really must be going."

"Thank you for the wine," Taye said making sure his manners were as perfect as Marshall's.

"Of course."

Watching him walk to the curb. Taye was barely able to restrain the laughter threatening to come out. Marshall got into his BMW and drove away.

"Is it safe now?" he asked.

She shook her head. "Let it out."

Taye laughed. "The look on his face was priceless."

She picked up the bottle and caressed the glass. "God, that was too easy. Paper cups, my butt."

She kissed the bottle. "Love it. I have to admit he has great taste in wine. And by the way, my wine glasses are Lalique and my parents bought them for me as a wedding present."

"Expensive?"

"Very, but I still let you drink out them." She hugged the bottle. "I can't believe he bought me this wine?"

Maybe he was being a dick head. "Don't you like it?'

"I love it. He hates it."

"He wants something from you." Back in her life back in her bed. Hell no. Now way was Marshall even going to get past Taye.

"Maybe his puppy wife slipped out of training." She headed inside the house. "Let's get drunk and fool around."

He was down with that.

Taye drove past Erica house and spotted Marshall's car parked on the curb. His hands tightened around the steering wheel as he made a u-turn to park. Damn this man was getting on his last nerve. Why couldn't he just leave them alone so that they could get on with their lives? He parked the car and turned off the engine. He took a deep breath, needing to be in his calm place to play mental games with this asshole.

Just as he was about to get out of his car he saw Erica and Marshall walk down the sidewalk to his car. They were arm in arm. Rage coursed through him. His woman shouldn't be touching him. When they got to his car they stopped and she stood on tip toe and kissed his cheek.

Taye hand fisted. Damn. This was so wrong. And in that instant he knew. He was in love with Erica. If he were a better man he would have laughed at himself, but his humor was nowhere to be found.

Marshall touched Erica's cheek and spoke a few words to her. Then he went around to the driver's side of the car and got in. Erica smiled and waved. Then the lithe BMW sedan roared to life and took off from the curb.

Erica started to walk up the side walk.

Taye couldn't move. Not until he calmed himself down. That was it. Whatever was between Erica and her ex husband was going to end today or he was out of her life forever. The house was done and she was completely moved in. She didn't need him anymore.

But he wanted her.

He wanted her with everything he had. How had he fallen so far so fast? Hell it just snuck up on him and hit him upside the head. Then there she was playing kissy face with the man who dumped her for a younger model. What the hell was wrong with her did she think he changed his ways.

Taye got out of the car and slammed the door. He took a deep breath to calm himself and headed to Erica's house. He was going to give her a choice him or the ex.

Like any man in his right mind he needed to know where he stood.

He took the steps two at a time. All four of them and banged on her door not even bothering with the door knocker that he put up for her.

After a few seconds the door opened. "Hi sweetie, I wasn't expecting you. Come on in." She opened the door wider and stepped aside.

"We need to talk."

Erica smiled. "Sure." She hitched her thumb over her shoulder toward the kitchen. "What a cup of coffee?"

What he needed was a drink. "No."

"What's up? You look a little upset."

Taye crossed his arms over his chest. "Are you getting back with your ex?"

Her eyebrows hit her hairline. "What?"

Was she just acting or did she really not know what he was talking about? Hell he didn't care he needed to say this. "Why was he here?"

"What is your problem?"

"You can't get back with him. You're mine."

Tilting her head, she held up a manicured hand. "Back up there for a second."

"You have to get him out of your life. Or we can't be together. I'm not playing second fiddle to that jack ass."

"Who said you were?"

"You kissed him." Was it just him or didn't he sound like a spoiled boy?

"So what?"

"He hasn't changed. How can you want to be with him when I'm in love with you?"

Her mouth fell open.

"When you make up your mind call me." He turned and headed out the door.

Erica stared at the slamming door. What the hell was wrong with him and what had she done to deserve that? Did she run after him? He was in love with her. It's not she wasn't in love with him, too. Marshall was out of her life. He reconciled with his wife and wanted to thank her for talking some sense in his head. Oh boy. Taye must have seen him at the house. Erica ran to the door and flung it open. "Hey! You get your butt back here."

Taye stopped and turned around. "Why?"

She thought she was going to handle this like a grownup. Apparently not. "Because I need to get a word in, that's why."

He started walking up the sidewalk and on to the porch. "What?"

This man was making her mad. She poked him the chest. Thank God she was standing on the top step so they were eye to eye. "Who the hell are you to dictate how I run my life?"

"The man who loves you, that's who."

Putting her hand on her hip, she couldn't stop tapping her toe on the step. "I just got rid of the last man who took control of my life, what makes you think I want another one."

"I've only asked you to get your personal life together so we can make a life together."

"I just got my life back."

"I love you we need to be together."

She loved hearing those words, but she couldn't let him think she was this easy. "Because you decided we need to be together."

"Pretty much."

Erica bit her lip to stop laughing. God she loved him. "That's very arrogant of you."

"It's what you want."

She smiled. "Maybe."

"Do you want to be with me or not? Because if you do you have to get Marshall out of your life."

"He's out."

Taye grabbed her shoulders. "What?"

She let a long breath. "I had a long talk with him andtold him some hard truths. I also told him if he didn't want to be a three time loser, he needed to make some serious changes. Beside Monica is pregnant and he needs to start being a grown up."

A look of disbelief crossed his face. "Run that by me again."

She laughed. "That was good-bye and have a good life."

"So he's not going to be around anymore."

"He got all weird because he's going to be a dad. Apparently Monica who is barely out of diapers was a hell of lot smarter than anyone gave her credit. She backed Marshall in a corner and is forcing him to grow up."

"Damn."

Taye beautiful face had that 'I feel stupid' expression on it. It was really quite amusing. "Yeah, well back to you and me." She poked him in the chest. "You're stuck with me and my house."

"You love me?"

What could she say? "Like crazy."

He rubbed his hands over his face. "So that was just like me a jerk."

She nodded. "Pretty much but I'm gonna forgive and maybe on our fiftieth anniversary forget."

"Say it."

"I love you Taye."

"I'm going to love you until my last breath." He bent over and kissed her.

So was she.

Made in the USA
Charleston, SC
09 January 2011